...ar of the Phoenix Park

Twenty Major was born some years ago in Dublin, Ireland. He lives on, or around, the South Circular Road with a dog called Bastardface and a cat called Throatripper.

He was nominated for the Nobel Peace Prize in 1984 but was beaten to the gong by Bishop Desmond Tutu who ran a vigorous dirty tricks campaign against him. His other mortal enemies include Daryl Hall, LL Cool J (who stole his rap) and any kind of clown.

He writes a daily blog on www.twentymajor.net

The Order of the Phoenix Park

TWENTY MAJOR

HACHETTE
BOOKS
IRELAND

First published in Ireland in 2008 by Hachette Books Ireland
An Hachette Livre UK company

A CIP catalogue record for this title is available from the British Library.

ISBN 978 0 340 95287 0

Typeset in Sabon MT and Gill Sans MT by Hachette Books Ireland
Cover design by Anu Design
Cover illustration Fintan Taite

Printed and bound in Great Britain by Mackays of Chatham Ltd,
Catham, Kent

Hachette Books Ireland policy is to use papers that are
natural, renewable and recyclable products and made from wood grown in
sustainable forests. The logging and manufacturing processes are expected
to conform to the environmental regulations of the country of origin.

Hachette Books Ireland
8 Castlecourt Centre, Castleknock, Dublin 15, Ireland
A division of Hachette Livre UK
338 Euston Road, London NW1 3BH, England

For Anne and Terry

Prologue

Monday Night

Renowned record-shop-owner Tom O'Farrell staggered from the store room at the back of his shop. Terrified and unable to understand what was happening, he only knew that escape was impossible. He had already locked up the shop, the shutters were secured in place ... he had nowhere to go. Nevertheless, he made for the door, frantically hoping that a passer-by might see what was happening and raise the alarm. With the lights off though, that was unlikely, and the darkness caused him to stumble over a display of Tears for Fears *Greatest Hits* DVDs. He lay on the ground, out of breath, looking desperately for somewhere to hide.

Then a voice spoke, alarmingly close, 'Stay very still.'

Crouched on all fours, the record-shop-owner shud-dered, turning his head very slowly, like some kind of retarded owl.

Just 14 feet away, bathed in the light that pushed its luminous tentacles out from the store room, loomed the enormous silhouette of his assailant, who stared contemptuously down at him with shining, pink eyes. He was freakishly tall and built like the offspring of a farmer and a professional wrestler crossed with an old-school East German female Olympic athlete. His skin was so pale it was almost translucent, and from under his flat cap sprung a shock of bright orange hair.

'No. It can't be,' gasped Tom, 'the ginger albino! It was supposed to be just a legend.'

Christ, this was bad. If only people knew.

The ginger albino pulled a pistol from his duffel coat and pointed it at his victim.

'You shouldn't have tried to escape.' His accent was a mix of nasal American and Wicklow council worker, with a strange northern twang that Tom thought might be Donegal. 'Now, you know why I'm here. You know what you must do.'

'I've told you already,' Tom stammered, 'I have no idea what you're talking about.'

'You lie,' said the hideous man, his gingerness seeming to ooze from his pores like stuff oozed from teenagers' faces. 'You and your brethren know of me. You know what I signify. And now you know that I am not a fabled monster. I am real.'

Tom felt a surge of adrenalin rush through him. Well, he hoped it was adrenalin.

'I will give you a final chance,' the towering figure said coldly. 'Do as I ask, or I shall kill you.'

'Never,' said Tom. 'What you ask is too despicable for any person to agree to. I have spent my life working in this business – apart from that time when I lived in London and I had to do things to get by, but that's not important right now – and I will not see it destroyed by the likes of you.'

'Very well. I had hoped you would see sense. What is to come is inevitable. Your pathetic stand against it will make no difference whatsoever. The wheels are in motion. This Rolling Stone is gathering no moss. Que sera, sera, and such. Your death will serve as a warning to the others. They won't be so foolish.'

In an instant, Tom knew what he had to do. 'If I die,' he thought, 'then it's all over. There's no chance for anyone.'

Instinctively, he tried to get up and run for the door. The gun thundered, and he felt a burning heat as the bullet penetrated his stomach. He fell again ... battling against the searing pain. He turned onto his back again and faced his attacker, who had the pistol pointed directly between his eyes. The ginger albino pulled the trigger, but there was only the click so reminiscent of the Russian roulette scene in *The Deer Hunter*.

'MAO!' said the man, laughing. He reached for more bullets but then saw the blood spreading across the floor from Tom's stomach. He pocketed the bullets and holstered his gun. 'My work here is done.'

Tom looked down and saw the hole in his Che Guevara T-shirt. As a veteran of the turf wars between the punks, the mods and the Val Doonican fans during his time in London, he'd seen people gut shot before. It was a slow and painful way to die. Worse than being starved to death in a room filled with Phil Collins music while being rimmed by a cat.

His hateful assassin regarded him for a moment. 'Your pain is as nothing compared to what the rest of humanity will suffer. Be thankful and die well.'

The ginger albino walked calmly over to one of the racks behind the counter, searched for a couple of moments, then took something. The next moment, he was gone, locking the back door behind him.

Alone and dying, Tom O'Farrell knew he had to act fast. Within minutes, the poison from his stomach would enter his chest cavity and render him immobile for the final, excruciating moments.

'I must warn them. I must find some way.'

Staggering to his feet, he tried to move, but he was too weak. His legs were like jelly beneath him. Close to tears and knowing time was short, he lay down on the floor. An idea came to him. He pulled his T-shirt over his head, wincing in pain, and summoned the last of his strength to do what he had to do.

When he was finished, he grimaced as he found his mobile phone in his pocket and flicked through the address book until he came to the name of the person he wanted. Too weak to make the call, he left the screen displaying this entry as the blackness enveloped him … and Tom O'Farrell died, hoping against hope that he'd done enough.

I

Tuesday Morning

It was early morning when the call came. I was up and about though. A hangover made sure of that. It felt like there were little brain dwarves drilling holes in the skirting boards of my brain. I hate dwarves.

'Hello, Twenty?'

'Yes. Who's that?'

'Detective Sergeant Larry O'Rourke, from Pearse Street.'

'Ah, Larry. How's things?'

'Not so bad, Twenty. Long time no speak.'

'You know me, honest as the day is long.'

'Yeah. A day in the North Pole.'

'Ever the card, Larry. What's going on?'

'We've got a bit of a situation here. Do you know a fellow called Tom O'Farrell?'

'Of course, Tom owns Vinyl Countdown, the record shop on Wicklow Street.'

'Owned, Twenty.'

'Did he sell it? The big corporate monsters and the online world have finally put paid to the little record-shop-owner man?'

'No, he's dead!' He laughed. Larry was never one for subtleties.

'Jesus. What happened?'

'Shot in the belly. Bled like a stuck pig, so he did. Bet it hurt like buggery, too. I read somewhere it's the most painful way to die. Even worse than being starved to death in a room filled with Phil Collins music while being rimmed by a cat.'

'Christ, that is bad. How come you're ringing me, though?'

'Well, it looks like he was trying to call you with his last dying act. Your phonebook entry was on his mobile. There's something else very strange too, but I can't go into that now because I'm dying for a piss and a smoke. Yes, at the same time. Can you come down here?'

I told him I'd be down within half an hour, jumped into the shower, had a smoke, then hopped on my Honda 50 and headed for town.

🎧 🎧 🎧 🎧 🎧

When I got to the station, Larry was standing outside. He acknowledged me with a nod of his head as he carried on his phone conversation.

'I don't care what he says. That's just bullshit. This time that little fucker is going down. He's not getting away with that shit anymore. We have him bang to rights. Just keep him there till I get back.'

He hung up.

'Sorry about that, Twenty. The missus caught the young fella looking at porn on the internet. We've always suspected but never been able to prove it.'

'Er ... right enough. So what the fuck happened here?'

'Cleaner found him this morning. Dead as you like on the floor. She's so shocked she's talking about going back to Poland.'

'Jesus.'

'Yeah. Come in here and have a look though. It's all very odd.'

I followed him into the shop, and there were all kinds of people in there. He explained the forensics officers had been in already and there was no danger of me contaminating the scene. As we went past the Classical section, I could see some bloodstains on the ground. When we came into the Male A–Z, I could see poor old Tom's feet.

Tom and I were old friends. He'd grown up on the same road as me and had always been into his music. He had wanted to get into managing bands, but his eye for talent-spotting was like Paris Hilton's – all crooked and deformed. He'd passed up the chance to manage a young, enthusiastic Northside band, saying the lead singer was 'a wanky little dwarf cunt with a stupid name,' and instead chose a punk band from Killester called The Unholy Flaps.

It didn't take him long to realise that he wasn't any good at decision-making when it came to new groups, so he moved to London. He came back about two years later, looking very thin, and never once spoke about what had happened to him there. I never really asked. When he came to me looking for financial help for his new record shop, I was a bit dubious, despite his earnest promises to pay me back every penny. Had it been anyone else, I'm pretty sure I'd have told them to take a running jump.

'You want to open a second-hand and rare items record shop on Wicklow Street, do you? Well, I suggest you think again because it would be a disaster,' I might say as I sent them away and turned to the window, silhouetted in the late evening sunshine, individual hairs from my beard shining as if under spotlights.

Tom was different, though. As kids we'd been through a traumatic experience together when, as part of somebody's idea to instill religion in children, we had been sent to a monastery on 'retreat'. When we got there, it was horrible. It smelt like a hospital. Well, a hospital whose walls were scrubbed with Jeyes Fluid and still-warm semen. Tom and I had to share a room. He got the top bunk, which suited me, as I really don't have much of a head for heights. After being told to go to bed very early we were still full of energy, young innocent scamps emboldened by the strange surroundings. So, we did what any typical lads of that age would do. We sneaked out of the dormitory room and went exploring. The corridors were dark and narrow, and the floors had diamond-shaped black and white tiles. We had no idea what might be around the next corner, so we moved as slowly as a government inquiry into anything that might be vaguely its fault. Soon, we found ourselves in a kind of atrium with a number of large doors leading left and right and the continuation of the corridor straight ahead. Not quite wanting to risk going in a door where we might find a tableful of monks, their helmets on, sitting around a table playing gin rummy or spin the bottle, we decided to go straight on. It was the worst decision we ever made in our lives.

We had just turned the corner when, from behind us, a voice spoke and stopped us in our tracks.

'Boys.'

We looked sideways at each other, gulped, and turned around to see a very ugly monk standing with his arms folded. He had the blackest hair I had ever seen, heavy stubble and shaggy eyebrows that almost met in the middle. When he spoke, you could see that his top gums were larger than his actual teeth, making him look like some kind of Hallowe'en mask. He had a strange, sickly sweet smell, and the look of him put chills down my spine. Even at an early age, I knew this was not the kind of person I should be around.

'You're here with the retreat, isn't that right?'

'Yes, Mr Monk,' said Tom.

'And you were told to go to bed and not come out of your rooms until morning, weren't you?'

'Yes, Sir Monk,' Tom stammered. I was now even more nervous as I watched the smile, small as it was, begin to spread over his face.

'Well, that means you two are in serious trouble. Your teachers will have to be told, then your parents, and Lord knows what they'll say when they learn how you have disrespected a house of God.'

Tom's parents were particularly religious, and if they discovered he'd been up to mischief in a monastery, they'd redden his backside for him and no mistake.

'Oh Jesus!' he said.

'Now you take the Lord's name in vain?'

'I was praying. I swear!'

'That's not what it sounded like to me. That's even more trouble if they find out that. Oh now, that's made you look very worried. Well now … what if I told you that there was something you could do that would make sure you didn't get into any trouble at all? Would you be willing to do it?'

'Oh yes,' said a now-panicking Tom. 'Yes, we would. Wouldn't we, Twenty?'

'Erm …'

'Well, that's settled it then. You two come with me, and I'll make sure you don't have any problems.'

He steered us towards a door that was almost hidden in the corner of the dark passageway. My nerves were screaming at me – every part of me knew this was wrong, this was a mistake, this was something I'd regret for ever, but I just walked on, too young to prevent it happening. I cursed myself for leaving to explore in the first place. If I'd just stayed in the room and played Top Trumps, none of this would have happened. I'll never forget the click of the door as it shut behind us, and we were made sit on a rock-hard sofa. The monk went into another room, and when he came back in, he efficiently but lengthily took our innocence.

I'll never forget his fingers opening the clasps, then rubbing up and down, then gripping the shaft before starting to strum gently. That bastard played folk music at us for over an hour, singing songs about idiot people who seemed to be far too fucking miserable to bother paying any attention to. The corny lyrics, the lethargic performance, the closing of the eyes when singing ... the whole thing was just utterly traumatic. When he escorted us back to our room and bade us goodnight, we both lay in our beds, rigid, violated, hollow inside.

After a long time, Tom spoke. 'Twenty. Would it be okay if we never talked about this again?'

'That's okay with me.'

'Epic. Goodnight, Twenty.'

'Goodnight, Tom.'

I'm not sure either of us slept, though.

Years later, with the money I provided, he was able to open his record shop and it became one of the most popular in town. If you found the door on Wicklow Street, hidden away on the curve, behind it you'd find a wonderland, specialising in rare vinyl that nobody else seemed able to get. Tom paid me back within the year, and I still got a small percentage of the annual profits for my trouble. Tom insisted, and I'm not a man foolish enough to turn down cash in my hand. Tom and I had a history. A good history, a history that could fill a bargeful of kegs. A history that ended now and went on for ever.

Tom was dead.

Larry was speaking again. 'Look, the reason we asked you to come down wasn't just because of the phone thing. People get shot in Dublin all the time. Normally though it's one drug dealer shooting another, and we don't really care about that. If you had a kitchen full of cockroaches, and one of them ate another one, you wouldn't be upset, right?'

'Right.'

'Well, this is different. Tom O'Farrell was no cockroach, and he surely wasn't eaten by another cockroach.'

'Police work is complicated, eh?'

'Joe,' he said, talking to one of the crime-scene guys, 'lift up that sheet and let Twenty have a look at the body.'

Joe did as he was told. There lay my old friend, his stomach caked in dried blood, bits of his guts hanging out. It was an ugly sight.

'Now, Twenty, this is why we brought you down here. As well as the phone with your address-book entry, it seems he left us another clue. Look.'

I moved closer to the body, and on his chest, with his own blood, Tom had written the number '60'.

'Any idea what that means?' asked Larry.

'Not a clue. Sorry. Maybe it's the start of a phone number, or the number of a house?'

'It could also be a registration plate, a time, a file in a numerically organised filing system, somebody's position in a list, the price of something, the number of times he's eaten steak-and-kidney pie. It could be anything.

We were hoping it might mean something to you.'

'I wish I could help, Larry, but nothing springs to mind. Tell you what, I'll check with the lads, see if they can come up with something.'

'Fair enough. Keep it quiet, though. We're not releasing that information to the press. We need to keep something back to weed out all the lunatics who'll ring up and claim to have done it.'

'Does that really happen?'

'Nah. It's just a good line. Get in touch if you figure anything out though.'

I walked out of Tom's shop, my head spinning. What was it that he'd wanted to tell me? Who would want to do something like that to old Tom? And why would they want to do that? If I could figure out those three questions, then we'd be closer to finding out what really happened in there.

I knew there was only one place I could go.

2

Still Tuesday Morning

I dropped my trusty motorcycle back home and wandered around to Ron's bar. Ron's is my local. I've been going there for years. It's not like your achingly trendy super-pubs, it's not even like a normal pub, it's an old-fashioned bar. There's no carvery lunch or Mediterranean fusion food. You're lucky if he's remembered to stock up on Tayto, and even then he never has Smoky Bacon flavour. There are no plasma TVs, just one old set bolted to the roof in the corner. We did make him get Sky in, though, so we could watch the football.

That's his one concession to the modern world.

Ron and I have an understanding. I pay him money for my booze, and he lets me smoke in his bar. He's never liked being told what to do, and the smoking ban, to him, was just another cunt telling him he couldn't do something. He would hold no truck with that. Once a busy little man came around, claiming to be from some government department, and told Ron he could lose his licence for letting people smoke. Ron paid him no heed, and nobody ever saw the busy little man again.

Me, I've been smoking since I was six. I had my first cigarette when Johnny Scanlon robbed three Sweet Afton from his grandfather's box. He said he'd never realise and he was right because it turns out he had Alzheimer's disease and died a few months later. Not from Alzheimer's disease. He contracted a serious case of gastroenteritis and, given his already weakened state, quite literally shat himself to death one afternoon when the rest of the family were out. They had to move house in the end, unable as they were to remove the stench of death shit from the walls. Anyway, me, Jimmy the Bollix and Johnny Scanlon (who would later become a heroin-addicted chef that added his arm scabs to his sauces) were hanging around down by the canal in Kilmainham, we had a box of matches, and we all had our first fag together. We coughed, we spluttered, we did our best to inhale, we puked. We thought we were cool. When I went home, I told my mother that the reason my T-shirt was covered in vomit and I was grey in the face was because I saw a man get his head run over by a bus. The simple lies of a child.

Ron likes his bar the way it is. Traditional. Quiet. Unclean. A while back, some Trinity students decided they'd start drinking there because it was so different they thought it made them cool. I don't know how they even found the place. He tolerated it for one night, but when even more of them came back the next night, he knew he had to act.

Up to the bar went the scarf-wearing, blazer-sporting student with the ripped jeans and the weird spiky hair. 'Foive points of Hoyno,' he said.

Ron poured the five pints, placed them on the bar, then said, 'That'll be sixty euro, please.'

'Sixty euro? Are you, loike, out of your moind or something?'

Ron assured them he wasn't out of his 'moind' and to make it quite clear what the lay of the land was, he produced a baseball bat, which he keeps under the bar for emergencies such as this, and told them their teeth would become well acquainted with the end of it if they didn't pay up, drink up and leave. He never had another Trinity student in the bar. He likes to keep control over his clientele.

Not being men of the conventional nine-to-five life, I knew at least a couple of the lads would be there, it was open after all, and I was happy to see Jimmy the Bollix, Stinking Pete and Lucky Luciano sitting at the bar. Jimmy is my oldest friend, and, as his name suggests, he is a bollix. Not to me though. Well, not often. He's a tough man who has come through some difficult times. Jimmy's father loved *National Geographic* magazine, and there were always copies lying around the house (in fact, Stinking Pete thought all women's breasts should hang around their waists after spending way too much time in the bathroom with a copy he'd pilfered). For years and years, he worked overtime in his job as a Guinness bargeman to save as much money as possible to bring his family on a once-in-a-lifetime safari trip to Kenya. Jimmy, his parents and his elder brother, Johnny the Bollix, had a wonderful time ... until the last day, when their jeep was attacked by wild animals and the guide dragged from the driver's seat and eaten. As more and more big cats surrounded the vehicle, the family knew their lives were close to an end. Mr and Mrs the Bollix looked at each other, and, without speaking, they knew what had to be done.

'Son,' said Jimmy's father, 'remember we love you very much. And Johnny, you're all right too, for the most part. Take advantage of the distraction we'll cause and make good your escape.'

'No, Dad!' said a terrified Jimmy, but it was too late. Hand in hand, they got out of the car and were set upon by the wild beasts. As he put his foot to the floor, the last thing Jimmy saw was his father being raped by a gay panther and his mother being torn apart by lions.

He's always carried a lot of guilt with him about it, but he works it out through committing acts of violence and sending people who ask him for directions the wrong way completely. The shocking safari incident should have brought the two brothers closer, but while Jimmy is a bollix, his brother Johnny is a complete fucking cunt of a bollix.

Shortly after the funeral service – in which they buried a set of clothes for each parent because their bodies had been eaten then passed as waste on the savannah – Johnny forged his parents' signatures and falsified their will so that he was left the entire estate and Jimmy got nothing. Distraught, Jimmy moved to London and got involved in the 1980s synth scene and starred in Howard Jones' 'New Song' video as the bloke dancing in chains. Later, he went to America and fathered a child with a member of a famous all-girl band. Jimmy Junior comes to stay in Dublin quite often and isn't nearly as much of a bollix as his father. He's still learning though, and we try and teach him something new each time he comes. Last time, we taught him to tell the difference between Lithuanians and real people.

Lucky Luciano isn't, as his name suggests, particularly lucky, although he did once win €100 on a scratch card. He comes from Livorno, in Italy, and he is a compassionate assassin. This means he'll only kill somebody if he feels they deserve to die. And if the price is right, of course. He claims to have killed, amongst others, Princess Diana, Michael Hutchence from INXS and Shergar. I once asked him what exactly the horse did to deserve to die, but he wouldn't tell me, only saying that if I knew, I'd agree with him. Despite his sinister profession, he is entirely henpecked by his wife, Elisa, who insists he bring her to the cinema at least twice a week even though he absolutely hates going to the movies.

'Cazzo! Why I a want to go to place to see film when all around me is a people who eat like is end of world and will never get more food? Why is not a possible for people to eat the dinner or the lunch and a then go to see film? These a porks, they make a me sick,' he says every time he comes into Ron's after leaving his wife back home after their latest cinematic jaunt. When we ask him why he doesn't just tell his wife he doesn't want to go, he looks at us as if we're simpletons.

'Howya, Twenty!' said Stinking Pete.

'Not great, Pete. Had some bad news this morning. Ron, pint please.' I watched as Ron put a glass under the Guinness tap. Despite being the biggest shithole in town, Ron's has the best Guinness in Dublin.

'What happened?' asked Jimmy the Bollix.

'Remember Tom O'Farrell?'

'The lad whose brother ran off and married a priest?' asked Pete.

'No, that was Tommy Farrelly.'

'Ahhh, you mean the fella who used to work in the chipper and deep fried his own hand one time?'

'No, you fucking clown, that was Tim Farrell.'

'Ahhhhh, Tom O'Farrell. His Dad owned the first ever mobile kebab van in Ireland, and he used to wait around outside Tamango's every weekend and—'

'Pete, shut your hole,' I said. Pete shut his hole. 'I'm talking about Tom O'Farrell, my old mate who owned the record shop on Wicklow Street.'

'Never heard of him.'

'Give me strength,' I muttered.

Stinking Pete, as his name suggests, smells very badly indeed. He is also as stupid as a shoe, and that is being unkind to shoes. We have all, over the years, grown used to his odour, but at first, when we were but lads, it was slightly distracting to be out and about with someone who smelt like a decomposing goat. Through the years, we have become experts at sending him on pointless missions that are designed to get him out of our company as much as possible. Once we'd worn out all the old classics – 'Pete, nip down the hardware store and get me a glass hammer/a bucket of sparks/a tub of elbow grease – ' we had to get quite inventive. One time, we managed to dispatch him to Turkey and told him that it was imperative that he shot the Pope. Luckily for him, some local nutjob got blamed, and I have to admit he's been a little more cautious since then.

'What happened to him, Twenty?' asked Jimmy.

'Shot dead last night in the shop.' I told them about the call I got that morning from Larry O'Rourke and how Tom had been trying to ring me. I also mentioned the fact that he'd taken his shirt off and, using his own blood, written the number '60' across his chest.

'What do you reckon the sixty is about then?' said Ron.

'No idea. It could be anything. I told O'Rourke I'd let him know if we could think of anything.'

'I a tell you one thing,' said Lucky Luciano. 'The person who a kill your friend no is a good assassin. Is not good for to shoot somebody in a stomach. Can take a time to die and can a call police or fire brigade, or coastguard like Davids Hasselhoffer. Is two possibilities. First possibility, is a crap assassin.'

'What's the second, then?'

'Is – how you say in a Ireland? – a big, mean fucking a cunt.'

A crap assassin is not a particularly big worry. Look at the bloke who tried to kill Reagan. His ignominy faded. A successful assassin, on the other hand, was a powerful figure. Another Mark Chapman would not be welcome on the scene, particularly as it seemed he wasn't trying to do the decent thing and wipe out the remaining Beatles.

I had a feeling in my stomach that had nothing to do with the eight pints I'd had the night before. Nor the five gins, two Jamesons and the battered sausage and chips on the way home. Something strange was going on.

3

Thursday Morning

The day after Tom's funeral, which was a very sad affair brightened only by Stinking Pete tripping over a gravestone in Mount Jerome and landing face-first into the headstone and breaking his nose, we were sitting in Ron's at lunchtime. I'd been in touch with Larry O'Rourke to tell him we had no ideas about the '60'.

'You're as much use as a fish on a bicycle,' he said to me. I never thought to ask why he'd want a fish on a bicycle in the first place.

We spent hours at the bar, thinking about what it could possibly mean. Dirty Dave, another friend with very questionable personal hygiene but not quite as stupid as Stinking Pete, actually managed to tie the whole thing into a vast conspiracy that involved Opus Dei, JFK, the fact that man never really landed on the moon, the Freemasons, the Jewish cabal that supposedly runs the world and the American government. What was worse is that it actually made some sense at the time. In the cold light of day, however, it didn't seem to ring as true as it had done the night before. I'm not entirely sure why.

Before the funeral, Jimmy and I had broken into Tom's house to see if we could find anything there that might point us in the right direction. After a good search, we hadn't found much apart from a few magazines and photos that he kept in a secret compartment in his bedside locker. We thought it best to tear them up and bin them. We also went through his record collection and took a few things to help us remember our old friend and certainly not to sell on eBay because they were so rare. However, we didn't find anything that gave us the slightest clue to what his dying message meant. There was no diary, no secret file on his computer, no safe, no nothing. It was all very frustrating, more frustrating than trying to teach the difference between 'their', 'there' and 'they're' to a class full of Spanish dyslexics.

In Ron's, Dirty Dave had his argument that politicians should be expected to do immoral things roundly countered by Jimmy, who hates politicians like a racist politician hates having to kiss black babies.

'Shut up, Jimmy,' said Dave.

'Tell me shut up again, Dave, and I will insert this pint glass up your arse, then kick you in the hole so hard it'll end up in your bladder, then I'll punch you in the stomach, break the glass, then laugh as you piss shards of glass for a week.'

'Sorry, Jimmy,' said Dave and picked up the newspaper.

'I had a look at the number 60 on the old internet last night,' I said to Jimmy, 'I Wikipediaed the shite out of it. The only things that happened in the year 60 were Boudica sacking London and some Roman emperor called Pubilus doing something.'

'Pubilus. Hahaha.'

He has a childish sense of humour.

'What about the number sixty?' he asked.

'Well, sixty seconds in a minute, sixty minutes in an hour, maybe something to do with time?'

'Sixty is also the diamond wedding anniversary, if you can make it that far without going insane and killing your wife or your wife going insane and killing you.'

'Diamond, eh? Maybe there's a Pink Panther-style heist being planned, but why would Tom give a shit about that? Hah, I know what it is. Neil Diamond is planning to release a new album!'

'Gobshite. What about 1960? Did anything happen in 1960 that might be relevant?'

'Adolf Eichmann got caught by the Mossad. Could it be a Nazi conspiracy? Oh! Oh! JFK was elected. Perhaps Dave was onto something after all.'

'Don't be soft. Dave has the brain power of a dinosaur on a life-support machine.'

'This is hopeless, isn't it? We'll never figure out what the hell he meant. Why couldn't he have written, "I was killed by X for Y reason"?'

'He'd have needed a very big chest for a start.'

'Here, Twenty,' interrupted Dave, 'have a look at this.' He handed me the newspaper.

'Man dies in fatal donkey rape tragedy?'

'No! Underneath.'

'Taoiseach admits ten-year affair with Archbishop of Canterbury?'

'No, more underneath!'

'Oh sweet holy mother of the sacred heart of the crucified Jesus! This can't be happening. Oh fuck.'

'What is it?' asked Jimmy.

'It's the worst thing I have ever seen in my life. A free concert in the Phoenix Park. It's called Folkapalooza, and it features all your acousticy favourites, such as Damien Rice, David Gray, James Blunt—'

'Isn't he a racing driver?'

'You twat, Dave, that's James Hunt. Plus special guest star Bob Dylan along with countless other no-mark cunts who think that if they get up on stage with an acoustic guitar and sing in a whiney voice about how miserable their lives are people will like it. This is despicable.'

After that, I didn't feel like awareness of the world outside the bar was good for me, so we spent the rest of the afternoon drinking. By around eight o'clock, I decided I had to eat something and volunteered to go to the chipper around the corner, still run by an Italian family whose surname ended in a vowel. As I strolled back with the battered sausages, fresh cod and steaming hot chips, I didn't even notice the busker, standing on a street with practically no pedestrian traffic, singing a Damien Rice song.

4

Friday

I woke the next morning with a very sore head. After I'd coughed up a solid nugget of Major-inspired phlegm, I padded my way across the wooden floors to the kitchen to make coffee. My house is an old Victorian cottage on, or around, the South Circular Road. I've lived here since the day I was born, and I inherited the house when my folks died all those years ago.

My parents were ordinary, decent folk. My Mam was a housewife while my father was a burglar. Well, he was once. I know this because the house he burgled was the next-door neighbour's, and he brought me along as a look-out. I was ten years old. His real job wasn't quite so exciting. He was an assassin for the IRA. Okay, he was a postman. He loved his job, though. How can anyone not love getting up ridiculously early in the morning, rain or shine (it's Ireland though, so it's mostly rain with some bright intervals and north to north-easterly winds reaching gale force 2 at times), picking up a fucking big heavy bag and going from house to house, bending down to post the letters, thus giving yourself a lifetime of back troubles? Exactly. He was a very big man. At least six foot two, and he wasn't what you'd call skinny. He wasn't a big fat bastard like Mickey Nakajumi's dad, though. We used to tease Mickey a lot about it.

'Hands up whose dad is not a fat cunt!' we'd say, all putting our hands up while Mickey stood looking at the ground.

'Hands up whose dad isn't going to drop dead of a heart attack because he's a big, fat bastard who drinks too much beer and eats more than a small army!' we'd mock as we raised our hands in the air. The irony of Liam Feeney's skin-and-bone dad dropping dead of a heart attack just moments after he gleefully put his hand up was not lost on us as we watched him and his weeping brother make their way home.

'Hands up whose dad is a sumo wrestler!' we'd guffaw.

Funnily enough, we never slagged Mickey off for being a slanty-eyed yellow bastard, but I suppose kids only see what they want to see. My da was strict at home. He taught me manners, how to respect my elders and how to look after myself. One day, I came home from school after a rough day. There was one lad who was a bit of a bully and was giving me a hard time. My da wasn't the kind of man who taught you to turn the other cheek.

You had to stand up for yourself, and I'll never forget his words of advice that day.

'Son,' he said, 'if somebody hits you, then you have to hit them back twice as hard. Or wait until they're not looking and cave the back of their head in with a big fucking plank.'

With that in mind, I have to say he wasn't as understanding as I thought he would be when he was summoned to the school to rubber-stamp my expulsion after bully boy came off the worst in a game of headers with a piece of a tree I'd found during playtime. It was only on the way home that he imparted the 'Don't let anyone see you doing it' bit that he'd previously neglected to mention. Still, with that one incident, my reputation in the neighbourhood was made. I wasn't the biggest, but the other kids knew I wouldn't be picked on, that I had easy access to heavy branches and I knew how to use them. It has stood me in good stead over the years.

As for my mam, well, she was just brilliant. She looked after me like a Mormon looks after his favourite wife, keeping beatings to an absolute minimum. I wasn't overly stressed when people scolded me for doing things wrong. At an early age, I developed a capacity to ignore authority and seniority and just get on with doing whatever I wanted. My mam was the only one who could make me feel bad about stuff.

'Oh, Twenty,' she'd say, 'you really shouldn't have set fire to that car which caused three houses to go on fire and all those children to be hideously scarred,' and I'd feel slightly rueful about it. Or she'd give out to me for shoplifting, and I would be penitent, even when I shoplifted nice things for her birthday and Christmas presents. There's a moment in every person's life that he can look back on with a clarity that he might not have if he thought about something that happened the day before. My moment is the day she caught me stealing a few pence from her purse. Not much, just enough to get a few bulls' eyes and a couple of smokes that they sold in singles out of an old glass in the local shop. To this day, I don't remember what she said. She probably didn't say anything, and that's what made it so bad. There was an all-encompassing shame that I could let her down like that. I can remember wanting the ground to swallow me up and eat me whole (not eat me hole), and for days she wouldn't look at me. I still cringe, and my face burns, even thinking about it. It did teach me an important lesson about life, though: if you're going to do bad things, don't shit on your own doorstep, and if you're going to steal, make sure you don't get caught. She taught me that, something I'll forever be grateful for, and if she was looking down on me now, she'd say, 'Get on with the story and stop being such a sentimental old tart. And clean up your room.'

I looked out the window into the back garden, which was paved and pebbled for maximum convenience. I do not mow. A large apple tree stood in the bottom half, its enormous branches ripening with fruit that tasted like you were taking a bite out of Satan's armpit. I turned on the kettle, then opened up the back door and gave a whistle. From a large kennel emerged an enormous head, blinking at the sunshine. The head was soon followed by enormous shoulders, an enormous back and the rest of my enormous dog, who is called Bastardface. He went across to the big tree in the middle of the garden and took care of his morning ablutions before making his way inside. He headbutted me on the hip, his normal morning greeting, as I made coffee and remembered how much I hate it when people take half a page to describe how they make a cup of fucking coffee. Yeah, we get it. You have an expensive coffee machine. Just don't waste my time telling me about it in your book. I don't fucking care.

I've had Bastardface since he was a very small puppy, although it's hard to believe anything that large could ever have been so small. I rescued him from a scumbag myself and Jimmy had to talk to about some money he'd been lent and hadn't paid back. He lived in an isolated house, out beyond the airport, and when we got there he was attending to something in his back garden. We came around the side without announcing ourselves, and when he saw us, he came running up the garden.

'Howdy Twenty, Jimmy,' he said. 'I've got an envelope for you right here.'

He handed the money to Jimmy who counted it and declared everything to be in order. I didn't like the look on his face, though, and wanted to know what he was up to. I have this innate curiosity about things, which I try to ignore but often can't. For example, if I see a queue outside a cinema, then I'm not bothered in the slightest. If I see a queue without any obvious explanation for what those people are queuing for, it bothers the shite out of me.

What if it's something amazing? Why don't I know about it? What if it's something so cool they haven't even put a sign up to tell the people queuing why they should be queuing because they're so cool they already know? It's a bother, I have to say.

'What are you up to down there?' I asked yer man.

'Ahh, a bit of pest control is all,' he said. 'So, your money's all there. I'll be seeing you, gents.'

'What kind of pest control?' I asked, looking over his shoulder.

'Just vermin. Nothing important.'

The look on his face, which said, 'Please get out of here and stop asking me questions,' was too much for me. I pushed past him, and, despite his cries, I continued down to the bottom of the garden, where a big black sack looked to be piled full of gardening crap. It was full of puppies. Puppies with their heads bashed in by the spade sitting beside the sack. Only one was left alive, with his mouth held shut with black insulating tape. He was afraid and trembling, having seen his brothers, sisters and runts beaten to death before his doleful brown eyes. He looked up at me. I'll never forget that moment. It was special. It wasn't quite Dr Doolittle, but it was almost as if he was speaking to me with his eyes. 'Save me,' they said, 'and give that cunt a beating too, would ya?'

So I did. I rescued him, and, while Jimmy held our friend, I showed him how it felt to be hit in the head with a spade. Repeatedly. We didn't kill him, but the fact that he's referred to locally as Drooling Mick should tell you enough.

On the way home, Jimmy asked me what I was going to call the dog. 'Rover? Patch? Spot?'

'Nah, look at him. He's got the face of somebody born out of wedlock. Hello, Bastardface,' I said.

After I finished my coffee, I fed Bastardface his breakfast of a leg of lamb and was on my way for a shower when the doorbell rang. I hate when the doorbell rings. I peeked out the spy-hole and saw it was the postman. I opened up.

'Hello, Posty,' I said, 'what has you ringing on my door this morning?'

'Registered letter for you, Twenty,' he said. 'And you might want to bring your cat in.'

I looked up, and in the cherry-blossom tree in the front garden, the cat Bastardface and I had rescued down on the canal while out for a walk was taking on a family of magpies who were determined to peck his eyes out. Throatripper, that's the cat's name, see, was lying on a branch, ears flat, making a sound worse than Ireland's last Eurovision entry and lashing out with his razor-sharp claws.

'Cheers, Posty,' I said and went over to the tree. The birds scattered, and the cat looked at me like I'd just put a thermometer up his arse. He does love to kill things, and cats do love to bring their masters presents. Many a cat owner has come out to find a bird or a mouse or a rat spat at them as a thank-you from their feline friend. One morning, I found an ostrich, dead as Princess Diana, on the back step. How the fuck he got it over the wall I'll never know.

'Get down off there,' I said to him, and he climbed down and jumped straight onto the back of the dog, who was seeing the postman out (he never so much as barks at Posty, but anyone unknown who comes through the front gate is in trouble. I do have a 'Beware of the dog' sign though. I must put it up one of these days) and the two of them took off through the house and out the back.

I opened the letter, which turned out to be from DHL, who had delivered something to me a few weeks earlier. Apparently, I should have paid duty on it, and I now owed them €12.17. Taxes are for cunts. I scrunched the letter into a ball, threw it in the bin and went to shower. Afterwards, I had another coffee, a cigarette and 1,200 milligrammes of Ibuprofen and sat down at my computer to write my blog. With Folkapalooza coming up soon, I vented my spleen at its general lameness but drew far fewer comments agreeing that it was crap than I would normally have expected. Odd.

Afterwards, I headed into town to meet Jimmy to consult about a very important upcoming business meeting. The people in question were about to call in a favour and we were in no position to turn it down. It was a nice day, so I decided to stroll in. Even though we've got more grey days than any other, when the sun is out in Dublin it makes everybody's mood better. Cab drivers keep the casual racism to a minimum, people lounge around on the grass in St Stephen's Green and even the tourists dispense with their umbrellas, rain jackets and galoshes. I strolled down past Patrick's Cathedral, through the adjacent park and made my way onto George's Street.

As I was meeting Jimmy in Mulligan's on Poolbeg Street (which has the second-best Guinness in town, after Ron's), I went down onto Dame Street, down the side of Trinity College and crossed over by the Screen cinema.

People were bustling around, laughing, enjoying the good weather, but something struck me as odd. I couldn't quite put my finger on it, although it nagged at me like a Jewish wife. Jimmy and I arrived at the pub at the same time, and I ordered two pints from the barman. As well as being my best friend, Jimmy and I are business partners. People often ask us what it is we do and when we do it. For the most part, I avoid answering those kinds of questions. When I tell people I'm a shepherd, that's as much information as I'm willing to give, and any attempt to get into a discussion about the mechanics of modern shepherding is shot down quicker than a Korean passenger jet in Russian airspace. I suppose you could call us 'consultants', but I don't particularly want to be associated with those lazy cunts who pretend to work in hospitals but most of the time send along some underling because they're in the middle of eighteen holes at the K Club. I don't want to be tarred with that brush. Suffice to say, we do things that people ask us to do and often do things despite people asking us not to do them.

'So, what are we going to do about this situation?' he asked.

'When's the meeting?'

'When they decide. Yer man's out of town now. It could be tricky, you know.'

'Well, after what happened previously we can't say no.

They know that. They're going to call in their marker now.'

'Seems like it. I wonder what they want.'

'Me too, man.'

We drank our pints and speculated what it might be. We were on the cusp of getting something together, which was probably so far off-course it might have been a Dublin bus driver trying to go around a tight corner, when it struck me.

'Guitars!' I exclaimed.

'What the fuck have guitars got to do with anything?' said a clearly disturbed Jimmy.

'So many guitars. When I was walking through town, I knew something was a bit different, but I couldn't put my finger on it. There were lots of people carrying acoustic guitars around with them. That's what it was.'

'Oh, it wasn't a slight change in the public mood then? Or the sky being a strange shade of blue that might mean some inclement weather or an attack by aliens?'

'Eh?'

'Just saying that if lots of people were going around carrying fucking guitars, it's not too difficult to spot, is it? It's not like everyone wearing odd socks or something. You are as observant as a government official inspecting extraordinary rendition flights and finding golf clubs and horses instead of shackled and badly beaten Arabs.'

'Yeah, well, it doesn't matter that it took me some time to work it out, the point is that I did work it out and now I know what it was, and now that I've told you, you know what it was too.'

'Jesus Christ,' said Jimmy and then finished his pint in one swallow. 'I'm off to buy some music that I can play really loud and annoy my neighbours, who are too afraid to ask me to turn it down. Something rocky, I think.'

'Soundtrack to *Rocky*?'

'You cunt,' he said and got up. 'See you in Ron's later.'

I watched him walk out, and, as I had nowhere else to be that afternoon, I ordered another pint and pondered the guitar-wielding types I'd seen around earlier. All aged around eighteen to twenty-five, all of them with a bit of scruffy beard, but the kind of scruffy beard somebody who can't really grow a beard grows. Not like my beard, which is mighty and bushier than any kind of bush you want to hold up against it. I was, deep down, a little uneasy though. Wispy beards weren't the 'in' thing with the kids these days. It was stubble or a chin stripe or one of those tufts of hair under the bottom lip that were trendy. 'Maybe there are a lot of recent Irish conversions to Islam,' I thought to myself, but I know the youth of Ireland. It's hard enough to get the cunts out of bed to go to school or work or college. There's no way you'd get them up at 4.00am for their first prayers of the day.

I put it to the back of my mind, took out my book (I carry a book with me at all times) and read about a detective covered in pond scum trying to impress a new client. I sat back in my chair and settled in for a while.

🎧 🎧 🎧 🎧 🎧

After I left Mulligan's, I strolled around the corner to Pearse Street garda station and popped in to see if Larry O'Rourke had made any progress with the investigation into Tom's death. As I got to the door, I saw him outside, talking on his mobile phone. He raised a hand to acknowledge me, listening intently, then began bellowing a reply.

'Look, they're a pack of scumbags, no two ways about it! We can either do this by the book, in which case we'll get ourselves kicked all over the place, or we can take the law into our own hands a bit. Fight fire with fire, if you like. They won't be expecting it from us, so from the off we go in hard. Elbows, knees, sly punches, possibly a bit of truncheon action, we'll put them completely on the back foot and take control of the situation rather than respond to what they might do. Understand? Grand. Well make sure they fucking know. Okay, talk to you later.'

He hung up.

'Sorry, Twenty, the young fella's football team are playing this bunch of toe-rags from Foxrock this weekend. Niggly pack of fuckers, they are. Always fouling and looking for trouble. Just making sure we're not caught out. Any news for me?'

'Not a thing, I'm sorry to say. What about you?'

'We've made as much progress as the government in solving the health-care crisis.'

'So, you've gone backwards then.'

We both roared with laughter until we simply couldn't laugh anymore.

'Seriously, though, it's a total mystery. The forensics people have been all over the scene and done all their hi-tech stuff with the evidence they collected, and they haven't found a thing. Obviously there were millions of fingerprints because of all the people coming in and picking up the records and CDs, but nothing came from that. There were all sorts of skin flakes and hairs all over the place, your pal's cleaner only came once a week, but nothing from them either. Tell me, though, did Tom have pets?'

'No, he was completely allergic to dogs, cats, turtles, budgies, goldfish, hamsters, gerbils, mice and pot-bellied pigs. The only thing he could have had as a pet was a rhino, but he felt they were a little too big and a little too stabby for him. Why do you ask?'

'Just something the forensics mentioned. They found some hairs they couldn't really identify. Not human and not from any animal they have in their database. They think it might be related to a sheep, but nobody keeps sheep in a two-bedroom house in Rialto. Not these days anyway. The hairs were a strange colour, too. Sort of white, but sort of ginger too.'

'White and ginger? Jesus, that sounds truly terrible. Perhaps a very old ginger person who hadn't quite lost all their gingervitis?'

'No, like I said, the techs couldn't identify the beast these hairs came from. Anyway, I'd best get inside. Crimes to solve and all that.'

'Yeah, good luck with that. You're top of the charts at the moment, eh?'

'Shove it up your hole, Twenty,' he said as the door slammed behind him.

Not having anything to shove up my hole and not being very much inclined to do that anyway, I headed to that place where everybody knows your name.

Home.

5

Friday Evening

(Elsewhere in Dublin)

The ginger albino sat alone in his spartan room. Only a formica table with a deck of Power Rangers Top Trumps and a cheap old radio broke up the space. There was a small bookcase in the far corner with old paperbacks whose paper has gone that gloomy yellow kind of colour. He sighed as he thrashed at his back with guitar strings. This self-flagellation was something he had learned during his time in that dark place, the place he had pushed so far down in his mind it was almost leaking out of his arse.

The pain comforted him, and he felt confident and

assured of his destiny. It was a long way from his childhood, which had been a difficult time. His name was not Seamus then, but he could no longer recall the name given to him by his parents. At ten years of age he had left home, never to return. His father, a bull of a man who worked his farm every day of his life, constantly beat his mother, blaming her for the freak of nature she had given birth to. His anger was fueled by locals in the village pub who made fun of him and his bizarre son, with his shock of orange hair and almost translucent skin. Whenever Seamus tried to defend his mother, he too got a hiding.

One evening, there was a terrible fight, and his mother hit her head on the side of the fireplace. She never woke up, and the boy felt an incredible guilt at what had happened.

'This is all because I'm a ginger mutant! Why could I not have been born with a mighty hump or some other hideous deformation, like webbed fingers, instead of the ginger gene?'

Later that night, after his father had come home from the pub and collapsed on the bed reeking of pink gins and cosmopolitans, he decided what he had to do. He went to the shed, took a large spade and returned to the bedroom where his snoring father lay. Looking back at the stiffening corpse of his mother, he raised the instrument and cleaved his father's head nearly in two. To make sure, he beat him until there was little more than pulp where the head used to be. Lost in the madness he picked bits of the brains from his hair and ate them like you'd eat a freshly picked yet deliciously crunchy snot.

After that, he left his house and flitted from place to

place, stealing to eat and drink, sleeping rough and doing what he had to survive (manual labour, mushroom-picking, karaoke host). The years passed, and he grew more intro-spective, shying away from human contact, until one day, in desperation, he broke into a big house south of Dublin. Little did he know that the house belonged to a very famous person who shied away from all publicity, despite their worldwide renown.

Safe behind her steel door, the celebrity looked on in wonder as her security system fed her images of Seamus gorging himself from the fridge, smoking cigarettes, drinking fine wines from the cellar and twelve-year-old Scotch from the drinks thingy, which was in the shape of a globe, before finally passing out many hours later.

When Seamus woke, he found himself in a warm bed, the fine sheets soft against his skin, the sun shining through the window. Sitting in a chair at the end of the bed was the owner of the house.

'I could have you arrested, you know,' she said in that curious voice of hers.

Seamus said nothing.

'I'm not going to do so. What is your name?'

'I … I … do not remember,' he said.

'Well, you look like a great big Seamus to me. So that is what I shall call you. Great Big Seamus. Do you know why I won't hand you over to the police, Seamus?'

He shook his head.

'It is because I have been waiting for you for years. I knew you would come one day and that you would become useful to me, like a lightbulb for a lamp. You will work for me, and I will reward you with money, clothes, food and from time to time I will allow you to lap at my vagina like a dog licks his own balls. Would you like that, Seamus?'

Thinking of the terrible things he'd done down the years to survive, Seamus figured this wasn't so bad at all. He nodded his head.

'Good,' she said. 'Now rest some more. Soon our work will begin. It will be long and difficult, like a contrary python, but you, and only you, have the skills I need.'

Since then, Seamus's life had been better. The money was enough to buy small things, but he did not care for material goods. Once he had warm clothes and a roof over his head, he was happy. The work was inspiring to him. At last, he was no longer just a 'ginger freak' now he was somebody they feared. Somebody who garnered respect. Somebody who would no longer be pointed at and laughed at. Well, children still pointed and laughed at him, but children were stupid. His mission sustained him. He took up the guitar strings again and began to self-flagellate, going, 'Oooooh … mmmmm … ahhhhhh' as he felt the blood begin to trickle down his back. Everything was on course. Nothing could go wrong. He turned on the radio to listen to the fat man who looked like a bulldog. That always brought him peace, and a mild erection.

He thrashed some more and smiled.

6

Friday Night

Sitting in Ron's, later that evening, I was in rare auld form, as they say. Having filled myself with a good gallon of Arthur's finest, I was holding court in style, telling the lads a story about my time as an artist in Barcelona many years before.

'So I had this studio apartment in an area called Gracia. It's all very bohemian up there, full of artists and actors and poets and various other kinds of people who don't wash very often. Not me though. I washed a lot. I was known as the most fragrant artist in all of Barcelona. Now, my work was rather abstract because of my working methods. For nine months of the year, I did nothing, then for three months I'd smoke all the amazingly strong marijuana I'd grown over the summer and ensconce myself in my studio and churn out the canvases like nobody's business. I didn't do boring stuff like portraits or landscapes though, I simply painted picture after picture of my own scrotum.

Now, Barcelona, being Europe's answer to San Francisco, was full of people who would hang enormous paintings of somebody's testicles on their wall and really enjoy looking at them, so I was never short of a buyer for my work. This meant I had a three-month working year and spent nine months smoking the rest of the grass and drinking absinthe cocktails in the Raval area of town. I'm telling you, you've never hallucinated until you've hallucinated on that stuff. Anyway, I kept my work fresh and "now" so my reputation as the finest scrotum artist grew and grew.

However, one year, it turned out I had competition. An Albanian artist had come to town and not only was he painting his ball bag, he was giving them pictures of his chopper, too. Now, there was really only so much of myself that I was willing to share in oils and acrylics, so this guy, whose name was Aidoof, began to eat a bit into my market, and this was not good. I only met him one time. I was sitting in a bar eating mussels and drinking a beer, and I was approached by a man who pointed out Aidoof to me and said he'd like to buy me a drink. "Tell him I'll have a pint of absinthe," I said, knowing artists are notoriously tight-fisted and he'd never go for it. Sadly, this cunt had to be the exception to the rule and there in front of me sat a pint of the green liquid. He came over to sit with me, sporting a tiny chupito of local brandy, and we spoke for a while about our rivalry.

"I will crush you, and all the world will know that Aidoof is the greatest painter of marbles and pogo-stick in the whole wide world. Globally. On an international level."

"Yeah, well, you talk all you want my be-helmeted friend. I've been around the block. I've got something you don't have and will never have."

"What's that then?" he asked.

"One testicle much, much larger than the other one. Cheers!" I said and raised my glass. He downed his brandy. I swallowed my pint in one go. There were audible gasps all around the bar at the sheer audacity, nay, lunacy of my action, but I couldn't let this fucker show me up.

"Now, I bid you good day, Sir," I said and marched out of the bar. I got about halfway home when gravity stopped working. I woke up, many hours later, face-down under a bench on Rambla Catalunya, clutching a battered umbrella I had no recollection of taking with me. I swore I would never drink again. Obviously, though, I came to my senses. However, the problem still remained. This rival artist could steal many of my clients, which would mean less money, which would mean I would have to work more, and no fucking Albanian ponce was going to make me work more.

As luck would have it, word seeped out onto the artists' grapevine that Bryan Adams, the world's biggest collector of paintings of scrotums, would soon be visiting Barcelona and was coming flush with cash because he had a brand-new house in the Hollywood Hills to deck out with artwork. So, with that in mind, I threw myself into my work. I painted night and day, all the while stoned off my head, and I have to say, in all modesty, that some of the pictures I created are up there with the very best scrotum pictures you've ever seen. Not even the offspring of Michelangelo and Picasso could have done better.

My sources were telling me that Aidoof was doing the same, working like a demon in his studio not 500 yards from mine. But I put him out of my head. I had to concentrate on myself. Then came news that many other testicle artists were coming to town and Adams would be casting his beady little Canadian eyes over all of them. Dammit, this wasn't supposed to happen. But I had faith in my work, and I was sure the quality of it would see me right.

What happened in the end was that Bryan Adams hired a massive hall in which all artists could showcase their work. On the day in question, I brought my best three or four pieces down, as did everyone else. I was heartened when I saw the competition though. Aidoof apart, the rest of them were shabby amateurs. The quality of their scrota were so poor, there was no way he'd buy them ahead of mine, but I had to admit that the Albanian's work was pretty damn good, even if it did feature his langer.

So, we all hung our canvases, and, eventually Adams arrived and wandered around, looking at everything. He hummed and hahed, tutted, shook his head and even laughed openly at a couple, but when he got to Aidoof's stuff, he took his time, examined the images carefully and looked very interested indeed. He had a few more to see *before he got to mine, and the reaction to them was negative as well. When he came around to view my works, I knew he was impressed by the way he kept saying, "Damn, I'm impressed." He spent a little longer with mine than my competitors', and I was feeling confident. I could see Aidoof across the hall, looking at me, slightly worried. Surely my reputation would win the day for me.*

"I can't decide, so I'm going to get me some tapas, have a think and then make a decision," Bryan Adams announced, leaving us to bite our nails and smoke anxiously. The wait was interminable, but eventually he returned and went straight to Aidoof's pictures. Then to my pictures. Then back to his. Then to mine again. It was like torture. Then he just stood in the middle of the room with his hand under his chin like some kind of thinker. I couldn't stand it any longer. I had to know, so I marched right up to him.

"Listen here," I said. "You've had more than enough time. I know a man has to consider which pictures of leathery old sacs he spends his money on, but you've got to make your mind up now. Whose pictures are you going to buy?"

He paused for a moment and then spoke.

"Everything, Aidoof," he said. My heart sank. "Aidoof or you."'

'Oh, Jesus Christ on a holy bike, Twenty,' said Ron, 'you are a fucking horrible cunt and no mistake.'

'I hate you, Twenty,' said Jimmy the Bollix.

And so the evening continued in such a vein, with raucous stories and high spirits until, around 10pm, something happened. Dirty Dave was explaining to us why he'd rather be an anteater than an ant when I saw Ron's face change. Normally stony at the best of times, it was like somebody had pissed in his chips. He was staring at the door. I turned to look, and I guess the look on my face made Stinking Pete look, and the look on his face made Jimmy the Bollix turn around, and that's when things got tense, for there, standing in the doorway, was Jimmy's brother, Johnny, who nobody, least of all Jimmy, had seen in over twenty years.

Even someone as stupid as Dirty Dave knew there was something up, and he stopped his inane tale to see what was going on.

'Oh fuck,' he said when he saw who it was.

Jimmy stood up, cracked his neck from side to side and finished his pint. He turned and walked towards his brother. The tension was unbearable. I was waiting for the first punch to land but without even acknowledging him, Jimmy just walked straight out the front door. Johnny didn't look back and came over to where we were.

'You're a brave man to show your face around here,' said Ron.

'What has you back?', I asked him.

'I have to make peace with him, Twenty,' he replied. 'The thing is … I'm dying.'

It took all my strength not to run around the bar going 'Woo hoo' as if I'd scored the winning goal in the last minute of the cup final.

7

Saturday

Jimmy lives not far from me, down behind the South Circular Road. Quiet roads, old Dublin, lots of houses broken into flats and, thanks to the nearby mosque, a large Muslim population. Jimmy knew all the local bigwigs: Abdul, Mohammed and the bloke with the crutches who spends all day walking up and down between the Headline Bar and the National Stadium. This was the house he bought when he returned to Ireland after some years away. It was quite minimalist inside, with the odd painting hung against the painted yellow walls. Upstairs, he had knocked two bedrooms together to make a pool room, but when advised the weight of the water and the tub would collapse the ceiling, he put in a snooker table instead.

I sat around in Jimmy's kitchen the next day listening to him rant.

'That fucking cunt. He's got some nerve coming back here. After all this time. I swore to myself if he ever came within six feet of me again I'd rip his fucking head off and shit down his neck. And what did I do? I walked out. Jimmy the Bollix? Jimmy the fucking great pansy, more like. Man, I hate him, but at the same time I can't be as horrible to him as I can to other people that I hate. Perhaps that's because he's the last family I've got left, and he is my older brother, after all. What did the fuck did he want anyway?'

'He says he's dying.'

'Haha, good enough for him. Did one of those fish that swims up your mickey while you're having a piss into a river swim up his mickey?'

'Nope. Leukaemia. He says he wants to make his peace with you before he dies.'

'Hmmmm, that's not as good as a fish swimming up his mickey but effective nonetheless. Did he say how long he's got left? A matter of days, hopefully.'

'Nah, he didn't say. He does want to speak to you though.'

'Fuck him. Seriously.'

'Well, he is your only family, as you say, and, if he's dying, what difference does it make?'

'What are you, his fucking agent? There's more to this than meets the eye, Twenty. That slippery bollix is up to something, or he wants something, you just wait and see.'

'Well, you can do what you want, man. I'm not going to try and influence you one way or the other. Not that I could anyway. He left me a card with his mobile number which you can use, throw in the bin, clean your fingernails with, whatever. You know how I feel about the cunt.'

I left the card on the table.

'So, did you pick up your collection of Gilbert O'Sullivan CDs yesterday then?'

'Ahhh,' replied Jimmy, 'funny thing that. I meant to say something to you last night in Ron's, but between your interminable stories and that other fucker showing up it went right out of my mind. I went into HMV on Grafton Street, and I was struck by how much hippy, drippy, acoustic shite there was there. All the other sections seem to have shrunk. I asked the manager about it, and he seemed curiously reticent to talk about it, and you know how much record-shop managers like to talk. Just muttered something about there being less demand for other types of music and scuttled off as quickly as he could. I tried a couple of other shops, and it was the same. Eventually, I found something in Freebird Records, but even in there there was lots of that other shite. Odd. Really odd.'

'Maybe it's like punk, techno, Estonian acid house music or some other craze. It'll die out, I'm sure.'

'I dunno, there's something very weird about it.'

'Weird like seeing a woman with a goat's head fucking a man with two cocks, or weird like how-the-fuck-did-anyone-think-Bryan-McFadden-might-be-a-successful-solo-artist?'

'Er … both? I don't fucking know which kind of weird it is. It's just weird. Leave it at that.'

'Maybe it's the kind of weird tha—'

'I said, leave it at that.'

Sometimes it's just best to do what Jimmy says, even if he is my best friend.

I left him to his hard-to-come-by new music and headed off. As it was Saturday afternoon and there was no football to watch, home was the boring option, so I decided to wander into town. Sometimes I like to just stroll around my city and pretend to follow people as if I'm a private detective. I'll let them see me, then follow them into a shop and stare at them, and, when they see me staring at them, I look away in a hurry, like I'm up to no good. Then I might sit in a café and read a newspaper but cut eye-holes in the newspaper and make sure they see me. It's all good fun. For me, anyway. The Central Bank on Dame Street is always a good place to start – a place where hundreds of people get off their buses every hour. There's always somebody worth following, and, while I am waiting for the perfect target, there are the hordes of Goths – or Emos as they're known these days – to amuse me. Boys with make-up on, leather trenchcoats down to the ground of which the Columbine boys would be proud were they not completely dead, baggy jumpers, piercings, girls who look more like Robert Smith from The Cure than Robert Smith from The Cure trying to smoke joints surreptitiously, and all manner of moping, misery and non-conformist conformity.

'We are all individuals,' they practically shout. 'Look how different we are from all of you!' their body language shrieks, as they scut about the place being exactly the same as each other.

I headed straight there now, but when I got there, it seemed some of them actually were individuals, different, properly non-conformist. Mixed amongst the Goths were guys and girls wearing blue jeans (some ripped at the knee, some not), white shirts and brown suede jackets. Some of them carried acoustic guitars, some of them played their acoustic guitars and, fucking stone me, with box of ancient rocks, some of them were singing along to the strumming weirdos. This was most odd. Normally, the kids who hung around at the Central Bank wanted everyone to know how miserable life was and all that shite, but they weren't prepared to sing out loud about it. That would have been lame and possibly a bit gay. Looking closer, it seemed that this lot even outnumbered the ones in the black clothes. Something very strange was happening. I approached a girl of about eighteen or nineteen, who was staring at the ground smoking a cigarette.

'What the fuck is going on here?' I asked.

'I'm staring at the ground to see if the mirror of my soul reflects the beauty inside of me.'

'Oh Jesus. Not with you. I meant, who are all these kids with the guitars? I thought this place was for Goths only.'

'Gorks.'

'Huh?'

'Gorks. My dad says we're Gorks. That's Goths crossed with dorks.'

'Right. Your dad probably has a very good point.

Anyway, leaving your father's astute observations to one side, why are they here?'

'They have always been here.'

'What, like the eternal spirits of your tormented soul?'

'No, you beardy old shite, they've always been here. They used to be like us. Then they changed. A couple one week, a couple more the week after, then more the week after that, then some more the following week, then seven days later—'

'Alright, I get you. Why did they change though? What turned them from miserable, introspective cunts wearing black clothes and make-up to miserable, introspective cunts wearing slightly hippy clothes?'

'I don't know. It's like a plague. They just say that one day we'll see the light and that the light will be all light and stuff, and not dark, but light light is crap light. I much prefer my light to be a darker kind of light or, more precisely, dark.'

'Yeah, you keep on keeping on there. Have you not asked any of them what made them change? Surely some of them must have been your friends. Well, perhaps not friends, but whatever approximation you lot make to that kind of emotional attachment.'

'They say that time will show us the way, but they make me feel a bit sick. They always want to talk about how depressed and terrible things are, and, worse than that, they want to write and sing songs about it, and in reality, most of them aren't miserable at all. They come from middle-class families, go to good schools and universities, have never really wanted for anything in their lives, go home to a full fridge, warm house, widescreen TV, internet access, PlayStations, Xboxes, Wiis, DVDs, two cars in the driveway, and the worst thing that ever happened to them was some freckly bird called Sorcha wouldn't get off with them at the school disco. Gimps.'

'Er ... fair enough. What's your name then?'

'Sorcha.'

'Oooookaaaaaaay. Thanks for talking to me Sorcha. Stay dark.'

'I will, Beardy.'

I left her there, staring at the ground, smoking her cigarette, still unable to see the mirror of her soul. Not unless there was something else in her cigarettes than PJ Carroll's finest tobacco. After looking around a bit more, I didn't really feel in the mood for making someone think they were being followed or stalked by someone who might possibly murder them. I figured I'd go look in some of the record shops to see if I could see what Jimmy was talking about. I wandered up from Dame Street to Wicklow Street to Tower Records then up to HMV, and it was exactly as Jimmy had said. The aisles were the same size, but the majority of the shelf space, in-store advertising and even the 'Top Twenty' sales charts were dominated by guys with varying types of bushy and wispy beards, with their acoustic guitars, singing about how their only love had left them and how life was so utterly unfathomable without this only love. Stupid cunts. There are lots of other girls out there, some of them so desperate they would actually have sex with one of these people, if only they'd get out to a nightclub of a Saturday night instead of staying home pretending to drink hard and smoking roll-ups because they're too fucking cheap to buy packets of real cigarettes.

It was more than I could take. I needed to feel the warm embrace of my stool at the end of Ron's bar, the idle, inane chatter of the lads, some pints, a good smoke and some quality chipper food on the way home. I span on my heels like a private dancer, a dancer for money, and headed out of HMV. On the way, out I saw the number one and two album positions were taken up by Damien Rice. Oh man, I really hated that guy.

As I left, something, like a thought being on the tip of your tongue – which is obviously not where you have thoughts, but you know what I mean – made me turn back and look at them again. Damn. It had gone. Whatever it was though, it was something. There was no question about that. It was something to do with something.

8

Monday

(One week PM — post-murder)

It was on a Monday, one week after Tom's death, when the first breakthrough came. It was lunchtime in Ron's, and, as none of us really felt like working, there was a good crowd of us in there, shooting the breeze, discussing politics, world economics and other important social issues (although Dave and Pete were discussing how much they'd have to be paid to get it on with the redhead from Girls Aloud. They'd agreed around €1.50 would do it for them). Ron had the TV on to catch the lunchtime news on RTÉ and during the break an ad came on the TV for Folkapalooza.

'Don't forget folks, on bank holiday Monday June 7th, Mega Gigs presents the biggest free concert in the history of free concerts. EVER! All your folk favourites all day long, playing all your favourite acoustic music. Join James Blunt, David Gray, Damien Rice, Brian Kennedy and special guest Bob Dylan and many more in the Phoenix Park for free. Absolutely free. That's right. It'll cost you nothing ... tangible [muttered]... so come down and join us for Folkapalooza. It's folktacular in folkstrousness. That's Folkapalooza with thanks to Mega Gigs.'

'Christ,' said Jimmy, 'that really looks like a load of interminable bollocks. Can you imagine the tedium?'

'It'd be even worse than that time Banal Billy came over one Sunday.'

Banal Billy was a guy we knew some years back, and, while he was a very nice chap, he was possibly the dullest person alive. One Sunday afternoon, I was lying on the sofa with my head pounding from the previous night that had turned into the very early morning. I lay there, inside the house, with my sunglasses on to keep the light from burning my retinas out when the doorbell went. Of all the people in the world it might have been – an axe murderer, Hitler's grandson, Pat Kenny, it was Banal Billy. I had no choice but to invite him in, and, after I'd made him a cup of coffee I lay back down on the couch as he whittered on about something or other. The next thing I knew, it was completely dark and he had gone. Looking at my watch, I realised that I'd been asleep for three hours and had fallen asleep while he was talking to me. That's how fucking dull he was.

'What I don't understand,' said Ron, 'is why this concert is free. I might be at odds with the modern world but I understand concert promotion well enough. What's going on there?'

'Good point,' said Jimmy. 'Let's not forget this Mega Gig crowd have a bit of a reputation as money-grabbing bastards at the best of times, so why on Earth would they go to the trouble and expense of putting on a free gig?'

'It's all very suspicious, I have to say'

We went back to watching the news in order to keep up to date with the main stories of the day. I drank beer while doing it. I'm a man of simple pleasures, really.

A little later, Splodge came in. Splodge is one of the regulars in the bar, and he got his name because he has an enormous birthmark on one side of his face. Some birthmarks on people's faces make them look a bit deformed, but some-how Splodge suits his one. It looks rough and menacing, and he does too. He's generally very quiet and rarely smiles, which adds to his threatening appearance, but when he does speak, it's worth listening to. Like the time there was a table full of lads shrieking and roaring at the top of their voices. Sure, they were drunk, but everybody could hear everything they said, and one of them had a very, very annoying laugh. Ron was about to go over and tell them to leave when Splodge got up and walked over to the table. We didn't hear what he said, but the lads immediately shut up, drank up and left within two minutes.

'Fucking hell, Splodge. What did you say to them?', asked Dirty Dave. 'Well,' he replied taking a slug of his pint,

'I just said that if they didn't shut up and leave I'd rub my birthmark on their faces.'

So, as you might imagine, it was a massive surprise when he came in and told us all how great it was to see us and how much he really enjoyed our company and how much he loved being part of our little group in Ron's bar and how Ron was the greatest barman the world had ever seen, and countless other things until eventually we had to ask him to shut up while we had an intense discussion regarding the pros and cons of Hilary and Obama. While we did that, he took out his iPod and started listening to some music. If we hadn't been so engrossed in the intellectual discourse, we might have noticed the strange head-wobbling he was doing as he tapped his fingers to the beat of whatever he was listening – which was quite obviously not the beat of the rhythm of the night.

Ron doesn't like the TV on, apart from football and the news, so as soon as the weather forecast was over he switched it off. It hadn't been off a minute when Splodge began telling us how sad he would be to ever lose us, telling us stories of girls he had been in love with who never loved him back and all manner of drippy shite. This wasn't the Splodge we all knew. I looked at Jimmy, who looked back at me and did that squinty thing you do when you're trying to say, 'What the fuck is going on here?' without using your mouth. I did that thing where you shrug your shoulders and make your mouth like Robert De Niro's as if to say 'Beats the shit out of me.' When he went off to the loo, we all just looked at each other in wonder.

'Mama mia! What drugs is he a doing?' said Lucky.

'Fuck knows. He's off his box though. Reminds me of the time we ground up three Es and an acid tab and put them in Dave's dinner,' I said.

'What was that?' said Dave, who'd been explaining to Pete why, if he was a roof slate, he'd choose to be one at the top of the roof rather than one at the bottom.

'Never mind. Do you reckon he's got something in his bag there that might be a clue? He never carries a bag.'

'We can't go through his stuff,' said Pete, who had tired of Dave's witless ramblings.

'Why not?'

'It's not right.'

'Well, when you compare it to some things which aren't right, like child prostitution, genocide, famine, rape and Bono's sunglasses, it's hardly the worst thing in the world, is it?'

'I suppose when you put in that way …'

'Right then, Pete, you open it up there.'

'Me? But I—'

'Just open it. He'll be back soon.'

So, Pete went over to Splodge's stool and from underneath took out a small over-the-shoulder bag. He breathed deeply and began to unzip it. We stared wide-eyed. He began to reach into the bag when a voice spoke.

'WHAT ARE YOU DOING?' roared Splodge who had just had the quickest piss in history.

'Erm …', said Pete. 'Erm …Twenty.'

'We tried to stop him, Splodge,' I said, 'but he insisted on going through your bag.'

'You absolute cunt,' said Pete.

'How could you do this to me? Me, one of your best and closest friends. I would have written poetry for you guys, and this is how you treat me?'

We all stared at our feet like school kids caught giving the fat lad in class a wedgie. I tried to explain.

'Splodge, we were just worried for you and thought—'

'It's too late for your excuses now. You have violated my privacy. If my privacy were an altar boy, then you are the priest's penis that went up its bum. It's been nice knowing you, lads. I might write a song about you one day. Or an epic poem of some kind set to minimalist organic instruments carved by natives with ancient knives made from the shinbone of a mammoth.'

He finished what was left in his pint, picked up his bag and span on his heels, heading for the door. He threw the bag over his shoulder in a dramatic gesture, and some of the contents flew out and landed on the floor. It took us a moment to realise what it was but when we did, you could have heard a pin drop.

'Oh no. Oh, sweet holy mother of the sacred heart of the crucified Jesus,' said Dirty Dave before vomiting where he stood.

There on the floor, between some flyers for Folkapalooza, lay two CDs. Two Damien Rice CDs.

'Holy fucking shit, Twenty. Do you see what I see?' said Jimmy.

I couldn't answer. Not just from the horror of having my personal space invaded by Damien Rice CDs, but there it was. The number we'd been trying to figure out.

9

Monday
(Just moments after the last chapter ended)

'That's got to be it,' I said. 'All this time we've been trying to work out what "60" meant, hypothesizing and coming up with all kinds of outlandish theories, but it was much more subtle and clever than that.'

Damien Rice's two studio albums were entitled 0 and 9. When the CDs landed side by side and upside down, that was the '60' that poor old Tom had scrawled on his chest in his own blood. That was the clue he was trying to give us. Somehow, there was a connection between Damien

Rice and his death, and not just from the point of view of listening to his music and wanting to kill yourself.

'Jesus. Something really weird is going on, Jimmy. Someone or something connected with Damien Rice is responsible for Tom's death in his own shop; all you can find in the record shops now is that kind of music; the Goths are turning into drippy shites. I bet even the radio stations are playing this kind of music.'

'I wouldn't know. I only ever listen to Newstalk, and I only listen to that because it makes me angry,' said Jimmy, before punching Dave as hard as he could in the side of the head.

'Ow! What the fuck was that for?', squealed Dave.

'Sorry, Dave. It was either punch you or go off on a relatively tedious rant about how the people that work on Newstalk offend me on so many levels, and nobody wants that.'

'True enough,' I said, looking around. 'Where's Splodge?'

In the time we'd spent talking about the '60' and offensive radio presenters, Splodge had slipped out.

'Gone,' said Pete.

'Look, you and Dave go find him. It's important. We need to find out what the fuck happened to him and see if we can fix him. We can't just leave him like that. He's been brainwashed somehow, and now we have to make his brain dirty again. Here are my keys. When you get him, bring him back to my house and sit him in the kitchen with Bastardface. There's no way he can escape then.'

'What are you going to do?'

'I'd better contact Larry O'Rourke, tell him we know what the "60" clue means. Go on then, see you back at my place.'

I tried Larry's phone but got no reply. I said I'd sit and finish my pint rather than go chasing around the streets for Splodge because, ultimately, I'm a lazy cunt like that. Plus, Dave and Pete needed the exercise, the tubby bastards.

'This is a more strange than a referee not giving penalty to Juventus in a big a match,' said Lucky.

'Aye,' said Jimmy, 'it's like he's been possessed but instead of being possessed by a demon or dark spirit, he's been taken over by a complete sap.'

I tried Larry again, and this time I got through. I could hear him shouting in the background.

'It's as simple as this. Either he bucks up his ideas and starts talking or he'll suffer the consequences. He'll be sent to bed early, denied all PlayStation privileges, no TV, no food for his budgie, last for dinner, and he'll get a good spanking. Right, talk to you later.'

'Hello?' he said into the phone.

'More trouble with the young fella, Larry?'

'Ahh, Twenty. Nah, some paedophile murderer in Mountjoy won't talk. So, what's up?'

'We know what the "60" is.'

'Well?'

I explained in great detail how we discovered, completely by accident, that 60 was just an upside-down 0 and 9 and who it referred to.

'Damien Rice, you say? He might be a boring twat but

I'd never have him down as the ruthless killing kind. What motivation would he have for killing Tom O'Farrell?'

Again I explained, in great detail, all about the proliferation of kids with acoustic guitars instead of skateboards, of suede coats instead of long, black trenchcoats, the situation with the record shops, and, finally, I mentioned Folkapalooza and our concerns about that.

'It all sounds a bit circumstantial, Twenty, but it's funny you should mention Mega Gigs. I met the head of that crowd one time. They had some kind of break-in at their offices. What's this his name was? Alan … something. Alan Smithee, that's it! Never even offered me a cup of tea, the miserable bastard.'

'Truly, he is history's greatest monster,' I agreed.

'Look, I'll dig into this a bit. Make a call to the record company, send someone to talk to the record shops. I'm up to my tits though. Maybe you and Jimmy can check out Mega Gigs, talk to that Smithee guy, see if he's got anything to do with all this. It can't be a coincidence that they're the promoters of Folkapalooza – a concert Damien Rice is headlining, Damien Rice CDs are selling like hot cakes, and the number 60 Tom scrawled on his chest points the very same man.'

'Sterling policework, Larry.'

'It is that. Look, I have to get back to this stake-out. There's a serial dog rapist upsetting the people of Donnybrook. They don't like their pedigree hounds being bummed. We're on his trail.'

'Right enough so,' I said, making that finger-by-side-of-head-twirly-twirly 'you're mad' gesture to Jimmy and Lucky, 'I'll give you a shout if we find anything out.'

'Do that, Twenty. Cheers.'

He rang off, and I put my phone down on the bar. I gave Ron the nod for another round of pints, and I figured by the time we'd finished them, Dave and Pete would have Splodge back in my house and we could try and figure out what the fuck was going on. Pints first though. A man, even in the face of adversity, must maintain some standards.

🎧 🎧 🎧 🎧 🎧

There was a ferocious roar as I shut the front door and we hurried into the kitchen to find Stinking Pete, Dirty Dave and Splodge all cowering behind the overturned kitchen table with Bastardface snarling at them all.

'Good man, Bastardface. You kept Splodge from escaping and those other two fuckers from going around my house looking in drawers like the nosey cunts they are.'

I gave him a snack of a side of Argentinian beef and sent him out into the back garden, where he growled at clouds that came too close to his precious meat.

'Right, first things first. We need a drink. Jimmy, there are some bottles of whiskey in the globe. A pint for everyone. Pete, get Splodge tied to that chair.'

I went into the sitting room with Jimmy, and Dave and Lucky followed us in. Jimmy poured the whiskey into the glasses, and we stood drinking for a moment or two.

'Right, the way I see it, we have two problems. Firstly,

Splodge is now a retarded Damien Rice fan, and we have to figure out a way of fixing him. Secondly, we have to find out what happened to him – unless we do this we're pissing in the wind.'

'Aye', said Jimmy, 'because what's to say that he won't be turned back again even if we do somehow cure him.'

'Why don't we just ask him?' ventured Dave.

'Like that's going to work. He'll just waffle on with some crap about poetry or unrequited love, and I may have to punch his throat in;I don't want to do that.'

'For me is a like when my a mother-in-law drink a too much wine. Is all I can a do not to smash her a fat face in. Cazzo! I hate a this bitch-face,' said Lucky.

From the kitchen, I heard the muffled ringing of a mobile phone and low murmuring as someone answered it and had a conversation. We drank in silence some more, contemplating what our next move would be.

'Where's that cunt Pete?' said Jimmy. 'It doesn't take that long to tie somebody up. I should know.'

We wandered back into the kitchen where we found a half-tied Splodge, and Pete sitting at his feet, gazing at him.

'Pete? What are you doing?'

'I am transmitting the thoughts of my inner soul to my great friend Splodge.'

'Insoles?' said Dave. "What have insoles got to do with anything?'

'Me and Splodge will go to Folkapalooza. Oh, what a time we shall have, and afterwards we will be sad poets for ever.'

'Oh fucking hell,' I said, 'now Pete's got it.'

'Jesus, maybe it's contagious. Like if you get too close to someone who has it, it jumps on you like nits in a kid's classroom.'

'Let's a get out of a here,' said Lucky.

'Pete. Wait there,' I commanded in a commanding fashion. I was confident that even though he was now a muttonhead he'd do what he was told. 'The rest of you, follow me.'

I closed the kitchen door, and we retired with our drinks to the sitting room.

'Right,' I said, 'somehow, while we were in here, Stinking Pete has now become Stinking Acoustic Pete. What happened?'

'Well,' said Jimmy, 'Pete was inside with Splodge. Perhaps Splodge injected him with something.'

'I don't think so. This thing is infecting a lot of people, that would explain all those people with guitars I saw, and I'm pretty sure it doesn't automatically provide you with a syringe and phial of infecto-juice when you get it.'

'Maybe is a like the AIDS, you a get it from the deep kissing?'

'Pete is a desperate man,' said Dirty Dave, 'but not so desperate that he would frenchie another man. Not at the moment anyway. There are times of the year when—'

'Shut up, Dave,' said Jimmy. 'Maybe it's a spell. He recites some magic words, and that does it.'

'This isn't Harry fucking Potter, Jimmy,' I said.

'Hmmmm,' he grumbled. Nobody else had any other suggestions. We sat in silence, taking the odd glug of whiskey, and then it hit me. Actually, I hit it. And, by it, I mean Dave, as I slapped him right in the face.

'Ow, you cunt. What was that for?'

'I've got it!' I said. 'It's the mobile phone.'

'But why did you hit—'

'Shut up, Dave. When we were in here earlier, I could just make out a mobile ringing in the kitchen and then someone talking. When we went back inside, the pair of them were vegetables.'

'You mean some kind of ringtone or frequency modulation can brainwash a person?'

'There's no other explanation. As Sherlock Holmes says, "When you have exhausted all other possibilities and you only have one thing left, or something, then that thing has to be the thing you're looking for."'

'That was George from the Famous Five who said that.'

'Whatever. The point is that's what it is.'

I ran into the kitchen and grabbed Splodge's mobile which was sitting on the kitchen table.

'Right,' I said. 'Somehow, we're going to have to find a way of making these two simpletons relatively normal again but I think then one of us is going to have to do something both hideous and brave.'

'You don't mean—' said Dave.

'I do.'

'Oh God … God, Jesus, Mary and Trevor help us all.'

10

Monday
(Still in my gaff...)

While Jimmy set about tying up Pete, I went into the room next to the kitchen, which was like my little office. My computer was in there, and during the summer it was a great place to be. The french doors opened onto the back garden, and I often sat in there smoking and drinking with music on, looking out into the night. Sometimes I'd see the cat prowling the back garden like some kind of murderous assassin waiting for his victim. Bastardface would sit at my feet, sometimes dreaming and twitching as he slumbered. I took my Bang and Olufsen stereo (bought for a nice price from Knock-Off Nick) and speakers and brought them into the kitchen.

I went back inside to the computer and put together a playlist, which I then burned onto a CD.

'What are we doing?' asked Jimmy.

'I'm not entirely sure, but somehow we have to try and make Splodge and Pete into normal human beings again. If that crappy music has twisted their tiny little minds, then we need to untwist them. We can do it two ways. One would be to completely twist their brains in another direction, which might make them forget but leave them twisted in a different way. The other way is to try and deprogram them with music.'

'I still think we should ask them what happened,' said Dave.

'It's pointless. You know those "This is your brain; this is your brain on drugs" things? Well, if they did one for Splodge now, his brain on drugs would be a picture of a freshly laid turd with some daisies growing out of it. If you did one for Pete, it would be the same, except the turd would be covered in a hard shell of pig's vomit. You won't get any sense out of them. If we can snap them out of it, they'll give us something we can work with, for sure.'

We went back into the kitchen. Splodge and Pete were now tied to a kitchen chair each, hands bound behind their backs, feet tied together. They looked at us with wide eyes, Splodge occasionally singing a few lines from a song under his breath, but neither of them said a word. I went over to the stereo and put in a CD. My theory was that we would have to deprogram them with music that was the opposite of the stuff they'd become so enchanted with. I went to Track 1, which was Metallica. I left it play for a while, but nothing seemed to happen. When it was finished, we asked Pete how he felt, but he simply smiled an enigmatic smile and said nothing. The smile told me all I needed to know. Metallica had failed badly – worse even than their cover of 'Whiskey in the Jar.' Something older might work, I thought, so next up was 'Smoke on the Water' by Deep Purple. Classic rock, surely the antithesis of the terrible acoustic stuff, but again, it seemed to have no impact. Glam, thrash metal, power ballads (not even 'I Wanna Know What Love Is' moved them), Christian rock, rockabilly, rock 'n' roll, garage rock, psychedelic rock, handicapped deformed lesbian dwarf rock, Brighton rock, I tried everything, but nothing worked. We decided that perhaps we needed to try different musical genres. For the next two hours, we tried classical, country and western, bluegrass, progressive house, techno, reggae, ambient, hip-hop, fusion, chamber music, soul, Motown, opera, ska and, God save us, we even tried as many kinds of jazz as we could dig up, but nothing happened. He remained vacant and distant, sort of like Bertie Ahern being questioned in the Dáil.

'This is very frustrating,' said Jimmy.

'Fucking right it is. We've got to help them though. We can't just give up like a Chelsea team in the semi-finals of the European Cup. And if we do find out what's going on, then we're closer to finding out what happened to Tom.'

'Perhaps a bit of thinking music?' suggested Dirty Dave.

'Not a bad idea,' I said and went to pick something out. At times like this, there was only one choice.

My favourite album of all time: *Now That's What I Call Music 4.* I began to ponder the next steps we could take as Giorgio Moroder and Phil Oakey's 'Together in Electric Dreams' filled the room with its gloriously chugging synthtastic melody. Bronski Beat's 'Why' had something on the tip of my tongue, but by the time Limahl was halfway through the 'Never Ending Story,' I was stumped again. We'd been at this for so long, and nothing seemed to be working.

'Twenty. Look. Pete.'

I looked down, and something had changed. His right foot was beginning to tap in time to the music. Bingo. Eighties music – why didn't we think of it earlier? I ran inside to the computer and quickly burned another CD, which I put on straight away. Each tune was like a punch in the old *Batman* series.

Men without Hats, 'Safety Dance' BLAM; Yazoo, 'Don't Go' KERPLONK; Howard Jones, 'New Song' SPLORG; Spandau Ballet, 'To Cut a Long Story Short BIFF; OMD, 'Enola Gay' FRAMP.

With each passing tune, they both seemed to raise a little from the mire, Pete's feet were tip-tapping in time to the music; Splodge moved his head from side to side and lost the sickly pallor which had come over him after he got infected.

'It's working! It's working!' shouted Dave.

'Right, it's the ultimate test. Untie them there,' I said and Dave and Jimmy cut the ropes that bound them. Turning the stereo up as loud as it went, I went to the last track, the one tune that would surely snap them out of it.

The tune that, if it was locked in the Ark of the Covenant and then buried for thousands of years and then dug up by some Nazis, would melt their faces off as it was released into the world once more. The tune that summed up all that was good and great about the 1980s. That's right, 'Maniac.' Whatever was infecting Splodge and Pete could surely not resist its sheer awesomeness. As the first bars filled the room with melody and rhythm, Splodge got to his feet and began to move from foot to foot, and within sixty seconds he was dancing like a Mancunian at the thought of hearing a Stone Roses song, having just scored some crack. Pete leapt around the room with such glee on his face you'd have thought he'd just been spared the fate of being starved to death in a room filled with Phil Collins music while being rimmed by a cat. By the time the guitar solo kicked in, he was spinning like a top with his arms outstretched and a massive grin on his face, shouting 'Oh, Kevin Bacon and Lori Singer, will your magical performances ever be topped by anyone in any film ever?'

Soon the music was over, but such was Pete's enjoyment he continued dancing to no music which, as we all know, is the purest form of dance there is. As Pete continued his silent dancing, I asked Splodge what it had felt like.

'Oh Jesus, it was awful,' he explained. 'It was like being possessed like that girl from The *Exorcist* except without cool bits like projectile vomit and shoving a crucifix up my gee. I was aware of what was happening, but it was like I was trapped.'

'Like a fool in a cage?'

'Exactly. I wanted to listen to sad men playing the guitar and I had this overwhelming need to make sure I went to Folkapalooza. I had to be there.'

'Yeah, I thought I heard you mumbling something about that. How strange.'

'Another reason to get Mega Gigs checked out', said Jimmy.

'Definitely. That's something we'll need to do first thing tomorrow, but now that we know how to cure the infection, we need to know for sure that it's being spread by the mobile phone. It's time for me, like the prettiest boy on the prison football XI, to take one for the team.'

11

Monday
(Even stiller in my gaff...)

I would really have preferred somebody else to do it, but I knew it had to be me. Jimmy was needed to put on the music and generally organise and keep control of things, Pete and Dave were cretins; Splodge had just been cured of it, and who knew what further exposure could do to him, and Lucky was Italian. Plus, we had to know what exactly happened, and perhaps my years of meditation and total hatred of Damien Rice and his ilk would harden my brain against the infection. In order to protect the rest of them, I went into a different room, well, the bathroom, because I was hanging for a poo, and took Splodge's phone with me. After giving me ten minutes to relieve myself and have a quick read of my toilet book (a book of strange questions which I had read cover to cover at least fifty times), they were to ring the phone then come and see what, if anything, had happened.

I gave them the soldier-about-to-go-into-war look and went about my business. I had just wiped (it was a four wiper, which possibly could have done with a fifth) and buttoned up my pants when the phone call came. I'm not sure I can accurately describe the sensations as the music started. In an instant, it felt like I was being punched in the stomach with a fist made from invisible baby vomit mixed with the piss of a cat in renal failure, while inside my head it was as if someone took out all the good parts of my brain and blended them in a food mixer with the essence of poems and Cecelia Ahern novels. Deep inside me, the 'real' me screamed to get out, but this newly mangled monster that possessed me was the dominant force. And I had a tremendous longing inside me to go see Folkapalooza. I couldn't wait for it. Deep inside me, the 'real' me tried to escape this poisonous demon, but I was as powerless as a knight turned to stone by the hideous Madonna. I mean Medusa.

The lads were horrified when they opened the door.

'Fuck me, did something crawl up your arse and die?', said Jimmy.

'Ooooh, Mama, it smell like a Berlusconi's armpit in here,' said Lucky Luciano.

Dirty Dave wandered in, then threw up into the sink. I stared at them with an expression that Jimmy later said reminded him of a retarded simpleton who had just been given a 'cuckoo's nest'-style lobotomy. He said his first thought was to make like a giant Red Indian and put me out of my misery before he realised that there was a cure for this thing. He then said he considered the Red Indian thing anyway. He's such a joker, that Jimmy. As they led me into the kitchen and tied me to the chair, I began to sing a Bob Dylan song in a high-pitched warble totally at odds with my normal rich baritone. A sort of protest folk song at the way this new me was being treated. The other me felt like punching the new me in the bollocks, and I willed the lads to put on the music that would get me back to normal. True to form, Jimmy was in charge and quickly put on the music that had worked for the other lads. However, the tunes which had them tapping their toes after a couple of minutes seemed to be having no effect on me. They turned up the volume, turned me around to face the stereo, showed me photos of people with enormous 80s hair but nothing seemed to be working. I remained steadfastly a drippy shitehawk.

'Dave,' said Jimmy, 'I think we're going to have to perform an exorcism here.'

'Right so,' he said, 'I'll get the eggs.'

'EXorcism, you fanny. Look, we can't use holy water because Twenty's allergic to it, and I don't think it'd work anyway. We need something from the 80s. A quintessentially 80s drink.'

'I know! West Coast Cooler.'

'Yeah, but you can still get that these days. It may not have the awesome power of something truly 80s. Think, what could we use?'

'Lilt, with its totally tropical taste?' said Splodge.

'Nah, that's still around today, even though its taste is considerably less tropical than it used to be.'

They stood there thinking, but every time they came up with an idea, it was thwarted. Tizer – nobody knew where to get any. Banana milk – still current. Club Shandy – far too delicious to waste. It was beginning to look like a lost cause, when all of a sudden, Stinking Pete jumped up and shouted, 'I know! I know!', and, before anyone could ask him what he knew, he had gone out the door at a rate of knots. A short time later, he arrived back to the house carrying a dusty holdall.

'I know it's in here somewhere,' he said, going frantically through it. He pulled out all kinds of stuff. A ticket for *Rocky III* from the Green cinema, a pool cue chalk with the Pierrot Snooker Club logo on it, a McGonagle's ashtray, a photo of the Diceman terrifying children on Grafton Street at Christmas time, a Radio Nova car sticker (original 88FM–738AM flavour) and all manner of items which had been gathering dust in his attic.

'Ahhh, here it is,' he exclaimed and took out an object which made us all gasp.

'Gasp,' said Jimmy, feeling that merely gasping on its own wasn't enough. 'Pete, you are a fucking genius. A stupid, disgustingly stinky genius though. That is just what we need.'

'What is it?' asked Lucky.

'This, my Italian chum,' said Jimmy, 'is a Sodastream. They were all the rage for a while. What happened was you got the machine, a gas canister, some bottles of concentrate and some glass bottles. You put water in, then put in some of the concentrate, then gassed it all up to make your very own fizzy drinks.'

'But a why you not just go to shops to buy fizzy drinks like a normal people?'

'Because going to the shops just wasn't as cool as having your own personal supply of fizzy drinks. Italians just wouldn't understand anything as sophisticated and fashionable as Sodastream. Old George Armani never had one of these.'

Jimmy looked at the assorted Sodastream paraphernalia that Pete had brought. There were bottles, the machine itself, the gas and one bottle of cola-flavoured concentrate. Unfortunately, the concentrate itself had solidified over the years, and any attempts to melt it just did not work. It was the hardest substance on Earth, and Pete wondered briefly if all the sponge fingers he'd dipped directly into the liquid and then greedily scoffed when he was younger would have any effect on him later in life.

'Bollocks to this. We're just going to have to make our own cola-flavoured concentrate from whatever the fuck Twenty has in his kitchen.

As they went through my cupboards, I could feel myself slipping further and further away from real life. This new persona was taking over, and it wouldn't be long before I was buried deeper than a politician's financial records at tribunal time, and there'd be no way back for me. I concentrated as hard as I could, and with all my strength, I tried to tell them what was happening to me.

'FUCK SHIT CUNT ARSE TITS WANK FLAPS GEE HORSEFISTINGCUNTBUTLER!', I exclaimed loudly.

'Shit,' said Splodge, 'it sounds like Twenty's in real trouble. We've got to hurry.'

'Look, give a me this,' said Lucky Luciano. 'I'm Italian. I can a cook. You Irish only know how to make a potato and boil ham. I mean, who the fuck boil a the pork. Is a disgusting.'

Jimmy could find no argument for that, and soon Lucky was at the counter-stirring the ingredients he found in my cupboard into a large pottery bowl.

'Sugar. Water. Salt. Golden Syrup. Basil. Soy sauce. Black pepper. White pepper. Juice from tin of a sweetcorn. Horrible runny watery bit a from top of bottle of a ketchup. Worcestershire sauce. Small amount of my own blood. Teabag. Powdery bits from bottom of a cereal box. Oregano. Curry powder. Soil from house plant. Two flogs. Olive oil. Thick-cut marmalade. Nutella. Fish paste. Coriander. Limescale from kettle. Bay leaf and final ingredient,' he said, digging around with his index finger, 'ear wax!'

He got a wooden spoon and started mixing it all together before putting it in a saucepan and boiling it down to a thick, viscous liquid.

'Is a ready,' he said.

'We need to try this out,' said Jimmy as he brewed up a batch of delicious Sodastream cola. 'Pete, you can taste it.'

Reluctantly, as he had viewed exactly what had gone into making it, he agreed. He braced himself for the worst and took a massive gulp.

'Jesus fucking Christ!' he shouted, spitting the foul liquid into the sink.

'Is it that bad?'

'Yeah. It's exactly the same as the real Sodastream cola.'

'Thank fuck for that.'

They all stood in front of me. Jimmy clicked on the stereo and, again, the pulsating beat of 'Maniac' came flooding out of the speakers. He breathed in to prepare himself for what could well be a titanic battle, looked across at the others, gave a slight nod and breathed out.

'Now!', he said, and, in unison, the four of them doused me with the foul liquid while chanting, 'The power of Sodastream compels you. The power of Sodastream compels you.'

At first, I thought it wasn't working, but it wasn't long before I could feel the drippy me recoil in horror. As the lads continued this most holy of rituals, I tried to get up but was still tied to the chair. One of them cut me free, and soon I was dancing like I'd never danced before. As the song ended, I let rip an enormous fart, expelling this malevolent presence from my hole, and fell face-first onto the floor.

'Is he all right?' said Dave.

'There's only one way to find out,' said Jimmy. He rolled me over and offered me two cigarettes. One was a delicious, full-strength Major. The other was a completely gay Silk Cut Blue. Without hesitation, I took the Major, and Jimmy lit it for me.

'Good to have you back', said Jimmy.

'Good to be back, old pal. It was touch and go there for a while. I thought at one stage I was lost, lost and alone in the dark, but thanks to you guys I'm back once again.'

'Like a renegade master,' said Pete.

'You know it.'

'What was it like?', asked Jimmy.

'Horrible. Really. It was so odd, like my body and brain knew what was happening was wrong but could do nothing to combat it. It's almost like you're just doing what you're told but nobody's telling you what to do, if that makes any sense. And the Folkapalooza thing. It's like you're five years old and they've just announced a month of Christmas Days, each one with Santa and with different presents.'

'You know, it sounds more like Folkapalooza is the danger here, rather than Damien Rice.'

'I think you're right. He could just be an unwitting tool.'

'He's some kind of tool, all right.'

'Hah. But I think the number 60 was the only way Tom could point us in that direction. There was no way he could write "Folkapalooza" on his chest in his own blood so the headline act, and one of Mega Gigs most high-profile stars, was his way of pointing us in the right direction.'

'Poor old Tom, imagine your last thoughts in life were about Damien Rice. That's very depressing. We owe him, Twenty. What a sacrifice he made for us all.'

'Well, we'll see what we can dig up when we go to visit

Mega Gigs tomorrow. Now, I'm going to grab a shower and clean this place up. Then, I think, it's time to retire to Ron's – we all deserve some pints.'

As I made my way down to the bathroom, I began to shake. Imagine if they hadn't been able to free me from the clutches of acoustic me. I'd have been a snivelling shitebag for the rest of my days. Having experienced it firsthand, I knew I had to stop this thing once and for all and God help anyone who got in my way. Even God couldn't help himself if he was the one who got in my way.

12

Tuesday Morning

Around eleven the next morning, I hailed a cab outside the house and picked up Jimmy at his place. We headed out towards Blackrock where Mega Gigs, offices were. Traffic was absolutely terrible, as always. We probably would have been quicker just walking into town and taking the DART out, but as a strong supporter of global warming, I was determined to make my carbon-footprint as large as possible. I probably wouldn't have been so vehement about it if they hadn't invented the whole carbon footprint concept, twats. Everyone knows the cause of global warming is cow farts, so this insistence on trying to pin it on humans to support the multi-billion-dollar eco-industry annoys the shite out of me. They have global warming in China, too, and every fucker there goes around on bicycles, so much so that their bicycles have been known to take on human characteristics, including, but not limited to, lying around doing nothing, standing on street corners and freewheeling through life.*

Mega Gigs' offices were on Main Street above a dry cleaners, which made me think about dirty laundry but I didn't take it too far. We went up the stairs and into the reception area. The receptionist girl was wearing one of those headset telephones and reading *Vanity Fair*. She was a vaguely orange kind of colour with her dark hair swept backwards and kept up by a hairband. She was nearly pretty and tried desperately hard to make up for it with make-up, make-up and some more make-up.

---

* During his explorations of China and its sprawling cities in the early 1980s, Des Elby noted that the Chinese were 'at one' with their bicycles in a way that no other nation was. Not even the Dutch, whose government gave free bicycles to any family that had more than four children or owned two children and any kind of pet that wasn't a turtle. In many ways, he reported, a man could become part of his bicycle and the bicycle part of the Earth due to its continued friction with the ground, and, in such ways, did the Chinese become closer to God or whatever their approximation of God in their fake religion was. It was the ones who insisted on travelling in different ways that you had to be careful of because if they weren't closer to God, they were closer to the Divil himself, and the Chinese who emigrated to other countries rarely used bicycles at all and, he estimated, were responsible for at least 17.45 per cent of all the evil in the world. The figure was unconvincingly countered by the country's tourist board, but scant attention was paid to them as peddlers and shysters went to town selling tokens and idols, designed to ward off Chinese evil, which, in the end, turned out to be little more than milkbottle tops wrapped around pipe cleaners and scorched with a kitchen blow torch – although many a quick-witted fellow had become very wealthy before the scam was uncovered.

She looked completely bored, like she couldn't wait to get off work and go into town for some drinks in a bar where she might meet a guy who works in finance or insurance and plays rugby to a decent level and has a nice car and can afford a house that isn't in a purpose-built new suburb. I put on my educated and polite head, as I have always found people really respond well to good manners and patience. It's just common sense, isn't it? If you ask nicely, chances are you'll get a nice answer. That wasn't always true of the people I had to deal with, but I was always happy to give them the chance.

'Good day to you, young lady,' I said, 'we would like to see Alan Smithee.'

'Do you have an appointment?' she said, without looking up from her magazine.

'Well, not as such. We're rather arriving on spec, I'm afraid, but if he had a few moments, I can assure you it is a matter of the greatest importance.'

'I'm sorry, but without an appointment, you can't see him. He's a very busy man.'

'Of course, I appreciate that but it is imperative that we see him. Lives could be at stake.'

'Yeah, right.'

'Honestly, we have uncovered some very strange goings-on, and somehow your company is linked to it. I'm sure Mr Smithee would be eager to ensure that no bad publicity were to befall such an august agency as yours.'

'Look,' she said finally putting down the magazine and honouring me with eye contact, 'I've already told you he's not available. If you'd like to make an appointment,

I can fit you in the week after next sometime. If not, then I'm afraid you'll have to leave.'

I looked at Jimmy. Now, Jimmy can be a very persuasive sort of a man. He can generally sway even the most stubborn of opponents, and, if the worst comes to the worst, he has a special mind-control move. It's similar to Obi-Wan Kenobi in *Star Wars* telling the stormtrooper he's not looking for these particular droids, despite them being exactly the droids he was seeking, although not quite as subtle. What he does is make a fist with one hand and smack it into his open palm very hard indeed and then say something like, 'You will have the money tomorrow, right?' or 'We'll take your car in the meantime as security' and it nearly always works. The only time it didn't was when we were chasing some money from a deaf, dumb and blind bloke who'd defaulted on payments for his pinball machine. That required a more fists-on approach.

'Look Emma, or whatever your fucking name is,' he said, 'we can do this the easy way or the hard way. The easy way is for you to just buzz his office and tell him we're coming to see him. The hard way is for you not to do that, and we'll still go and see him, but you'll have two broken wrists. I'm not one for violence against women, but I'd only do to you what I'd do to a man sitting there. I'm no sexist. Now, what's it to be?'

She picked up the phone and dialled.

'Er, hi,' she said, 'I know you're busy, but there are two "gentlemen" [she said 'gentlemen' like you might say 'shit covered cockroaches'] out here who want to see you.

I know. I told them that, but I really think you need to see them. What? I don't know. Okay, keep your knickers on. Jesus. I'll ask. What are your names?'

'I'm Twenty Major, and this is Jimmy the Bollix.'

'Twenty Major and Jimmy the … erm … Bollix. No, really. I swear! I'm not making it up. Look, can I send them down to you? Right. Okay.'

She put down the phone.

'He'll be with you in about five minutes. You can wait over there,' she said pointing at a glass-topped coffee table covered with magazines like *Vogue*, *Hot Press* and *OK!* 'Would you like a coffee?'

'No thanks, we're fine.'

'I'll have a black coffee,' said Jimmy, tutting. 'Nine sugars, please.'

She went off, eyebrows raised, to get the coffee for Jimmy, while I eschewed the low-quality publications. I read for a few minutes about cellulite-covered celebs and *Big Brother* rejects who still make headlines for no good reason I can possibly think of. Still, given the choice between these vulgar irrelevancies or *Hot Press* there's really only one winner. She returned with Jimmy's drink, and, after a little while, a strange-looking square-faced man came through the reception.

'Gentlemen,' he said, not offering his hand for us to shake, 'what can I do for you?'

'Perhaps we could go into your office,' I suggested.

'Perhaps your mum.'

'What?!'

'I've got only a short time, so if you wouldn't mind,

please tell me what's going on.'

So, I explained to him about Tom O'Farrell, the clue he'd left on his chest in his own blood and how we'd discovered that it was pointing to Damien Rice who was being promoted by Mega Gigs as one of the headliners of Folkapalooza.

'How awful. Truly, truly awful. But what does any of this have to do with me?'

'Well, you're putting on this Folkapalooza concert, and Damien Rice is one of the headlining acts. We're just trying to find out how he links to the murder. We're investigating, *if you will*.'

'I can't imagine Damien Rice as a murderer, can you?'

'I didn't say he was, just that the clue Tom left pointed to him. I'm curious as to why you're putting on this enormous free gig though. It must be costing a fortune, and I've never known any concert promoter willing to take a loss like that.'

'Mega Gigs has made a lot of money over the years from the people of Ireland. This is our way of giving something back, if you will.'

I went on to explain to him about how all the record shops were chock-full of Rice and his ilk at the expense of real music and how all the little Goths around the Central Bank were turning into little acousticies.

'You don't think there's anything strange about that?'

'No. I don't think there's anything strange about it at all.'

'Why did you say strange like that?'

'Like what?'

'Like you know there's something strange about it and you know more than you're letting on about its strangeness.'

'I'm sure I have no idea what you mean.'

Jimmy, who had been looking on and drinking his coffee, suddenly dropped his cup right into the middle of the glass table, shattering it into lots of little pieces. Well, he didn't exactly drop it. He threw it as hard as he could.

'What the Hell are you doing?!' shouted Smithee.

'I'm sure I have no idea what you mean,' he said.

'I think it's time for you to leave.'

'Yes, perhaps it is,' said Jimmy, 'but we'll be back. Back like a 60s rock band on their final ever, honestly this is the last time we'll ever play these songs, world tour.'

'Yeah, we'll be back. I just have a few mobile-phone calls to make,' I said, stressing the words 'mobile phone,' just to let him know we might know more than we let on.

We left him staring at the table and went down the stairs onto the street. I lit a cigarette and had a think. Despite his denials, it was obvious this Smithee chap knew more than he was letting on, sort of like a politician at a tribunal. We'd have to keep a close eye on him. As the summer breeze blew down Main Street, Blackrock, we clearly had much to discuss, and men can only discuss things over a pint or two, so we retired to a local inn.

🎧 🎧 🎧 🎧 🎧

Meanwhile, across Dublin...

In his room, Seamus listened intently as the man on the phone ranted about the disturbing visitors he'd received.

'Stinking bloody men, they were. Who do they think they are, coming here like that? Not only that, they're suspicious, and if they get more suspicious, they might investigate more, and if they investigate more, then they might find more out, and if they find more out, they'll get even more suspicious and investigate some more and that will lead to them finding out more, and this will continue until they know everything, and that cannot happen. They might even know something about the ringtone. So, you understand what needs to be done?'

'What are their names?' asked Seamus. 'I know somebody who can take care of them.'

'Twenty Major and Jimmy the ... erm ... Bollix,' said Alan Smithee. 'I can trust you to take care of this?'

'Yes, Sir. I know somebody who can take care of them.'

'You said that already. I assume you mean you will take care of them.'

'No, I said I know somebody who can take care of them, not that I would take care of them personally. If I had meant I would take care of them personally, I would have said "I will take care of them personally" and not "I know somebody who can take care of them."'

'Jesus, if there's anything worse than a ginger albino, it's a pedantic ginger albino. Just make this problem go away.'

'Which problem? The one where you seem to misunderstand my very straightforward English or the two men who are bothering you?'

'The men! The men! Christ. Keep me informed, you hapless freak.'

The phone went dead. Seamus didn't like dealing with this man. He had such a superior tone, as if he was somehow better. But who was the important one – the one who thinks of what to do or the one who actually does it? Smithee would do well to remember who was really pulling the strings, and, if she found out, she'd be less than impressed. Obviously, these men were a problem though. If they discovered too much, it could put his whole life at risk, and he wasn't going to let that happen. He didn't want to end up back on the streets, or in a place where the streets have no name, because that would mean the streets weren't really streets at all but barely functional strips of land between ramshackle houses. There were too many bad memories. Memories that made his anus twitch. They had to be dealt with, and Seamus knew just the man. He picked up the phone and dialled a number. Then there was a ringing tone, which stopped when somebody answered.

'We need to meet,' said Seamus. 'I have a job for you. The usual place, 11.22am.'

The person on the other end hung up abruptly. That was twice inside five minutes that somebody had hung up on him. Seamus's cheeks burned with anger, but he knew he had to stay calm. Nothing calmed him like some haunting, echoey vocals, so he pressed play on the CD player and let the serenity pass over him. When he was less irate, he made another phone call, and the man on the other end gave him information and promised to email him some pictures. It had been worthwhile doing that thing in that alley that time. A contact in the Gardaí was always handy.

🎧 🎧 🎧 🎧 🎧

I looked around after Jimmy and me got ourselves a couple of pints and a decent table. There was rugby memorabilia everywhere. A big poster of some fat ginger bloke pulling what appeared to be the entire English team over the line for an Irish try. There were signed shirts and rugby balls in cases and pennants and scarves. You could barely see the peach, silky wallpaper in places.

'That Smithee bloke knows more than he's letting on,' said Jimmy, 'and that fucking receptionist only put six sugars in my coffee, and I specifically asked for nine. They are evil to the core in there.'

'No question about it. I think we might need to pay that office a visit again. And by "visit" I mean "burgle" and by "again" I mean "tonight".'

'Aye, good idea. There's bound to be some kind of documentation or computer file detailing all kinds of stuff. I don't know anything about computers, although I'm pretty good at Pong. You're the blogging guy, you can do that stuff.'

'Ahh, wait on. Any old cunt can blog. You don't need any kind of technical expertise. All you need is a belief that anyone might possibly be interested in anything you have to say and vaguely passable writing skills. In fact, writing skills aren't really a necessity. After that, you just type and click Publish and wait to become really important. We'll have to bring Dirty Dave along. He's good at the nuts and bolts of 'puters.'

'Jesus, do we have to? He smells so bad, and he's as clumsy as a camel on rollerblades. I guarantee you that as we stealthily make our way around the place, he'll trip over something that will hit something else that will set off some kind of alarm.'

'Well, if we want to get into their computers, we need him.'

'Shite, well at least we can—'

At this point, we were interrupted by a blond-haired, white-toothed bloke wearing a light-blue and white striped rugby jersey. He seemed quite drunk despite the early hour.

'Look, ladsh, you're in my seat, roysh.'

'Your seat?'

'Yeah, my seat. Every time I come in here, thash where I sit. Everyone knows it, apart from scobies who don't come from round here. Now, I'm going to the toilet to have a Jimmy Riddle and wash the old Brendan Grace. I'm sure you'll be totally gone when I get back.'

And off he went. I looked at Jimmy. He looked at me. I shrugged my shoulders. A few seconds later, Jimmy got up as if he had felt the need, all of a sudden, to relieve himself. He came back a few minutes later.

'Everything all right?' I asked.

'Not a bother,' he said.

'Bit of blood there on your sleeve.'

'Here?'

'No, other side.'

'Ahh, cheers.'

'And is that a tooth stuck to the bottom of your trousers?'

'So it is! Funny where those things end up, eh?'

'It certainly is.'

We finished up our pints, and, having decided to come back later that night with Dave, we headed back into town. By taxi, of course. On the way, Jimmy got a phone call from the people we were due to meet the following week.

'They've made it very plain that they expect our complete commitment to the "upcoming project", as he kept calling it. You heard me ask, but he wouldn't give me any more details.'

'Right enough. This could be anything, and it probably won't be "We need you to pick up a package from the Caribbean and sure you might as well lie on the beach for a couple of weeks drinking mojitos before you come back with it."'

'I'd say you're probably right there.'

I told Jimmy I'd see him in Ron's later, then jumped out in town to go stroll through the streets and have a think about everything we'd discovered. I strolled up from Trinity College, whistling a happy tune as I went. Avoiding people with clipboards trying to get me to sign up to donate to some charity or other and the Gypsy women thrusting their obviously drugged babies under my nose and asking me for change, I turned onto Wicklow Street.

Passing poor old Tom's shop, I felt something harden in my heart. He had been a good bloke who just loved his music, and now he was dead. I felt a rage build inside me that I hadn't felt since that time a lounge girl put my fresh pint on the table instead of the beer mat. I mean, that's what beer mats were invented for. Why would you put it on the table?

I swore an oath there and then, walking down Wicklow Street. I was going to find out exactly what had happened to Tom, why it had happened, who did it, for what reason, and which person carried out this terrible thing, and, not only that, I was going to uncover their motives and discover the identities of the culprits. That the kind of music involved in this whole thing was the same kind that Tom and I had been raped with as youngsters just made the whole thing more personal. Tom wouldn't want other people to be subjected to the same thing, he'd cared about other people a lot more than I did. I could almost hear him talking to me.

'Don't let them away with it, Twenty,' his voice whispered.

I felt sad for my friend, and I felt sadder for me because at least Tom was dead and couldn't feel anything anymore. As I continued on my way, I stopped whistling a happy tune and started whistling a Leonard Cohen tune instead. That's how downbeat this whole thing had got me.

13

Tuesday Night

(Ron's bar)

I had already briefed Dirty Dave on the plans for later that night, so he arrived in the pub wearing black pants, a black polo-neck and black bomber jacket.

'Here, it's the fucking Milk Tray man!' chortled Pete.

'You seem to have forgotten something, Dave,' I said.

'What's that?'

'A big fucking bag with SWAG written on it. Jesus.'

'Hahaha, Twenty. You do make me laugh.'

I left him to his own devices and went to talk to Splodge, who was sitting at the bar and back to his usual contemplative self.

'All right, Splodge? Feeling better?'

'Yeah, a good night's sleep and I felt right as rain. A bit fuzzy in the head, I have to say, but otherwise grand. Thanks again for saving me from that terrible affliction.'

'Not a problem, man. If we couldn't have fixed you, we'd have put you out of your misery. It wouldn't have been fair to leave you like that. A feckless wretch addicted to shite music.'

'You'd have done it quickly though, right?'

'Sure … er … yeah, as quickly as we could. Still, it's all okay now thankfully, and we can get on with things. Catch you later.'

I went back to the end of the bar to talk with Jimmy about how we were going to break into Mega Gigs' offices without being seen.

'I got a lend of Lockpicking Lorcan's skeleton-key set. That'll get us in.'

'Sweet, that is very handy in so many ways. Does that key set even open Chubb locks?'

'He says it'll open any lock on any door in the world.'

'Even a door to another dimension?'

'If it has a lock, then it will open it.'

'Cool. What about a door—'

'ANY door.'

'Right.'

Dave, Jimmy and I left a sulking Stinking Pete in Ron's. He was upset that he wasn't allowed come along, but we told him it was only Dave's computer skills that had him involved. We hailed a cab outside on the main road.

'I think I have to urinate,' said Dave.

'Well, you should have gone before we left,' I replied.

'I didn't need to go then.'

'Shut up, Dave.'

It was a quiet taxi ride until the Middle Eastern driver spotted another taxi ahead of him.

'Look at that taxi!', he roared.

'What's wrong with it?'

'Is Saab.'

'So what? Saabs are nice cars, aren't they? If I had to spend twelve hours a day driving cunts around I'd want to drive a nice car,' I said, looking at the grotty interior of the fifteen-year-old Toyota Camry we were travelling in.

'Yes, is nice car, but what happen when something go wrong, eh? Is very hard to get part.'

'Yeah, but what difference does it make to you what car he's driving?'

'Look, before, I have Mercedes. Before, I have BM—'

'Before you had a Mercedes, you had a bowel movement?' asked Dave.

'No, BM. Is German car.'

'Oh, BMW.'

'Yeah, BM. Is expensive car but is easy to get part when car break. Saab. Pffff. Is easier to find Al Qaeda member in Texas than part for Saab. You have BM, and car break is easy to find other BM to get fix. Saab break is impossible. Stupid fuck.'

'So, if you have had a Mercedes and a BMW, why the fuck are you driving round in this piece of shit?'

'Fucking Irish girls. Dirty bitches. Is always falling

sleep and go piss on seats. Me, I like piss as much as next guy, but other passengers not like.'

'Right. Any chance you could just put the radio on and shut the fuck up?'

'Is my car. I do what I want.'

'Yeah', said Jimmy, 'this is my fucking fist. It does what it wants.'

'You fucking guy,' said the taxi driver, before clicking on the radio. Instantly, I wished we'd walked when the non-dulcet tones of David Gray spewed from the tinny speakers.

'What station is this?' I asked.

'Is Spectre FM, playing Dublin's hardest rock 24–7.'

'Doesn't fucking sound like hard rock to me.'

'I change.'

'No, leave it for a few minutes.'

Hard as it was to endure the terrible music, I had to hear what was next, and it was disgusting but no real surprise when this so-called hard-rock station pumped out more of the same miserable crap. Why would a station which built its reputation on Nine Inch Nails play David Gray? Why weren't their listeners trying to burn down the studios in protest? Just more proof, if any were needed, that the something I thought was going on earlier was definitely an important something and not just a workaday run-of-the-mill something like everyone in Galway getting the squirts from dodgy water. Eventually we got to Blackrock's Main Street, paid the driver and hopped out. It was quiet enough around, bar one very drunk student who passed us by and for some reason called me a camel before making a very strange noise with his tongue. We made our way to the office, and Jimmy took out his skeleton-key set and tried the first key. Then the second. Then the third. Then the fourth. Then, amazingly enough, the fifth, followed by the sixth. Then he forgot which keys he'd already used and had to start all over again. At this point, Dave was practically dancing he was so bursting.

'Hurry the fuck up, would you?' he squealed.

'Just go down that lane,' said Jimmy.

'Can't,' he said.

'Why not?'

'I can't piss outside. I have this obsessive fear that a rat will run out and bite the top of my cock off.'

'What?!'

'JUST HURRY UP!'

After about five minutes, Jimmy found the right key, and we got inside the front door. At the top of the stairs, there was yet another door, which took yet more time to open. By now, Dave was practically weeping tears of his own piss, and when we got inside, after another few minutes of trying the locks, he was at the end of his tether. He ran inside, looking left and right for the toilet. When it became obvious he was never going to make it there, he simply unzipped, stood on a chair and relieved himself into the fish tank in reception that looked like it was home to many expensive tropical fish. They didn't much like the splashing, but Dave wasn't bothered.

'Thank fucking God for that,' he said, with a beatific smile on his face. 'Now, let's get down to business.'

We made our way to Alan Smithee's office. We knew it was his because of the minimalist furniture, the glass and chrome, the anal neatness of everything. That and the sign on the door that said, ALAN SMITHEE. We checked his desk drawers, but they were locked. No hassle to us though, as we had the skeleton-key set, and Jimmy set about getting them open. It was likely that all of his important documents were kept on his computer, which was a large-screen iMac.

'I knew it,' said Dave. 'All these arty-farty media types use a Mac. Let's see what we've got.' He booted up the machine but was presented with a password screen. He tried a couple of obvious ones, like 'iamcool', 'nocomment' and 'norefunds', but we didn't get that lucky. That would have been simply too implausible.

'Are we not completely fucked now?' I asked him.

'Not at all, Twenty. You see, despite their lack of viruses and the common perception that they're a very secure machine, your average Mac is a very simple machine to get into. All I have to do is start up from an OS CD and then reset his master password and we have complete access to his computer. Here I have a CD of the new operating system, Pougar.'

'Pougar?'

'Yeah, they ran out of giant cats to name them so they combined them. This is a mix of panther and a cougar.'

'I have no idea what any of that means, but make it so.'

Within minutes, we were looking at his desktop picture, which was a hi-res image of Tom Cruise playing volleyball in *Top Gun*. I mean, super hi-res. I mean, you could see the sweat glistening on his nipple. Dave started clicking around.

'What exactly are we looking for?' he asked.

'Not sure exactly. Anything that relates to Damien Rice or this Folkapalooza thing, I suppose.'

He did some searching and came up with a few documents, but they were all purely administrative: hiring of equipment for Folkapalooza, artist contracts and riders (James Blunt demanded a dressing room full of fresh carnations, twenty-four bottles of Volvic, a book of poetry by Pam Ayres and three models to scream whenever he came in the room so he could feel a small bit like The Beatles). Various other technical piffle was all we could turn up. Hopes of finding a document that explained a dastardly plan in total detail – like a baddy at the end of a film giving the temporarily restrained hero the speech about how he was doing something and how to stop it instead of just shooting him in the face – were fading fast. Jimmy had gone through the drawers at that stage and had found nothing of any use either, although he did steal all the staples and left the tops off the highlighter markers.

'Maybe there's something in his email,' said Dave.

It was full of the usual stuff. Emails to the girl at reception asking her to bring him a coffee, editions of Popbitch and Holy Moly, threats from Elton John's agent to begin legal action if he didn't stop emailing, press releases and alerts from something called Gamedar, I think. I didn't have him down as a gamer, but you can never tell with people, can you? Then, in a folder within a folder within another folder, Dave found something interesting.

'Look at this,' he said, 'I've found something interesting.'
'What is it?'
'A series of emails from someone who's just called "MC".
Looks like they could be talking about something important.'
He opened one up.

From: MC
To: Alan Smithee
Subject: Re: Important

>>>Things proceeding well. It is spreading. Sales are good and will get better. Excellent. Just ensure that nothing changes. Continue as planned.

Dave opened the most recent one.

From: Alan Smithee
To: MC
Subject: Re: Small problem

>>>Was paid a visit by two ruffians. They're suspicious of link between that record guy and Damien Rice. Have told our Hucknallesque friend. He assures me he knows somebody who can take care of it. Will update asap.

I'm sure I can count on you to make this go away. I do not like when my harmonious life becomes, how do you say, less harmonious.

'Wow,' I said, 'I knew there was something to this. And it looks like there's a hit out on us, Jimmy.'

'Fucking hell, not again.'

'Yeah, it's all getting a bit tiresome now. How many is that this year?'

'Three already. That's nearly twice as many as last year, but still not as many as 2001.'

'Ahhh, 2001. What a laugh a minute that was!'

'God, it was too. I miss killing people when they sleep.'

'Dave, print off some of those emails, will you? Especially the ones about the "record guy". I reckon Larry O'Rourke would be very interested in them.'

'Will do.'

'Also, is there any way of finding out who that person is by their email address?'

'Doubtful,' he said, 'it's a pretty anonymous address: MC08009@gmail.com. It's a shame it's not alansmitheefrom21lawndrivetallaghtdublin24@hotmail.com, but that is probably expecting a bit too much. I can probably find out the location of where they sent the email from, though.'

'Grand, do that so.'

A bit of clicking around later and he told us.

'It looks like it's south Dublin, perhaps Killiney or Dalkey.'

'Hmmmmmm,' I said.

'Hmmmmmm, what?'

'I dunno. Dalkey. Harmonious life. It's setting off alarms in my head.'

'Do you think …? Nah,' said Dave.

'What?'

'Well, MC. It's obvious, isn't it?'

'It is?'

'Yeah. It must be MC Hammer. Who else's name begins with MC?'

'Oh. Just shut up and print those out.'

A few minutes later, Dave had printouts in his hand, and we were all set to go. Naturally it would have been remiss of me not to cause a bit of mischief, so I replied to Elton John's agent, telling her I would never, ever stop emailing and to bring on the legal action, as well as sending a memo to the girl at reception to advise her to wear long pants as the smell of her fanny was making me feel sick and I was unable to concentrate on my work. Then I got Dave to take a photo of his balls with the built-in camera and set it as the desktop picture. With that, our work was done. As we left the office, I glanced over at the neon-lit aquarium. All the fish were floating on their backs, as dead as dead can be.

'That's a powerful rod you've got there, Dave,' said Jimmy.

'I'd love to see yer man Smithee's face tomorrow. Eel come in and go mad altogether,' I quipped wittily.

'I wonder does he drive to work or cycle his pike?' said Jimmy.

'I dunno,' said Dave, 'but I'm having a whale of a time!'

'You cunt, Dave,' I said. 'Whales are mammals. Way to spoil the fun.'

We travelled home in silence. It was better that way.

14

Wednesday Morning

(In town)

Seamus travelled into town on the DART. He had slept
fitfully the night before, concerned after his inside man in
the Gardaí had told him they'd found a ginger/white hair
they could not identify. He'd had no choice though. The
man he was due to meet had been away when that job had
to be carried out, so he'd had no choice but to do it himself.
Because of his distinctive appearance, he preferred to
outsource the killings whenever possible. But sometimes a
man just didn't have a choice. He looked around the
carriage at the people. Many of them, he knew, were now

infected with the virus, and the more people that were infected, the quicker it would spread. He smiled uneasily, like a man with an upside-down mouth.

He got into Pearse Street station and walked up Westland Row. He was wearing a baseball cap and dark glasses, despite the weather, and his pale skin could have been that of an Icelander or Scot, but nobody paid him any kind of attention. They were all too busy getting somewhere, talking or texting or listening to music on their iPods. He stopped at an Italian coffee shop a short way up the street and bought himself a double espresso. He sugared it up inside, stirring it with a wooden stick, then sat outside to smoke, watching the busy people on their way to work.

As he was early, he had brought along a book to put him in the mood. Despite everything, he was a gentle soul underneath it all, and he sometimes needed stimulation to carry out his duties effectively. The two ruffians, Twenty and Jimmy, had irked him because he'd had to listen to Alan Smithee giving him lip and, although he knew there was no other option, he'd still had to get himself worked up in order to sort it out. After four pages of John Banville's *The Sea*, he was so furious at the supercilious, tedious prose about a man he couldn't care less about, no matter how much of the book he read, that he'd have beaten himself about the face had he not learned so much self-restraint over the years. The background info he'd received on the two men left him in no doubt that they had to be disposed of. Not just because they might interfere with the plan, but because of their history and the atrocities they had carried out in the past. It was unbelievable that they weren't rotting in jail already. He was seething away to himself when a man sat down beside him. There was no greeting. He just spoke.

'Who?'

Seamus handed him a file, and the man took some moments to read it.

'Why?'

'They are a threat to the very important work the people I represent have been doing over the past number of months.'

'How much of a threat?'

'Well, imagine if the work is The Beatles, then these two are Yoko Ono.'

'Ouch.'

'Exactly. I assume the normal price is sufficient.'

'Wrong. Double.'

'Why double?'

'There are two.'

'Okay, that makes sense. The sooner, the better. Time is of the essence. There is not a moment to lose and such. I can count on you, can't I?'

'Of course.'

'You are sure you have no more holidays meaning you're not around to do the work I have for you?'

'I'm sure.'

'In that case, I will await your call to let me know that everything has been done. Like your other work, I am sure it will be exemplary.'

Seamus got up and left and headed back towards the

DART station, pleased that everything had gone so smoothly. His mistress would be pleased at how quickly he had arranged for this problem to be put to bed. With luck, she would smear her lady patch with peanut butter before allowing him to lap it all off. That was his favourite. He smiled to himself, glad that his work gave his place in the world some meaning.

Meanwhile, back at the coffee shop, the man with the file looked at the documents he'd been given, rolled his eyes to Heaven and set off on his way home. He had a big decision to make.

15

Wednesday
(A little bit
later that morning)

I phoned Larry O'Rourke to let him know what I'd found out in Mega Gigs.

'Meet me in Ron Black's on Dawson Street,' he said.

'I can't. I'm barred.'

'Right then, Café en Seine.'

'Barred.'

'Samsara.'

'Barred.'

'Sinnotts?'

'Barred.'

'The Porterhouse?'

'Double barred.'

'Well, you tell me then.'

An hour later, I found him sitting at the bar in McDaid's on Harry Street. He was shouting loudly into his phone.

'Look, just tell the fucking slimebag that we do things on our terms, not hers, the jumped-up fucking bitch. If it comes down to it, I'll put her fucking head through the window. I don't care. I'll just do it. I swear to God. Right, well make sure.'

He hung up.

'Sorry Twenty, mother-in-law invited herself over for Sunday dinner. Just telling the missus to sort it out.' He put his phone away. 'How the Hell did you get barred out of all those places?'

'Ahh, just a series of intense personal disagreements one night. Nothing to worry about.'

'So,' he said, 'what have you found out?'

First off, I told him about the ringtone and how it was being used to spread this virus and the monstrous effect it has on people. I sent it to his mobile phone and told him that under no circumstances was he to expose anybody he had any regard for to it. It was also important to make sure he didn't expose himself to it. Obviously, he'd need to test it out though, so he promised to round up some prisoners and illegal immigrants and use it on them when he got back to the station because they weren't real people. As well as that, I told him about the link between the ringtone, Folkapalooza, Mega Gigs and Tom's murder.

'How did you get this information?' he asked, looking at the printouts of the emails.

'Let's just say a "little birdie" broke into their office last night, hacked into the computers, printed off the emails and killed all the tropical fish by pissing in the fish tank.'

'Erm, isn't the "little birdie" supposed to be a bit more circumspect than that?'

'Yeah, it probably should be, but what can you do?'

'Well, I probably can't do a thing because this "evidence" has been procured by illegal means and there's no way I can get a warrant to search the place. As well as that, if they're as dastardly as they seem, they'll have gotten rid of any evidence before we get there so there's not much point. You know, the sensible thing to do would have been to cover your tracks and not make it blindingly obvious that somebody had broken in and ransacked the place.'

'Yeah, hindsight is a wonderful thing. Still, there's a definite connection to Tom's murder, surely there's something you can do …'

'Leave it with me. In the meantime, just stay away from them in case you cause more trouble.'

'You wouldn't even know who "they" were without the trouble we've caused. Larry, Tom was my friend, and he died in a nasty way, and somehow it's related to a terrible pack of guitar-playing cunts who appear to be hell-bent on some kind of world domination. I'm going to get to the bottom of this with or without your help. I thought your motto was "to protect and to serve"?'

'That's the NYPD, I think.'

'Well, what's your motto?'

'Erm … don't pick it, it'll never heal.'

'Not your personal motto, the Garda motto.'

'Oh, that. I have no idea. "Be excellent to each other"?'

'Fuck me. Look, I'm going after these people. If you can help, great. If you can't, then stay out of my way.'

'You do what you have to do, Twenty, I'll be there to mop up and take all the credit.'

'I wouldn't have it any other way, Larry.'

I finished my pint in one large gulp, put on my hat and left. If the police weren't going to help, then we had to get to the bottom of this ourselves. Where once we had been the detected (long story) we were now, like the Thompson Twins, the detectives. Except without the ridiculous ginger fringe.

I wandered down Grafton Street, ignoring all the people coming out of HMV with their glazed eyes and simple smiles on their way home to play acoustic air guitar along to their latest purchase. It suddenly hit me just how dangerous it was to be out and about in public with so many of them around, unaware they were being used to spread the virus. We had to have protection because even standing beside somebody whose mobile phone went off would be enough to infect us, and without us, the whole country was doomed. I shuddered a little at the responsibility. It was huge, and I was just one man. I have a reasonably quiet existence, bar some occasional violence and all that stuff I do that I don't want the police to know about. Having the fate of the entire nation in my hands was just a little out of the ordinary for me. Believe it or not, I'm a man of routine. I like things the way I like them. I even like the stuff I don't like the way I don't like it. To now have a load of new stuff to not like was bothersome, and to know that that new stuff could change everything for ever was a real threat to my way of life. I just wanted things to go back to the way they were before – when the stuff I liked was simple and the stuff I didn't like was all around but I could cope with it. Adventures are for the Famous Five, Nancy Drew and the Hardy Boys and anyone who chooses to walk down Sean MacDermott Street in the dark. They are not for Twenty.

I was up against it, that was for sure. Ireland has more mobile phones per person than any other nation on the planet. A hundred million phones are sold every year, each person owns at least five (apart from this strange but delightfully ankled lady I know who simply refuses to purchase one) and six bazillion phone calls are made every day, which made the odds of avoiding the infection very small indeed. Smaller even than Bono's ego. At first, I thought me and the lads might have to puncture our own eardrums and deafen ourselves, communicating only by sign language, text message and that really weird talky voice deaf people have, but then I had an even better idea. I went into HMV going 'lalalalalalalala' to try and drown out the *Acoustic Covers* album they had on and shoplifted a load of iPods. Sadly, none of them came with pre-loaded 80s music, so I hurried back to my house and spent the afternoon charging them and filling them with top tunes. Now when the lads went out, they could use the iPods to block out the ringtone if it went off nearby and enjoy some classic stuff from the greatest decade in musical history.

I figured the sooner I got them out there the better, so I fed the dog, fed the cat and threw them out the back. I put the iPods into my bag and headed out the front door. As I was closing the gate, I could see one of my neighbours approaching. It was Detaily Darren from up the road, and the last thing I needed to do was to get talking to him. He was unable to just tell you something without going into the most extraordinary detail about it. Once I remember asking him about his new car, and he replied, 'Well, I had to get a new car because my old car was making some funny noises. I tried to get it fixed, but the mechanic said it really wasn't worth it, so I then went to a garage, and in the garage I spoke to a salesman, who was wearing a blue tie, and I told him I needed a car. He said I was in the right place because new cars were their speciality. So, we discussed various types of new car and the payment plans for them and the pros and cons of each particular vehicle. Firstly there was a Mazda, but he said that this—' ... no joke, he spent twenty minutes going on and on and on about it. Eventually, I had to tell him I'd soiled myself just so I could go inside. To avoid him this time I put on my iPod and fired it up, meaning I could no longer hear him calling my name. Pretending I couldn't see him, I took one step to the left, meaning he wasn't standing right in front of me anymore, and headed for Jimmy's house.

🎧 🎧 🎧 🎧 🎧

When I arrived at Jimmy's, I opened the garden gate by moving the lock slightly to left, then providing forward pressure on the gate itself. I then closed the gate by pushing it back in the opposite direction and slid the lock back into the position it was in when I first found it. I put one foot in front of the other in order to walk up the path to the front door. First left, then right, then left, then right. This action was repeated seven and a half times until I reached the front door. Then, aided by the motor cortex and the cerebellum, my brain sent signals to my limbs to move and to extend my index finger, which then pressed on the doorbell. An electronic signal in the doorbell travelled down some wiring and caused a bell to chime, which alerted Jimmy to the fact that somebody was waiting outside.

'Ahh, Twenty,' said a smiling Jimmy, 'come on in. I have a visitor.'

I walked into the house, wondering who it could be that would have him smiling. Jimmy never has visitors , and he really doesn't like letting strange people into his house. I could only assume that he had been holding some rapscallion who owed some money to someone and was convincing him to pay up. Imagine my surprise when I discovered Jimmy's brother, Johnny the Bollix, sipping coffee at the kitchen table.

'Hello, Twenty,' he said.

'Hello, Johnny,' I said, furrowing my brow. I have never really liked Johnny, and that's leaving aside what he did to Jimmy after their parents' death. He's a few years older than us and used to hang around with the older kids in the neighbourhood when we were growing up. This meant they had to torment us at every opportunity. If we were playing football – and honing the skills that would have enabled us to play for one of the top clubs in England if we'd wanted – they'd arrive and steal the ball. I blame his constant interruptions for my lack of a top-flight football career. They'd kick it back and forth and then make us ask for the ball back, and just when we thought they'd give it back, they'd kick it into old man McKeown's back garden. Now, Old Man McKeown had two Jack Russells which existed on a diet of old bread and young lads' ankles because his house faced the green we played on and sometimes his wall was used as a goal. So, it was natural that his garden was a ball magnet. One of us would have to climb over the wall, leg it as fast as possible to the ball, chuck it over, then scramble back over the wall (helped by a handy woodpile in the corner) before the dogs ate too much of his lower leg to stop him playing. I remember once Tubs Holloway, so named because he was a fat cunt, was struggling back over the wall when it collapsed under his weight. He landed on his back, and one of the flagstones from the top of the wall landed on his head, rendering him unconscious. Of course, being lads, we left him lying there and ran away as fast as we could due to the damage to the wall. We heard later that Old Man McKeown had taken him into his house and touched his special area until he woke up.

My main problem with Johnny was that one night when we were about ten and he was eighteen or nineteen, he caught a load of us looking through the front window of Barbara Hession's house as he furiously fingered her on the sofa. Dirty Dave, the clumsy fucker, managed to get his feet tangled up and went flying, knocked me to the ground and then got up and ran away as Johnny chased after us. I got a few digs in the head from a fishy-smelling hand. I couldn't believe the lads had just run off on me, didn't they know the 'one for all, all for one' code of the Muskahounds?

'You fucking little pervert,' he yelled at me.

'Me?!', I answered. 'I'm not the one fingering a thirteen-year-old.'

I got a few more digs after that and decided from that point on that, although Jimmy was my best friend, his big brother was a shitbag who I'd have as little to do with as possible. And I'd managed quite well until now.

'So, how's the terminal illness going?'

'Great! You'll be delighted to hear that Jimmy has agreed to help me out and donate bone marrow.'

'Nice of you to ask. Surely you could have forged some documents and stolen it from him while he was asleep.'

'Always so bitter, Twenty. Since you were a kid too. What a shame you never grew out of it.'

'What a shame you never got hit by a fucking bus.'

'Ooooh, get her,' he said, doing that hand motion that looks like you're a posh person holding two cups of tea in front of your nipples. 'I think it'd be best for me to head on, Jimmy. Thanks again, you have no idea how much this means to me. I always knew you could forgive. Unlike some people. Remember, make sure you fast on Monday night.'

'Yeah, see ya, Johnny,' said a curiously happy-looking Jimmy.

With that, he upped and left, and Jimmy went to see him to the door. When he came back, I raised an eyebrow.

'I know what you're thinking,' he said, 'but he's my only brother. He's all the family I've got left. I'm beginning to think seeing my father raped to death by a gay panther might have adversely affected me and my ability to be a bollix. I may have to do something overtly bollixy to make up for it.'

'Isn't it all happening very quickly? Don't they do counselling and stuff before you make a big decision like that? And don't they probably need to do tests to make sure your bone marrow is actually compatible?'

'Yeah, but he's already got that sorted. When I was a kid I had a piece of bone removed from my knee and I kept it in a jar at home. It was cool. Then one day it disappeared; I was gutted. Turns out Johnny had taken it just in case we ever had a serious falling-out and he needed a piece of my bone to determine whether or not I could donate to him in the event that he was suffering from some kind of terminal illness.'

'Damn, that is what you call foresight. Look, whatever you want to do is fine by me. I mean, if you want to undergo surgery, painful surgery, in just a few days' time, to help one of the biggest cunts on Earth to live, then that's entirely your perogative.'

Jimmy said nothing. I decided to drop it because we had more important things to worry about than whether or not Johnny the Bollix got a bone-marrow transplant. Like global warming, Dublin traffic and what was hot and not hot this week according to the various magazines in the Sunday newspapers.

I handed Jimmy an iPod, explaining to him that we had to ensure we didn't get infected when out and about. Assuring him that the music already installed on the device was 'gift' and 'capital', not to mention 'epic', we set off down to Ron's to meet the rest of lads. We walked in silence, Jimmy obviously thinking about the huge commitment he'd just made to his brother, while I thought about what sort of creature you'd make if you crossed a giraffe with a Polish person – something with a flat head and a long neck, probably. On arrival, we found everyone there: Dirty Dave, Stinking Pete, Lucky Luciano (who was looking rather agitated), Splodge and Ron. Nobody else. This was obviously a good omen.

'Ron, turn down the music for a sec, would you?'

It was disco night, and Ottawa were blasting out of the speakers. When the music was down to a normal level, I told them all about my plan to stave off the evil effects of that ringtone and about Folkapalooza, which had turned Ireland into a nation of mental Gollums, desperately waiting for their Phoenix Park precious.

'You've got to wear these at all times when out in public. This thing is spreading like chicken pox in a kindergarten, and we have to stay on top of it. Ron, if anyone comes into the bar, you have to make them turn off their mobile phone. Ask them in that way you ask things which nobody would dare disobey.'

'Will do, Twenty.'

'The rest of us are going to have to try and find out what's going on. It's all linked to this concert, I'm sure of it. Let's get a few pints down us to clear the heads, then we can come up with a plan.'

'I like the way you think,' said Pete and ordered a round for everyone. Ron's was an oasis of normality in the desert of madness that was enveloping us. My father had taken me to Ron's for my first pint all those years ago. I suppose it was a rite of passage, a father taking his son to the local bar, buying him his first drink, watching in amusement as the beer went down and the face scrunched up a bit at the sour taste when the kid had only ever been used to Miwadi orange. We sat at the bar together, my Dad and I, and chatted not so much like father and son but like two friends. I never felt closer to him than that day. We had a few drinks, not too many as it was my first time and he was conscious of that, until it was time to go.

'We'd best head off, Twenty.'

'Awww, do we have to?'

'Yeah, you know we do. Your Mam will have the dinner on and we can't have you hungover as a cunt on your Communion day.'

Memories. Not like the corners of my mind, as that would imply my mind was square or rectangular-shaped when it is, in fact, quite circular. I liked remembering those moments.

Just then, a hand tapped me on the shoulder. I span around quickly with my hands in the classic ju-jitsu pose, ready to pretend to know ju-jitsu to whoever it was.

'Twenty,' said Lucky, 'I must a talk to you.'

'Okay, my Italian chum. Talk away.'

'No a here. In privet.'

'Privet?'

'Yes, you know, privet!'

'Erm … pri-vet … uhm …'

'Only you and a me.'

'Ahhh, *private*. Okay. Let's go over there,' I said, pointing at the other end of the bar. So, we did. Now imagine, if you can, this is a film and this is one of those montage scenes with some cheesy music playing. You would see Lucky talking to me, trying to explain something, and me, because of his hilariously Super Nintendo Italian accent, pretending to not get it. I'm a cunt like that sometimes. Then he'd gesticulate more wildly than normal and hand me a brown dossier file, which I open. The camera would be on a close-up of me now, with my mouth agape, and I might even put my hand to my mouth to show just how shocked and surprised I was. Then, after speaking with Lucky some more, I'd rub my chin in a way that showed you I was thinking very deeply about what I'd just learned. Then I'd gesture, and Jimmy the Bollix would come over, and the music would probably stop at that stage, and I'd say something like, 'Hey Jimmy, you know that hit that's out on us?' and Jimmy'd say, 'Yeah,' and I'd say, 'Well, guess who's been hired to carry it out,' and Jimmy'd say, 'Carlos the Jackal?' and I'd nod my head in Lucky's direction, and Jimmy'd go, 'No way!', and I'd go 'Way!' Then things would go back to normal.

'Look, Twenty, Jimmy, this is big a problem for me.'

'I can understand that, Lucky,' I said, 'having to turn down a job like this because you can't kill your mates must be one of the toughest things a man in your chosen profession can come up against.'

'Is a not that so much. Is a big problem because if I no a kill you, then my reputation is, like a the Irish football team, fucked. I have to think long a before I tell you this.'

'You mean, you were considering it?' said Jimmy.

'Well, work is a work. But you know me. I am compassionate assassin and only a kill those who I think a deserve to be killed.'

'That's cool, man, you think we don't deserve to be killed. That's kinda touching.'

'No, I'm a not say you don't deserve to be killed, more that the reason this man give me is not good enough.'

'And what was his reason?'

'He say that you meddle with a big project they work on. I don't care shit about his project. Unless project is big a plan to blow up cinemas in Ireland. I hate a going to cinema. Also, is a difficult decision because part of me think you probably do a deserve to be killed, but I don't a have the evidence.'

'Hah! If the cops can't find it, then you have no chance.'

I turned to Jimmy. 'It's got to be our friend at Mega Gigs and whoever's in league with them. This could be just the breakthrough we need.'

'How do you mean?'

'Well, Lucky can go back to them and say he's killed us, and they'll think we're out of the way. Then we can sneak around and find out more stuff.'

'Lucky, when you do a job, how do they pay you? Bank transfer?' asked Jimmy.

'No, I'm a operate only in cash, so I a meet with them when job is done.'

'And do they need proof?'

'Like a what?'

'Like one of our hands, or a mickey, or a photo of the dead bodies?'

'No, they a trust me. Have done jobs before for this man. If I say you are dead, then he will a believe you are dead.'

'All right then,' said Jimmy, 'what we'll do is arrange for Lucky to meet with this bloke, then we'll kidnap him, put him in the back of a van, drive him up the mountains, beat the information we need out of him, then, depending on our mood, we can kill him slowly or we can just shoot him in the face. It'll be fun!'

'I like the general idea of it, but perhaps he might be more use to us alive so he can tell the cops what's been happening. Witnesses who can back up your story are good. I suspect this is one of those times we'll need all the evidence we can get.'

'Fair enough so, but I'm only promising to not kill him on purpose. If he dies while I'm beating the info out of him, I'm not taking any grief.'

'Lucky, when do you have to do this by?'

'Normally, I say five a working days.'

'Hah, working days. I like your style.'

'Is not me. Is a Mrs Lucky, she don't a like me work at weekend.'

'That's even funnier. Okay, we'll work out the details later.'

Just then, Stinking Pete called from the other side of the bar where he had the TV on as Ron had called a halt to disco night because he'd inadvertently played 'MacArthur Park' by Donna Summer, and the song sent him into rages every time he heard it. We went over to catch the end of a TV promo:

'... *so don't miss Folkapalooza. If you can't get to the Phoenix Park, then you can watch it live on RTÉ 1 and 2, TV3, TG4, Channel 6 and BBC1 Northern Ireland. As well as that, it'll be live on Today FM, RTÉ Radio 1 and 2FM, FM104, 98FM, Spectre FM, Cork FM, Radio Galway, Termonfeckin Radio and Newstalk, so there's no reason for you to miss it. Folkapalooza live and in your living room. THIS BANK-HOLIDAY MONDAY!'*

'Fucking hell,' said Splodge, 'that's what you might call unprecedented, isn't it?'

'It certainly is. How the fuck did they manage to do that?' said Dirty Dave while examining a rather crunchy-looking rock of snot he'd just mined from his nose.

'Obvious,' I said, 'they've used the ringtone to take over all the executives and decision-makers, and you know that people who work in TV and radio are a bunch of arse-kissing sheep. Nobody will ever disagree with the boss because there's so much competition for their jobs.

That means the ones that haven't been infected are just going along with it out of fear. And brown-nosery. Plus they're all cunts.'

'There's got to be some reason they're getting the concert on so many channels and giving away free tickets. Do you think they're going to play the ringtone and infect everyone in the country?'

'That sounds plausible,' I said, 'but given the fact this is Mega Gigs, Damien Rice, David Gray and many, many more, I think it's going to be something much worse than that.'

Now, I'm not one to blow my own trumpet, too many ribs you see, but you have no idea how right I was.

16

Saturday Morning

(TWO days PF –

pre-Folkapalooza)

Seamus admired himself in the mirror. He'd spent the morning gamboling around the Phoenix Park like a new-born lamb. He liked to go at night too and spy from the bushes at the deer rutting. At least, he thought they were deer. Sometimes the deer spoke to him. He shook his head vigorously.

He showered and began to make himself a sandwich, then remembered he hated sandwiches because they reminded him of a time in a town called Callan when a sandwich had nearly cost him his life. He'd been wandering from town to town, doing odd jobs. A little farming here, a spot of manning psychic hotline phonelines there, even though he was no more a psychic than a fat housewife from Ballyfermot. He did what he had to. In Callan, County Kilkenny, a town with a heartbeat so sinister and black that Stephen King himself couldn't imagine it, he sensed something was wrong. He had decided to move on as quickly as possible, but he needed some food. Spotting a shop just about to close, he entered.

'Excuse me, could I prevail upon you to make me a sandwich?' he asked the old crone behind the counter.

'I could that. What'd you like?'

'Ham. Cheese. And some onion. And some boiled egg, if it is not too much trouble.'

'Brown or white?'

'Brown, please.'

'Tough. We've only got white. D'ya want butter on it?'

'Yes, please.'

'Tough. All we have is Flora.'

'Okay.'

She made the sandwich in silence. Seamus looked around him. The shop was small, with everything stacked on shelves that looked like they could fall over at the slightest touch. There were brands of sweets he'd never heard of and some odd cakes. Soon she finished and handed it to him wrapped in tinfoil.

'That'll be £1.50,' she said.

Seamus handed her the money and was just about to thank her when she took his hand and said, 'Stay on the path, y'hear? Don't go on't moors tonight.'

'I will do my best to remember that,' said a clearly shaken Seamus, who left the shop as quickly as possible. There was something off about this town all right and his instincts were humming like a tramp's arsehole. He threw his meagre possessions over his shoulder, which were handily contained in an old sports bag, and set off on his way. Just as he was nearing the outskirts of the town, he remembered how hungry he was and unwrapped the sandwich. He took a bite. It was good. Then another bite. Greedily, he took another. It was delicious. Then, disaster. Due to his avaricious consumption of the sandwich, he was now choking-and-having left the shop so quickly, he never bought a drink to try and wash it down. As he chewed, he bit into a large crumbly yolk from a hard-boiled egg, and all the moisture left his mouth in a flash. With the food already caught in his throat and a mouth dryer than Mother Teresa's gee, he was choking to death.

He tried to cough, but nothing happened. It just made food get even more stuck. Then he remembered. Despite being born with the most hideous of mutations, nature hadn't totally overlooked Seamus. He was double-jointed and could manipulate his limbs and fingers in many weird and often disgusting ways. He knew he didn't have much time. Unlocking his shoulders, he flipped them over his back, then reached around and grabbed himself under the diaphragm and gave himself the Heimlich Manoeuvre. Once. Nothing. Twice, a little bit. Strength waning. Will to live fading. He summoned all his strength and gave one mighty effort, and a torpedo of sandwich came flying out and blasted a hole through the now-solid wall of egg yolk and cheddar cheese, allowing him enough of a passageway to get air again. He fell to his knees and sucked in air like he was Paris Hilton under a green night-vision camera. Righting his arms, he scraped the food out of his mouth and lapped up water from a nearby puddle to wash away what was left. It had been a close call. After he had recovered, he vowed to never eat another sandwich again. For the very same reason, he could never again eat Shredded Wheat, butterscotch Angel Delight and most varieties of crisps.

Back in his room, flashback over, he boiled the kettle and made himself a Pot Noodle. As he sat there, still thinking about how close he had come to death that day in Callan, his phone rang. He looked at the name display. It was him.

'Hello?' he said.

'It is done.'

'That is good news.'

'Yes. Now you must pay.'

'Of course.'

'Usual place. Tomorrow evening at sixteen minutes to nine. The PM nine. Not the one in the morning.'

'Thank you. I will see you tomorrow,' said Seamus, and, just as he was about to ask if it had been difficult, the line went dead.

🎧 🎧 🎧 🎧 🎧

'Okay, is a done,' said Lucky, no longer having to pretend to be able to speak English properly. We were in my house.

'What happens now?' I asked.

'Tomorrow we a go meet in usual place, he give me money. I take a the money, count a the money, then I go.'

'You count a the money there and then?'

He just looked at me.

'Well, where's the usual place? Somewhere quiet and inconspicuous, I bet.'

'Gate of Trinity College.'

'The gate of Trinity College?'

'Yes, is a perfect.'

'But there are so many people there …'

'Yes, but he is a, I don't know word in English so I say in Italian, albino.' He pronounced it al-bih-no.

'Al Banim, famous Dublin comedian?'

'No, al-bih-no, al-bih-no!'

'He's an Arab?'

'No, you a crazy cazzo fuckpig. He is a like a the fucking snowman. He is whites. All whites. Skin. Hair. Pubis.'

'Ahh, albino. Fair enough. But it's hardly a big deal these days, is it? If someone looks like a rabbit, then people are big enough to get over it without terrifying *Watership Down* flashbacks.'

'Yes, but is a strange. This is why he like a to meet in Trinity because there are so many people and weird students. He can, like a you say, get blended in.

You see, is not just only albino. Is a also ginger.'

'Say that again.'

'That again.'

'No, repeat the last thing you said.'

'Is not just only albino. Is a also ginger.'

Something clicked in the back of my head. What was it Larry O'Rourke had said about forensics? I closed my eyes, and soon I was looking at a flashback of that scene in Chapter 4 when he tells me, 'Just something the forensics mentioned. They found some hairs they couldn't really identify. Not human and not from any animal they have in their database ... The hairs were a strange colour, too. Sort of white, but sort of ginger too.'

As his voice echoed away, I knew we were close to something here. Garda forensics, the most technologically advanced forensics department in the entire world, had found this rogue hair at the crime scene. White, but ginger too. Not human and not really animal. Manimal. And now this. A ginger albino hired Lucky to kill me and Jimmy: He had left behind one of his ginger albino hairs at the scene of Tom's murder. It had to be connected, but how? I'm joking, of course. I knew fine well. Tom's killer and the man who hired Lucky to kill us were one and the same. I told Jimmy and Lucky what Detective Larry O'Rourke had told me and how we had a chance to find out what was really going on.

'Okay, it all makes some kind of weird sense to me,' I said. 'The problem is that if this meeting is taking place at the gates of Trinity College, it doesn't make it easy for us to get hold of him. We can't park there, and, anyway, there are too many people around.'

'Right then,' said Jimmy. 'That means when Lucky concludes his business and picks up the money for the job he didn't do, we're going to have to follow him and take it from there.'

'We'll have to be super-inconspicuous though. Remember, he thinks we're dead. He can't see us.'

'Well, regardless of that fact, we don't want him to see us, so it makes no odds, does it?'

'*Touché*. Lucky, when you say you did work for this person before, what exactly did you mean?' I asked.

'I a mean what I say. I have worked for a him before.'

'I know you probably have some client confidentiality thing going on, but this is important. How long have you been doing jobs for him?'

'I a cannot tell you. Is confidential.'

'Come on, man. You know how important this could be.'

'No,' he said and stared straight out the window. I looked at Jimmy, who rolled his eyes in that way people do when they mean, 'Oh, Italians eh?'

Then Lucky laughed. 'I'm a get you, stupid Irish pig! I do four jobs in a the last nine months for him.'

'You remember who they were?'

'Sure, are all managers of a big a record shops.'

'Fucking hell.'

'Yes, is a the manager of HMV, of a the Virgin Megastores, of a the Golden Discs and of a Tube Records in Rathfarnham Shopping Centre.'

'Dammit, those are the four biggest and most successful record shops in Ireland. But I'm confused. You've always said you were a compassionate assassin. That you'd only kill those who deserved to be killed.'

'Is a true, don't a question my morals. The man from HMV, he like a the films of Tom Hanks. He deserve to die. Virgin man, he always wear a the shirt tucked into the jeans. This I don't a like. So he die. Golden Discs one, he support Tottenham Hotspur. Must a die. And Tube Records bloke, he is worst of all. He use, on a daily basis, cosmetics for men like a thing they call concealer to make a the spots go away. Any man who wear a the make-up is a dead man to me.'

'This makes me deeply suspicious, like a skeptical lake,' I said.

'Well, while you are suspicious, I am hungry,' said Jimmy. 'I need some breakfast. Lucky, fancy a fry-up?'

'You mean fatty food fried to within an inch of its life in fatty oils and dripping and smothered in fatty ketchup, washed down with fatty sweet tea and which is a nothing like a healthy Mediterranean breakfast? Count a me in.'

'You coming, Twenty?'

'Nah, I'll stay here. I already had eight Pop-Tarts this morning. I'll catch up with you later on.'

I took the names of the record shop managers from Lucky, who, thanks to his photographic memory, never forgot a name or a face. That really was handy. I let them go and rolled a joint from the very smelly and sticky grass

Jimmy had brought over (which he'd confiscated off some young lads outside the off-licence who asked him to go in and buy beer for them) and smoked it for a bit. I felt a bit stuffed after such a big breakfast, so I decided to do some exercise. Sitting down at my computer I fired up Addams Family Pinball and played for two hours solid, until my two index fingers were aching. No pain no gain, as they say.

17

Saturday Afternoon

After a short nap, during which I dreamt of giant guitars being played by even gianter monks with their enormous gums, I got up, showered, taking great care to shampoo and condition my pubic hair, and did some research on the internet. Actual proper research, not the kind of 'research' you'd say you were doing when the boss looked over your shoulder and found you reading a website you shouldn't have been reading during work, and you know he doesn't believe you because your research into the area of home insurance shouldn't really feature Japanese amputee midget women dressed as schoolgirls and being sodomised by a three-legged horse. First, I googled the deaths of the record-shop-owners, using precise and exact search terms, and soon I had found them.

MAN SLAIN IN GOLF CLUB CAR PARK

Gardaí were today looking for witnesses to the murder of Mr Alan Cassidy, 35, from Baldoyle. Mr Cassidy, who was boss of Virgin Megastores Ireland, was found in his car by a passing jogger, who alerted local gardaí. Forensics teams have completed their initial investigation and have said cause of death was, what appeared to be the biggest wedgie of all time. It is believed Mr Cassidy was pulled up by his own underpants with such force that his custom-made Lycra boxers ripped him open up the middle as far as his chest cavity.

Jesus Christ! Lucky was some deadly bastard all right.

The Irish Times, 8 January 2007

RECORD CHIEF GOES WAY OF EIGHT TRACK AND 78s

HMV Ireland was today in shock as like-able Chief Executive Carl Allen was killed in what Gardaí say was a robbery gone wrong. Despite the fact that the assailant did actually get away with the victim's wallet, therefore making it quite a successful robbery, Detective Sergeant Andy Lyle says the intention wasn't to kill him.

'Sure why would he do a thing like that if he already had the wallet, like?'

Classic, Lucky. Making it look just like a robbery so they wouldn't see the pattern.

Irish Independent, 14 February 2007

3 KIDS LOSE DAD, AND WIFE IS ALREADY BEING TREATED FOR DEPRESSION

Three young children (pictured left, weeping) will never see their father again after Golden Discs top dog Jeff Tyrell was brutally cut down right before their eyes. Having accompanied their dad to the Farmer's Expo in the RDS, they could only watch in horror as an out-of-control combine-harvester harvested him into lots of tiny little pieces. A Polish man was later arrested and questioned in Ballsbridge Garda Station, and, despite pleading his innocence to anyone who would listen on top of having a watertight alibi, he is expected to be charged with first-degree murder.

My respect for my Italian chum was growing. This time,

he'd pinned it on an immigrant, who people would naturally be suspicious of. Genius.

Southside Express, 1 March 2007

OH DEAR JESUS, IT'S HAPPENING AGAIN

The local community is in fear this morning as well-known businessman and owner of Tube Records in the Rathfarnham Shopping Centre, David Coleman, was discovered dead in his shop. Gardaí say that the murder weapon was a recorder inserted up Mr Coleman's anus and then played at such a high pitch that his internal organs exploded. At the scene, Detective Larry O'Rourke would neither confirm nor deny rumours that Brian Hanlon had come back to wreak his terrible revenge on the community like he promised to all those years ago after the incident which cannot be spoken of. We at the Southside Express take that silence to mean 'yes' and urge you all to live in fear and terror. And remember, only the Southside Express has the inside track on this shocking story.

My God, he was even making it look as if the baddy could be someone with a motivation Lucky knew nothing about because of an incident he'd never heard of.

Amazing. And look at that, a link to Larry O'Rourke. This really was getting interesting, especially as Larry had never mentioned the fact Tom wasn't the first record-shop-owner to be killed. I needed to talk to him, but that could wait. I had to think. That required some thought. Eventually, I got it. Why would someone have Lucky knock off four record-shop chiefs? I don't believe in coincidences, except for that one time I was listening to the radio on my walkman and 'Baker Street' by Gerry Rafferty came on and where was I standing? That's right, outside the Brennan's Bread factory. That's pretty fucking indisputable. Wracking my tired and slightly hungover head, it came to me like a toddler to a bowl of chocolate ice cream – unsteadily and a disturbing brown colour. They obviously installed their own men in there to further their despicable agenda. But I needed proof.

Luckily for me, everyone lives their lives online now. Some searching around the various corporate websites gave me the names I needed, and then it was off to Facebook, where I signed in as John Murphy. As I suspected, each one of the recently installed managers had a profile, and I asked to be added as a friend, giving such reasons as 'We attended school together' and 'We both did that really boring course that time, remember? With that guy! Yeah, that one.' Within twenty minutes, I had been approved by each of them as they were all, like the rest, desperate to have as many 'friends' as possible, and I set about exploring their profiles. Ignoring schools, colleges and irrelevant crap like that, I immediately went to the careers section, where they each listed their previous jobs. It was all there. They had all worked for Mega Gigs at some stage. Facebook might be a big load of self-indulgent boring shite, but it had its uses.

William Langhammer, the new chief of Virgin, had worked at Mega Gigs as an advertising executive. Timmé Mangonio, the newly crowned head of HMV, had been responsible for sticking the holograph thing to each ticket Mega Gigs produced. Mark Carlisle, now the man in charge at Golden Discs, had previously worked as 'PR stormtrooper'. And finally, Gordon Hunt, a former office runner at Mega Gigs HQ, was now in charge of the multi-hundred-euro-a-week business at Tube Records in the Rathfarnham Shopping Centre. I printed off screenshots, then realised I might need to back them up in case mysterious hackers got at my computer and destroyed the evidence, so I emailed them to an old Hotmail account. Then I remembered I couldn't remember that password, so I set up a new Gmail address and sent them there. Despite a nagging voice in the back of my head saying that I had no reason to suspect Google would be anything less than completely secure, I also sent the pictures to my mobile phone using Bluetooth, burned them to an encrypted CD, a 100-MB zip disk and took photos of them with one of those cool, thin spy cameras that people always take pictures of documents with. I always knew that thing would come in handy one day.

At my feet, Bastardface sighed. I had been neglecting him over the past few days, and he wasn't getting his exercise. A big dog like him needs it. Sometimes I liked to take him into town with me. As he was large and fearsome, I found myself with plenty of room to walk up and down crowded shopping streets, but it wasn't exactly convenient these days. New laws ensured it wasn't just a muzzle for Bastardface, he had to go in one of those things they transported Hannibal Lecter around in. That wasn't even an option for me this time. I had to get this evidence to Larry O'Rourke as soon as possible, so that meant leaving the dog alone again. To make myself feel less guilty, I left him with his favourite game: I put a weeping, terrified orphan in a Liverpool shirt out the back garden for him to play with. He seemed to give me a look that said, 'Thanks, boss. This'll do for now,' while I locked the back door.

Before I left the house, I tried Larry's mobile, but there was no answer. He must have been off investigating something or apprehending criminals for him not to answer. I put on my iPod as I left the house, lit a full-flavoured Major cigarette and strolled into town in time with the music. Passing the Headline Bar, I clicked my fingers in time to 'Yah Mo Be There', shades on as the sun was shining. Past that great Indian takeaway just down from the pawn shop, the right-hand side of the road like it has been for years, the left crammed with red-brick modern apartment buildings and giant Spar convenience stores underneath. Christchurch, Lord Edward Street, down Dame Street, peering down into Temple Bar at tourists with maps looking lost and searching for somewhere to eat that didn't cost a month's wages in their country, and before I knew it, I was at the Central Bank again. The statue, which everyone uses as a meeting place, was like an enormous golden gonad glinting in the sun.

It being a Saturday, it should have been full of the Gorks and the suede-wearing acousticies, but looking around I could scarcely believe my eyes. The dark ones were gone, and a great Dublin tradition was broken. From Cureheads to Goths to skater punks to modern-day Emos, there had been a presence of dark, pseudo-existential misery in front of the Central Bank for years, and now it was gone. Not one remained. They were all wearing the same kind of clothes, but it was like going to a football match and seeing the opposition, who you hate with all your might, in a completely different-coloured shirt than you expected. Why had the kids who loved to wear black, and only black, now started wearing white shirts and jeans and possibly some blouses too? Parents were just glad that little Johnny or Mary had finally grown out of that awful phase and glad they looked like you could bring them to a restaurant without dying a little bit with the shame each time. Other adults were already under the spell of the virus and knew them as their own, while the rest of the world just didn't give a shit about them either way so never thought about it for a second.

I scanned the crowd, turning up the iPod a little bit for extra protection, looking for the girl I'd met before. What was her name? Sorcha! Surely it hadn't got hold of her too? In the end, I only recognised her from the way she was smoking her cigarette. Gone were the black clothes, the dark eyeliner and lipstick that would have made Robert Smith chuck a jealous hissy fit. I wandered over to her. She looked up at me. Something flickered in her eyes. I took her by the elbow and led her away from the main throng, and only there did I dare take out one earphone so I could hear her.

'Hey Gork. What the fuck happened to you?'

'Are you going to Folkapalooza?' she asked, eyes wide, mouth agape. I thought about dropping my cigarette into it to put it out, but didn't. That would have been mean. Funny, but mean.

'Oh fucking hell. I thought maybe you'd have been able to resist.'

'It's going to be great. Folkapalooza will bring us all together.'

'What do you mean?'

'Folkapalooza. Finale. Sweeeeeet,' she said, with a dreamy look in her eye. I wasn't getting any sense out of her at all. Should I slap her in the face like they do in the movies? It might bring her around a bit, but more likely somebody would call the Gardaí because a man with a white beard was beating the shite out of a young girl in public. I couldn't very well take her back to my house and deprogram her because somebody would have reported me for kidnapping. Then the Gardaí would break down my door just as I had her tied to a chair, playing 80s synth music at her in what would appear to be a situation a lot more serious, and possibly depraved, than it actually was. It all just made me mad, and I vowed, there and then, on top of everything else that had happened, that I would make these fuckers pay for snuffing the shoe-gazing, slack-jawed, moping, miserable life out of this girl. I let go of her arm, and she stood looking at me. I walked away, upset at what she'd become. I wanted to help her because if she could get back to normal, then so could everything else. As I headed away, she called my name.

'Beardy,' she said, obviously struggling to force her real self to appear.

'What?'

'This is really shit. Finale, Beardy. Finale.'

After that, it was too much effort, and she returned to drippiness and blandness and sterility. I watched her skip over to another group who were standing around practicing their David Gray head-wobbling and reading each other poems they'd written, using little flower symbols to dot their 'i's. They were like a litter of puppies all stricken with distemper and meningitis and running around in circles until you're forced to put them down. Maybe one of the puppies will survive, but he'll be so brain-damaged he'll try to chew water for the rest of his poor life, and every single time he's let into the house, he runs under the kitchen table, completely forgetting the head-height wooden bar underneath it. It was no life for a dog, let alone for a person who wasn't a dog. As I walked away, I thought of her words.

'*Finale, Beardy. Finale.*'

I knew immediately what she meant. Which made for a nice change. Whatever the final solution was, planned by these abominable miscreants, it was going to happen at the end of the Folkapalooza concert, at the last song. But what was this fiendish final curtain to be? Could we find out what the evil encore was before it was too late? No doubt there would be lighters in the air, and that was enough for me. Lighters were meant for lighting cigarettes, cigars, joints, fires, people and, possibly, the odd car for the insurance money, but they were not designed to wave back and forth at concerts. It was time someone put a stop to this lighter abuse once and for all.

I tried calling Larry O'Rourke again, but his mobile just rang out. As I wasn't too far from Pearse Street, I figured I'd just wander down to see if he was there. The classic melody and awe-inspiring lyrics of the Tom Tom Club's 'Wordy Rappinghood' played in my ears as I strolled down past Trinity College, and, at the 15B bus stop I could see people of all ages, of all shapes, sizes, colours and creeds, infected by this thing. You could tell by their eyes. They were dull and lifeless, but somewhere in the background there was a tiny spark that represented the pain they were in. It had now definitely reached epidemic proportions, and it was indiscriminate. It didn't matter if you were an inner-city street urchin blowing married men in an alleyway for a sawbuck or a well-to-do debutante from Howth riding your pony: This thing would get a hold on you and not let go; it would take your heart, and you wouldn't feel it. And, for all we knew, it could be getting stronger and more difficult to deprogram people. We just had to hope that wasn't the case.

I walked into the Garda station, turned down the iPod and asked the young, rosy-cheeked officer behind the counter for Larry O'Rourke. He looked at me vacantly and didn't answer. I asked him again. He just kept staring. Damn, now the police were infected. The Gardaí, the most efficient, well-trained, dynamic police force in the entire world, a force that had spent a fortune on anti-brainwashing training for its members, were powerless against this virus. What would it be like in other countries where they had police forces without such specialised training? Christ, this could just be the start of a diabolical plan to take over the world. Another garda came in from the street, and I was about to ask him, when it became obvious, from the way he was singing 'Babylon' at the top of his reedy voice, that he too had fallen victim. I then spotted a third one coming in the door who looked relatively normal, but when I spoke to him, he merely regaled me with anecdotes about the time he spent living in the Congo and how he'd had four wives there and survived an assassination attempt by a local chief who took umbrage at the fact he had led his village to a 4–1 triumph over the chief's men in the annual football tournament and how he'd invented a machine that could turn potatoes into gold. Knowing I'd get no help in there, I was about to leave and headed for the front door. As I turned the corner, who should I see walking towards me, talking on his phone, but Larry!

'Okay, well you just tell him that I love him and that everything will be all right. Despite the fact that life is made up of a series of crushing blows that would break the spirits of even the strongest men, once we can write poems and acoustic songs about it, everything is bound to be fine. I love you so much that I wish you'd leave me for another man so I'd have awesome material for a twenty-one-minute song on my three-hour-long concept album. Right then, see you later.'

I stared at him. Larry, too. Oh, no. But then I realised Larry was a bit crap, and we were probably just better off without any gardaí hassling us at all.

'Ah, hello Twenty,' he said.

'How do, Larry? Feeling okay?'

'Never better. There's a fire that burns inside me, Twenty. It's the fire of unimaginable loneliness and misery. Are you going to Folkapalooza?'

'Not sure that I am, I have to say. Do you remember what we've been working on the past few days?'

'Work? What is work at the end of the day? It's just more stuff that's not Folkapalooza. It's not important. Folkapalooza is important.'

This was good. It meant that this Larry was not conscious of the work we'd been doing behind the scenes, and, therefore wasn't going to try to stop me by using that knowledge. He also seemed completely spell-bound, which was unusual. The most sinister thing about this was how people could operate normally, for the most part, but Larry was gurning like it was 6.00am on a Sunday morning and he'd taken his seventh yoke about fifteen minutes previously. That meant it was fresh. I'd seen the same look on the face of Pete when he'd been infected in my house that time. Shit! That meant his phone was infected, and all the others too. I had to get out of there as quickly as possible, there was no time to waste. If one of those phones went off, I'd be done for.

'Well, I'll tell you what, Larry, if yer man gets back to me about that thing I'll give you a shout. Got yer mobile number here. Of course, he's waiting to hear back from the other fella, and you know what he's like. Blood from a stone, isn't it? Jesus, do you remember that time a few years back when the lad from Dundalk came down, and yer man says "Here, you might look like a cunt but if there's a cunt around here, it's me," and nobody had a fucking clue what he meant. It was only a few days afterwards when we were chatting about it in Ron's – oh, by the way, we're trying to get him to get a new plasma in for the football, the scabby fucker, you should come around for some of the matches. Where was I? Yeah, chatting about it in Ron's, and it was Dave, of all people, who reckoned it was all tied in with that TV show we were watching the night before. Remember, it had yer man from whatchacallit in it. You know the fella, he's got a head like someone smacked him from behind with a shovel. His wife was the one with the arse who went out with the little fat one from *NYPD Blue* in real life. Sipowicz! He was cool. Andy Sipowicz. He was on *Hill Street Blues* as well, wasn't he? God, I remember that. That's when TV was fucking good, not like this old reality shite these days. *Big Brother*? Big Bollocks, more like … erm … right … anyway, I'll be off, Larry.'

I quickly turned up the iPod and headed for the door.

Just as I was going through the door I felt a hand on my back.

'Argh, Zombie!' I thought before I remembered where I was. It was Larry. I turned down the music.

'Are you going to Folkapalooza?' he said.

'I think I might just have to, Larry. I might just have to.'

18

Saturday Evening

That evening, we had a lock-in in Ron's. Not the traditional lock-in where the riff-raff are sent on their merry way and the regulars are kept behind for some after-hours and deliciously crafty pints. This happened at nine o'clock, at which time we'd all arrived in the bar. Ron told the other two customers, a couple of old lads in caps sipping Guinness at the far end of the bar, that they couldn't leave for a while and not to listen to anything that was said, and, if they did listen, to forget it straight away. He put two fresh pints and two Jamesons in front of them so they wouldn't disturb him for a bit. The old lad on the left turned to the old lad on the right, pulled at the hair sprigging out of his ear and raised his left eyebrow as if to say, 'Who'd be bothered with his shite anyway?', before taking a mighty gulp and finishing his drink.

At the other end of the bar, I sat with Jimmy, Dirty Dave, Stinking Pete, Lucky, Splodge and Ron, and the topic of the evening was what the buggering fuck we were going to do.

'I've never seen anything like this in all my years,' said Ron, who has had his bar as long as anyone can remember. I once met an old drunk who claimed to have been drinking in Ron's one night with Éamon de Valera and Brendan Behan and that Ron was the barman back then. That would make Ron older than one of those giant trees in *The Lord of the Rings*. Orcs, what cunts. Outwitted by giant trees when the introduction of one Dutch Elm would have sorted the whole thing out. Anyway, Ron was still speaking and holding his iPod disdainfully in his large, scarred hands.

'You know, I hate these modern things and only for the fact I have *Now That's What I Call Castrati VII* I'd just say, to hell with it. Well, that and the fact that everywhere you go people are all changed. Shells of their real selves. Now, don't get me wrong. People are cunts. I hate every single last fucking one of them, but at least some of them have the bollocks to hate me back. This lot would just write a song about how mean you were to me as a child or something equally insipid. It has to be stopped. Obviously, they're still cunts at the moment, but I prefer the old kind of cunts. I want those cunts back, you cunts.'

I recounted my day's work to them, bringing them up to speed on the evidence, the fact that even the cops were useless to us now and how, from the subtle clues I'd been given, the finale of the Folkapalooza concert seemed to be the thing we should be concentrating on. They must be planning to detonate something. I mean, wasn't that what all evil geniuses wanted to do in the end? You work your way up to a position of enormous power and wealth and then you decide that you want to destroy the world. Wouldn't it be better to just use your money to play enormous and elaborate practical jokes on members of the public? I know that's what I'd do. Jimmy wasn't convinced about the 'exploding everything' scenario, though.

'I don't think this is about blowing everyone up and leaving the city in ruins. If you're going to do that, you'd make sure everyone was aware of what you were doing. You'd want them to feel the fear, fear worse than waking up in a strange bed and feeling an arm over you and the arm belonging to someone you really don't want it to belong to, such as an accountant from Bristol called Clive or something, but you want them terrified. You don't put them all in a stupor first.'

'That does make sense,' I said, 'leaving aside the bit about Clive, of course. So, what is it then?'

'Maybe this is a plot by the Moonies, and they're going to have the biggest mass wedding in the history of time, and then they'll get in the The Guinness Book of Records and also receive some kind of commemorative plaque to mark the occasion, which they'll hang in their main Dublin headquarters, which is where the old Hideout video arcade used to be on South William Street,' ventured Dave.

'It's good, but it's not quite right,' said Splodge.

'Personally, I reckon that the finale of the concert will do something like make it impossible for the people to be deprogramed, thus making the acoustic retardation they're suffering from permanent, which, when you get down to brass tacks, means it's no longer temporary.'

'Those evil bastards,' I said. 'Obviously, we need to get as much information from this ginger albino as we possibly can. Hopefully, once we get our hands on him, he'll squeal on the big bosses, and we can stop it like we stopped *Self Aid 3* all those years ago.'

'I honestly thought nothing could be worse than that,' said Jimmy. 'A concert for the unemployed featuring Ireland's premier unemployed acts, such as In Tua Nua, Something Happens and No Sweat. Lives were lost, and we'll always remember our fallen colleague, Malodorous Malachy, ripped to pieces and consumed raw by Leslie Dowdall and Tom Dunne. This, however, is far more serious. The entire city of Dublin and, less importantly, the rest of the country is under the kind of threat that only comes once in a million thousand and three years, and we are the only ones who can stop it. We'll probably never get the recognition and fame and reward and treasure we deserve, but there's more to life than recognition and fame and reward and treasure.'

'You're so right, Jimmy,' said Pete, 'there is more to life. There's being able to go to bed at night knowing you've helped mankind, that you have stood up and been counted and have done the right thing. That's what's important.'

'No, that's not what's important. What's important is that we may be able to kill Damien Rice and his ilk and get away with it.'

'Yes, but helping people and acting nobly is also important.'

'Maybe it's important if you're a charitable king, but I couldn't give a shit. I just want to smash his head in with his own guitar. Although I would use any handy six-stringed instrument, if it comes down to it.'

'Look, let's not squabble,' I said. 'There's every chance we can do the right thing and still murder them. That way everyone's happy.'

As we sat, using beer mats and salt shakers to plan our strategy for the capture and interrogation of the ginger albino, it struck me how much life had changed in such a short space of time. Previously, I was a happy-go-lucky character, my only real worry being the morning after a night on the Guinness when your bowels clench and hot lava flows from your arse, making that inimitable splattering noise as it hits the toilet water. Has it stopped now? Is it safe to fart once my pants are up? Those were the tough questions back then. Now, I was worried about the future of millions of people, a confrontation with a hideous mutant, a massive outdoor concert and an evil genius boss that would make anything at the end of a video game seem like small fry. I figured this really was too much for one person to be fretting about, so I lost myself in the pints and the chasers, and, by the time Ron had served the fourth tray of his delightful mojitos, I don't remember worrying at all.

Seamus walked through the darkness, unafraid but still feeling rather discomfited. Tomorrow he had to meet the hitman, and, while nothing in terms of the arrangements was out of the ordinary, he felt uneasy. Perhaps he should have asked for proof; none of the news bulletins or newspapers would report the crime if the bodies were found. The deliberate and early infection of those in the media plus the twenty-four-hour blanket coverage of Folkapalooza would ensure that, but he calmed himself further when he thought of the exemplary work 'Hitty', as he liked to think of him, had done before. The record shop chiefs had been knocked off perfectly, and nobody had suspected a thing. The handover of money had always been hassle-free, and there was no reason to suggest it would be any different this time. He'd stay alert though, a highly trained operative like him had no choice. It was just so close to the end now, the work that they'd been doing for so long was finally about to come to fruition, so he put his sense of unease down to the project moving into the endgame phase. He was sure the corpses were buried just off a path in Enniskerry or the Sally Gap, or somewhere like that. The only way they'd be found was by pure chance. Perhaps a basset hound snuffling around the undergrowth might discover them, but at that stage it'd be so unimportant it might as well be a date-rape victim in a garda station.

He made his way towards the Wellington Monument, a giant phallus erect on the skyline, and then beyond, towards the gallops, where the enormous stage and sound system was almost complete. In two days, the Phoenix Park would be filled with people and music, and, once the finale took place, there would be no turning back. Suddenly, he heard a noise behind him, and he span around, ready for a fight. There was a scrabbling noise, leaves were kicked, and from the bushes emerged a large stag. It stood there, looking at him, then winked.

Seamus waved a hand dismissively at the beast. It continued to look at him before leaping into the air and lolloping off back into the bushes. He stood in front of the stage, which would soon be packed with people singing along to the music, waving their hands in the air, loving each other, spending a fortune on Folkapalooza T-shirts, flight jackets, concert programmes and all the other merchandise on sale that day – and that didn't even take into account the post-gig CD and commemorative Director's Cut limited edition DVD and the Director's Cut of the Director's Cut special edition remastered double-disc blue-ray edition.

Folkapalooza was going to be a seminal event in the history of mankind, and now that the beardy smoking thug and his cohort were out of the way, nothing could stop it. Seamus lay down on the grass, looking at the stars, the constellations twinkling: the Saucepan, Orion's Belt, the Big Dipper, Dana's Quim, the Ferris Wheel. The bright lights spread into one, ever-dimming glow, and he fell asleep. He never even felt the stag, some half an hour later, nuzzling hungrily at his crotch.

19

Sunday

I woke up after midday on Sunday with my head pounding more than a porn star's arse after filming *Backdoor Black IV: The Widening*. Rubbing my eyes, I shuffled out of the bedroom in my shorts and T-shirt and promptly fell over a traffic cone handily placed just outside the door. Traffic cones again, eh? Those fuckers were always following me home when I was a teenager, but after I'd had a strong word with their leader one night, the problem seemed to have gone away. This was just more proof that the universe was on the brink of going topsy-turvy.

I went into the kitchen and opened the back door, and, before long the two animals came in. I gave Bastardface his traditional Saturday breakfast, thirteen rings of black pudding, and put some milk out for the cat. He'd surely eaten his fill during the night. I hoped it was that yappy little dog that lives across the back somewhere and yelps all day long when nobody's home. You'd think he'd just pull the washing off the line or something, but he was relentless. I opened the fridge to see what I had for my own breakfast. Some old cheddar cheese that had gone hard. Butter. Half a tin of coconut milk. A cola-flavoured yoghurt and a couple of rashers that had that oily sheen off them. That was it. Grocery shopping hadn't been high on my agenda in recent days. Oh well, I'd have to make do. I poured some olive oil into the pan and fried up the bacon. I threw in some chunks of cheese and some fresh basil, and, when the cheese had melted, I stirred in some coconut milk and ginger. Then I broke up five slices of slightly stale white bread and let them soak up all the juices. I put it into a bowl and ate it in front of the computer, checking on the news. I don't take a newspaper, you see. Fifteen minutes later, after I had finished vomiting, I was beginning to feel slightly human. I brushed my teeth and washed down some Ibuprofen with a glass of crème de menthe, which I prefer to use in place of Listerine.

The end of the previous night was a blur. I didn't remember coming home or what time we finished, but that homing beacon that we all have, the one that ensures we find our way back to our own house no matter how drunk we are, had obviously been in overdrive. I checked. I didn't have the fear. You know the fear. The fear when after a night out something just goes 'ping' inside your head and you can't remember what it is yet, but you're pretty sure it's something bad. Parts of conversations will come back to you, and you'll cringe, and your toes will curl, and all the while the fear is still there, and it won't go away until you talk to someone else or, even worse, you remember. If something did happen, you pull the curtains, ring for a Chinese and don't answer your phone for days. If it's nothing, it still might need confirmation from more than one person. That's the fear. But, as I say, I didn't have it. The important parts of last night's conversations were still right there.

Later on, we were to meet in town in a place where nobody would ever expect us to be. If there were spies around, the places like Mulligan's and McDaid's and The Long Hall would be the first places they'd check. Having thought about it for a little while, we'd come up with the bar in the Fitzwilliam Hotel on St Stephen's Green. A posh hotel bar. Nobody would ever think of looking for us there. The plan was for Lucky to go and meet the ginger albino as per usual, then Dirty Dave and Stinking Pete would follow the mutant when he took off. We figured he might be slightly wary and more alert, so, if he spotted me or Jimmy that early, the whole thing could be blown. So, Jimmy and I would be waiting inside Trinity, posing as Norwegian tourists looking for the Book of Kells. Once Pete and Dave had figured out which way the ginger albino was going, they would call my mobile and we'd catch them up and take over the pursuit. In the meantime, I had the afternoon to recover. I decided to read, and what better than Sherlock Holmes, given the circumstances? We were in the middle of a mystery so mysterious even the great Holmes himself would have been confounded, flummoxed and quite possibly a little bewildered. I lay on my couch, did a load of opium and began to read.

It was around three hours later when I woke up to the sound of my phone. Not a terrible infectious ringtone like the one that had enslaved so many, but the theme tune to the greatest detective show of all time: *The Rockford Files*.

'What's up?' I said, when I answered Jimmy's call. That's Jimmy the Bollix, not Jim Rockford.

'I'm grand. How's the head?'

'Humming a bit. Some night.'

'Yep. Sure was. Uh-huh. Yes, sir,' he said, in a voice that really said, 'I know something you don't'.

'What?' I said, immediately consumed by the fear.

'You don't remember, do you?'

'Oh fuck. What?'

'Jesus, man. We've been friends a long time, and we've done a lot of stuff, terrible stuff, but that was something I've never seen before.'

'—'

'Twenty?' said Jimmy, with a note of sympathy in his voice.

'No.'

'Twenty?'

'What?' I sighed.

'Gotcha.'

'You cunt.'

'Haha, you just fucked off home without saying a word. One minute you were there, the next you went into the toilets thinking it was the way out, then came back out and straight out the front door.'

'Thank fuck for that. I can't believe I let you reprobates lead me astray again. All sorted for tonight?'

'I am, yeah. You can ring those other two gobshites. I haven't the time or the patience to explain anything to them. It'd be like trying to teach a puddle how to jump.'

'Fair enough, I'll talk to them. See you in the hotel then, eight o'clock. Don't forget your iPod.'

'Will do. Laters.'

He hung up. My heart was back from its visit to my mouth, and the relief at not having the fear anymore perked me up no end. I found a bag of frozen scampi in the freezer and fried them up. I covered them in vinegar and salt and dipped them into tomato ketchup, imagining myself eating an entire scampi family with each bite. Cheerio, Pops. Adios, second son. Goodnight, Granny Irene. Eventually, I was down to third cousin on your mother's first husband's side. It was quite a big bag of scampi, you see. After I'd eaten, I went to the bathroom, where I trimmed the excess hair from various orifices and had a shower. I had to alter my appearance slightly for this evening's shenanigans. If we were following the ginger albino and he caught a glimpse of my distinctive hat and coat combo, then he'd be on to us immediately. As well as that, we were going to a posh hotel tonight and couldn't look too out of place. That reminded me. I rang Dave and Pete and told them to both make sure they showered (to which Dave went, 'Awww, do I have to?') and wear the most respectable clothes they had. We could go over the rest of it in the bar. And I told them not to forget their iPods.

After I had dressed, I looked at myself in the mirror. The Hugo Boss suit still fitted perfectly, despite the fact I'd had it so long. A plain white shirt underneath and a pair of black leather Adidas sneakers on my feet. Reservoir Twenty, so I was. On the way out the door, I set the alarm and the various booby traps I've had ever since that night I looked out the window to find a woman going for a shite in my garden. When I'd asked her what the fuck she thought she was doing, she scuttled off, clutching her baggy trackpants and muttering something about being caught short. I couldn't even give her a kick up the hole, I mean, she hadn't even wiped. Now there are precautions in place, so if you ever get caught short in front of my house, make sure you go in next door's garden. Fuck it, it's just flats and absolutely full of Muslims. They couldn't care less if someone poos in their garden. I prepared my iPod and was just about to turn it on when I saw a cab coming. I put out my hand and tried to untangle the headphones to put them back inside my jacket. I hate when they stick out. Still wrangling with the pesky cables, I opened the door of the taxi and got in.

'Good evening. I'm going to—' I said, before I turned around. 'Oh,' I said as I came face to face with the driver. Being totally convinced in my head that I was going to see some fat old lad wearing a cap and stinking of sweat and sweet Major cigarettes, I was taken aback to see a very striking black woman with a Grace Jones haircut. I couldn't help but laugh.

'Sorry about that,' I said. 'I wasn't expecting … you know … erm …'

'Bwa ha ha ha ha ha,' she roared like Dr Hibbert. 'Everyone say that. Where we goin'?'

'Stephen's Green, please. I have to say, you're a lot more pleasant to travel with than what I was expecting.'

'Bwa ha ha ha ha ha,' she roared again. 'Everyone say that too!'

If I were to tell you it was the quickest taxi drive of my life, you might think it was because she was such great entertainment that the time just flew by. And you would be right, to an extent, but the real reason would be more to do with her driving like she was Ayrton Senna, and we all know what happened to him. She flew up the Green and spun the car around hard, clipping a horse in the leg with the bumper.

'Bwa ha ha ha ha ha,' she went. 'Stupid horse. 500 points! That'll be €6.50.'

I gave her the money and thanked her for the pleasant ride. I'm sure I heard her shriek, 'You welcome, Beardface!' as the bloke who owned the now-lame horse that was supposed to pull his carriage of tourists around town came thundering over. She put the car into first and ripped back down before turning left onto Dawson Street. 'God bless you, Grace Jones Taxi Driver,' I thought to myself as I headed over to the bar.

🎧 🎧 🎧 🎧 🎧

Seamus and Alan Smithee sat on opposite sides of a table in Dakota on South William Street. They'd wanted one of those nice curved booths, but there were none, and some pack of Spanish students was sitting around two of them, with one cup of coffee between the lot of them. They each had a pint of a fancy Czech lager, which came in a nice glass that somehow seemed to make the beer taste much nicer.

'Now, you're 100 per cent sure it's all taken care of?' Smithee asked him.

'Yes. It is the same one who did the record-shop-owners. He has always been perfect. I am meeting him later to pay him.'

'Just be on your guard.'

'I am always on my guard. I am like a twenty-four-hour nightwatchman moving through the twilight.'

'What?'

'Nothing. You would not understand. The important thing is, everything is in order. You can relax.'

'I can relax? *I can relax?* There's just over twenty-four hours until we unfold the final part of our dastardly plan, and you're telling me to relax.'

'Everything planned perfectly, is it not?'

'Yes, of course. I planned it. With the great leader, of course. But it wouldn't have been possible without the foot-soldiers and cannon-fodder like yourself. You should be proud.'

Seamus was grateful for his new life and regretted

none of his work, but, for a moment, he'd have traded it all in just to land a sucker punch on that primping, condescending little man.

'. . . and the finale,' Smithee droned on, 'once that goes down without a hitch, this whole damned country is ours. And once you have one country, sure you'd want another, and being the ambitious sort anyway, I quite fancy a few. I think I'd like Paraguay. Just because, you know. And Cuba. Oooh, oooh, and Canadia. They talk funny there. But I digress. We need you and your work to make sure everything goes okay tomorrow. You know what these people are like. They'll try and do an extra song or ignore the lights on stage telling them to come off. You'll speak to each act beforehand and warn them. None of them will argue with a hideous mutant like you. They'll be scared to death of the sight of you standing there in your Y-fronts, your pasty white skin and pink and ginger bits for all to see.'

Seamus pulled the cap down tighter over his head and told Smithee he needn't worry. He'd do whatever he had to do to make sure the plan went without a hitch, but he felt like he used to feel as a boy when his father constantly belittled him for his disability. 'Why, Daddy, why?' he'd shout as his father administered another thrashing to his backside. 'Because ... because ... well, just fucking look at you. Not only an albino. But ginger, too. You're an abomination of God's holy law,' his father would reply, paddling away at his son's red raw bottom. He hated feeling like this. He had grown past all that, now he was strong and feared by men. The great leader never made him feel like this, even though there was never any question that she was far more important than him. Now he was body-conscious again.

'Right then,' said Smithee, finishing his pint, 'I'm off backstage at the Point. We've got David Bowie on tonight. The Rise and Fall of the Last Time I'm Ever Playing These Hunky Dory Songs so Let's Dance tour is opening tonight, and I'll be getting my picture taken with important people, and David Bowie loves me. Loves me, he does. He may not know it yet but it's true. It'll be a nice evening and some R&R before the big day tomorrow. You just make sure you get what you need to get done done. Check back in with me before midnight, or I'll know something's wrong.'

'I will.'

'And Seamus?'

'Yes?'

'Get a receipt.'

After Smithee had gone, Seamus ordered another pint of the Czech beer. His mind was wandering, feelings and emotions he hadn't felt for years were bubbling up inside him. He couldn't allow that to happen. He had to concentrate and ensure everything went as planned with Hitty. It wasn't easy, though. Now, with everything so close to the end, just when he needed his mind to be strong, he seemed to be falling apart. Alan Smithee's cruel jibes had opened up old wounds, and no amount of emotional Elastoplast could stop the bleeding.

20

Sunday Evening

(In the posh hotel bar)

We sat at the bar, the four of us, and were served by the young Spanish barman, who seemed very keen to practice his English. As this was a posh hotel bar, mobile phones were not allowed, so we were safe to sit and converse normally, rather than using little notebooks to write messages to each other while listening to our iPods. Dirty Dave and Stinking Pete had done quite well with their apparel, looking less homeless than usual, and neither one of them was visibly smelly, which made it rather a rare occasion, I have to say. Jimmy, like me, was in a suit.

Except his was cream linen, and he was wearing a Panama hat.

'What the fuck are you? Pierce Brosnan out of that film where loads of blokes come out at the end looking all the same but at one point he's on his island and he's going around in a linen suit and a Panama hat?' I asked.

'James Bond?' said Dirty Dave.

'No, you clown. If it was James Bond, I'd have said the James Bond film where he wore a linen suit and a Panama hat. He was a really rich guy.'

'Remmington Steele!' said Pete.

'Jesus.'

'Thitomaskrownisfair,' said the young Spanish barman.

'Ahh, that's it. Cheers, have a Paxtaran on me, chaval.'

'Gracias. I mean, thank you.'

'Right, Dave and Pete. Explain to me what your job is tonight.'

'Easy. We go down Grafton Street. We wait outside Pamela Scott's, pretending to look at the fine collection of shoes, until we see Lucky come down Duke Street. He'll give us a nod. We follow him, at a discreet distance, down to Trinity College. We watch him give the money to the ginger albino, then we follow him wherever he goes.'

'Do we follow Lucky or the ginger albino?' asked Dave.

'You jamrag, Dave,' said Pete. 'We follow Lucky first, then we follow the ginger albino.'

'Right.'

'Then what?' I asked him, testingly.

'We see which way he goes. He might go up Dame Street. He might go around onto Pearse Street. He might go up Westmoreland Street and catch a bus somewhere. He might go up Grafton Street. Or around onto Nassau Street and then up Kildare Street. He might go down Suffolk Street and then back onto Dame Street before crossing the road and going down the side of the Central Bank and then—'

'Yeah, he's got options. But what's the important part?'

'Stay with him until we've told you and Jimmy where he's going, and then we fall back once you have him in visual sight with your eyes.'

'Good man, Pete. We got it right!' said Dave. 'To celebrate, it's my round. Twenty, what'll you have?'

'Midleton, Dave. Cheers.'

'Righto!'

The others all had pints, but I had to drink shorts. If we were on for a long chase, the last thing I needed to have to do was stop for a piss. I was okay with a couple of pints, but once the seal has been broken, I have to go every fifteen minutes, on the button. I once did a test, and, for each pint of beer I drank, I produced three pints of urine. I'm not sure why, it's just a cross I have to bear, and I do so with stoicism and a very well-developed thumb and forefinger on my right hand from the constant unzipping and unbuttoning of my fly. I very often 'forget' to do my fly up again, it just saves time in the long run and provides the odd exciting moment for passers-by. So, Dave went up to the bar and got three pints of Guinness and the whiskey and handed over a €50 note. The young Spanish barman went across to the till then came back.

'Erm, I am sorry, but this is not enough.'

'What do you mean it's not enough?' asked Dave.

'Well, the three pints are €16.80, and the whiskey is €65.'

'The whiskey is €65?!'

'Yes, sir.'

'Is it made from solid gold and melted into whiskey form?'

'No, sir. Is just very expensive whiskey.'

Dave turned to me. 'You couldn't have just asked for a Jamey?'

'You asked me what I wanted, and I had a look, and that particular bottle was almost singing to me. How was I to know it was €65 a shot?'

'Perhaps the fact that it says it in the little menu of whiskeys they have thoughtfully placed here on the bar, right in front of you?'

'Drinks menu, Dave? Who really looks at a drinks menu? If you go into a bar and you need a menu to decide what it is you feel like drinking, then you're no drinker. Anyway, if it's that much of a problem, I'll pay for my own drink.'

'Oh no, don't worry. I'll get it. I'll use the last of my money to get you one small drink.'

'Fair enough.'

'Gah.'

As I sipped my delicious whiskey, and it was very delicious indeed, I thought about what the night ahead might bring. There might be violence. That'd be okay. I can live with that. Torture might be on the agenda, and who can argue with that? It really is the best way to get information out of people who don't want to give it to you. I remember once trying to find out an address from some young rascal who had gotten himself involved with the wrong people, and it wasn't until we threatened him with a twenty-four-hour Tom Hanks movie marathon that he started to spill his guts. The fact that we'd cut his stomach open with a Bowie knife also made him spill his guts, but that's beside the point.

There was pressure, too. We only had one chance at this, and if we didn't get it right, they'd continue unstopped. Folkapalooza was just a day away, and if what they had planned for the finale took place, whatever it was, then we might as well unplug our iPods and just join in. Or we could become a bunch of renegade mercenaries like the A-Team, but, of course, the problem would be lack of clients. With everybody under the spell of the ringtone and the terrible music, there'd be nobody with any motivation to hire us. They'd all just go along with their day-to-day lives, happy because they were miserable, miserable because they were Damien Rice fans, and we'd starve in our funky red-and-black van. I'd rather survive a nuclear war and be last man on Earth, existing on a diet of dead rats and bits of tyre, than live the rest of my life surrounded by Damien Rice fans.

I've had the fate of nations in my hands before, but mostly nations I didn't like too well, so, if it had all gone pear-shaped, I wouldn't have been that bothered. But this was home. My home town was under the kind of threat it hadn't suffered since the Spanish student invasion of 1993 when nearly 6,000,000 of them descended on Dublin over a three-week period. Only last-minute legislation banning sitting on the ground in giant circles saw them move on to somewhere their talents were appreciated. This, on the other hand, this could mean the end. And the end of something means the start of something else, and I hate new things. I'm totally resistant to change. Dublin may not be the perfect city, but by the slippery bride of Christ I was going to do my utmost to make sure Dublin was populated by the funny and objectionable people it always has been home to and not these robotic-minded gimps. And, by saving Dublin, I'd be saving the rest of Ireland, even those towns that have massive chips on their shoulders and jump up and down in outrage if you make even the smallest stereotypical joke about them. Oh well, rough with the smooth and all that. No doubt about it, we were heading into the endgame now.

21

Still Sunday Evening
(But not in the posh bar anymore)

Jimmy and I left the hotel first. Putting our iPods on, we headed for Trinity College. On Grafton Street, we could see the small percentage of normal people getting infected as we walked. A phone would go off, their eyes would glaze over, their eyelids would droop, and you could see the stench of misery begin to emanate from their pores, like ooze from a dead work colleague who had just been wrapped in carpet and put into a supply cupboard. Those few remaining unaffected souls would be under the spell in no time at all. I marched down the street to the strains of Matthew Wilder. Nobody was going to break my stride. Oh no. I had to keep on moving. We entered Trinity by the side door on Nassau Street, and, making our way through whatever room we came into, we found ourselves outside in that nice cobbled area where students in flared jeans were practising their peace signs and playing hacky-sack with each other. It was summertime, but, as you all know so well, being a student is a full-time occupation these days. We had little notepads to write messages on because we still couldn't risk turning off our iPods. Any one of these unkempt popinjays could have a mobile phone and the ringtone of death instead of their ever-so-cool homemade ringtone, which was the organ bit from the start of 'Light My Fire' by The Doors. 'It's so cool I just don't want to answer my phone,' they might say, which would make me mad if I ever heard anyone say that. So mad, I might take their phone and demonstrate to them how recently browned Nokias can fly.

We wandered around for a bit, and then I took out my pad and wrote.

'This is boring now.'

Jimmy took out his pad and checked his pockets for a pencil. His pants, inside his jacket, back pockets, he patted them all and came up with nothing. I offered him mine.

'Yes, it is boring,' he wrote back.

'Why didn't you just give a thumbs-up or something? There was no need to write a response to that, and even just "yes" would have done,' I scribbled frantically.

'Well, excuse me for being polite, but I was brought up to answer a question properly and you, of all people, should be the last to criticise somebody for behaving correctly and with good manners. Isn't the lack of manners in everyday people one of your biggest bug-bears?' he wrote back, in less than a minute.

'You're right. I'm sorry. In future, I will endeavour to act in a more appropriate fashion and respond better to your written communications.'

'Thank you,' he wrote, 'I appreciate that, and I am sure this, going forward, will improve our day-to-day relationship on the occasions when we have to write notes to each other instead of talking because of a terrible audio threat that nobody seems able to control.'

'Fair enough. PS, you're a cunt.'

This time, he gave me a thumbs-up-and-at that moment, a security guard came over. I looked at him as he mouthed words at me and then raised my hands in the classic 'I don't understand you' gesture. He seemed to take it that I was doing the 'I can't hear you because I've got music on' gesture and gestured at me to take off my earphones. I wagged my finger and shook my head. 'Why not?' he signalled. I rubbed my arms as if I was cold, then gave him a bye-bye wave, and we walked on. The last thing we needed was anything out of the ordinary, beyond the ginger albino, the ringtone and the upcoming horror of Folkapalooza. I kept checking my phone because, with the music on, I couldn't hear. I did have it on vibrate, but I think my left arse cheek is now so used to it vibrating, as that is where I keep my phone, that sometimes I don't feel it. At least, I assume that's what it is and not some numb area because of an arse tumour. Just as I was putting it back in my pocket, I got a text from Dave.

'Here, Twenty. Just one thing. How will I know the bloke?'

'No idea,' I replied. 'Apart from the fact that he's a ginger albino. Shouldn't be too hard to spot. Oh, and the fact that you'll know him when he meets Lucky, you stupid twat.'

I got no reply, which wasn't a surprise. What had I done to deserve such a friend? After thinking about it for a couple of seconds, I figured it was all the really bad stuff I'd done in my life. Stupid karma. The waiting inside Trinity really was a bad idea. There was nothing to do, and we'd have been much better off in a nearby hostelry where we could have enjoyed another drink, or two, or five. I really had a bit of a goo on me for a few pints. No. Don't give into temptation. I had to be quick-witted. But then there was that part of my brain that was very convincing when it assured me that a couple of drinks would actually be beneficial. I struggled with the goo for a while, but, as we were already inside Trinity, I'd have to just make do. Eventually, having put the phone in my breast pocket, I got the call from Dirty Dave. I took out one ear of my iPod and began to talk.

'What's going on?'

'Right, well, he's made the drop with Lucky a couple of minutes ago. He came down Dame Street and just met him at the gate there. They barely spoke, there was a little nod of the head, but that was it.'

'And which way is he heading?'

'Well, he turned right out of Trinity and looked like he was heading towards Pearse Street.'

'Looked like?'

'Yeah.'

'But, of course you, and Pete are following him, so you can tell me exactly where he is, right?'

'Erm ... fuck.' He put his hand over the earpiece of the phone, thinking that would give him some privacy, and I could hear him saying to Stinking Pete, 'Shit, come on, run. We've got to catch up with him.'

He came back to me. 'Yeah, we've definitely got him. Call you back in two minutes.'

'You stupid—' I didn't have time to finish before he hung up. How rude. There was no time to waste. I wrote a quick note to Jimmy.

'Dirty Dave + Stinking Pete = Mong central. Let's go.'

We went through the courtyard and out the gate onto College Green, turned right and headed down towards Pearse Street Garda Station, where now the finest police force in the world was as much use as Stephen Hawking's genitals. We blemmed down Pearse Street like Olympic walkers, except without the gay walk. I felt the phone vibrate again. It was Pete this time.

'What?'

'We have him in visual contact. Heading into Pearse Street DART station.'

'Okay, stay with him. We're not far behind you. Just stay inconspicuous.'

'Come on, Twenty. I'm not sure what my inability to hold on to my bladder has to do with this.'

'Christ. Just don't let him see you, okay? Act natural. Like two blokes heading out for a few pints or something. And ring me if there's any more movement.'

'10-4, good buddy. Over and out.'

Pete has never quite gotten over the CB fad and regularly watches films like *Convoy* and that one with Burt Reynolds. No, not that one with the canoe and the rednecks. You don't get CB radios on canoes, do you? Fucking hell. As the street around us was clear of pedestrians, I motioned to Jimmy to take one earphone out and told him what was going on.

'What the fuck were we thinking having those two anywhere near this?'

'Fucked if I know,' I said. 'Booze makes a man make some bad decisions from time to time.'

'Damn if I wouldn't like some booze now though,' said Jimmy.

'I hear you.'

We put the music back on, picked up the pace and got to the station. There was a massive queue of people with backpacks at the ticket window, so we went to the machine. Choosing the cheapest destination going southside as that's where the Mega Gigs offices were, I put in all the change, but it kept spitting out one of the 20 cent coins. Each time I tried, it'd just come straight back at me. I checked my pockets and had no other change. Jimmy shrugged his shoulders to say he had no change either. A line was beginning to form behind us.

What the fuck were we going to do? In the distance, I could hear the rumble of a train. Shit. I looked around frantically, then it hit me. I gave Jimmy the American Indian flat-palm signal, which an American Indian might interpret as 'How' but at this moment meant 'Wait' and ran outside the front door. There, sitting in her own filth, was a young Gypsy girl playing the accordion.

'LOOK OVER THERE!' I yelled at her, and, when she looked, I reached down into her cardboard box and stole a 20 cent coin. Then I figured I might as well go the whole hog and stole the whole lot. Get a real job, bitch. I legged it back inside and lashed the final coin into the slot, and it spat out our tickets. We ran upstairs and got three feet away from the doors when they closed and the train pulled off.

'FUUUUUCK!' I shouted.

A nearby priest tutted at me. I gave him the finger. Knowing that the two lads had to keep a low profile, I sent a text.

'Assume you're on the train with the gingino. Don't lose him.'

I got a reply a couple of minutes later.

'Yeah, it's all home.'

'You mean "good". Turn that fucking predictive text off if you can't use it properly.'

We had no choice but to wait for the next train, and it being a Sunday, the clock said it was going be nineteen minutes. Of course, with Irish Rail, that could mean anywhere between nineteen minutes and a quarter of a century. What a load of shit. If I was supreme ruler of the country, there'd be trains going wherever you wanted to go and leaving at five-minute intervals. Sure, it'd be expensive, but I figure you could pay for it using the money the Government hands to its construction-industry friends in kickbacks and brown envelopes. As for places without rail track, that's simple. Pass a new law that says that anyone who wants to move to Ireland from an eastern European country has to spend a year working on the railroads. You pay them, feed them, house them and then after they've done their year's work, you give them a residency visa. Easy as fucking pie. The public transport system is massively improved, and it'd separate the people who genuinely want to work hard from the spoofers and shysters who are here to claim benefits. I mean, it's not as if we don't have enough of our own of that sort.

Amazingly, nineteen and a half minutes later, we were sitting on the next train and speeding, as much as the DART speeds, southwards. I'd had a further text from the lads saying they'd gotten as far as Blackrock and everything was still in order. I told them to keep on his track, to let me know where he got off and to make sure they followed him when he did. They assured me they would, but then they had assured me they'd follow him from Trinity in the first place. That said, there was nothing else we could do from our train but pray that they and their goldfish memories could cope with the simple instructions they'd been given. I wasn't especially hopeful.

22

Sunday Evening

(Slightly later, on a DART)

Belouis Some's 'Imagination' was playing when I got the next text. I was doing my very best not to think about the video to that song in case I had to stand up all of a sudden.

'E gt of n Dlky. Fllwng. Headn up thru vlg. Pasta Kweens. Will keep u updtd.'

I showed the text to Jimmy. He hadn't the first idea what it meant either. It appeared to be some kind of primitive language, but what the hell was it? I made a quick phone call, risking my very soul, and Pete translated.

Apparently, the ginger albino had gotten off in Dalkey, and they were following him. At that time, they were heading up through the village, past the Queen's pub, and they would, from this moment on, keep us updated.

'Look, just keep following him. If he goes in somewhere, don't be heroes and go in after him. Wait for us and we can decide what to do then. And if that's the best you can do with the texting, just turn the predictive back on. At least those are real words.'

'Right so. G'luck.'

As we were only just at Salthill & Monkstown, home to the largest collection of free-range monks in all of Europe, it'd take us a while to get there, and I was worried about leaving Dave and Pete on their own. Their capacity to fuck things up was beyond compare. Like the way Dave put the bishop in hospital on the day of his Confirmation. As the man on the altar smeared the crunchy paste on his forehead, Dave passed out, toppled forward, knocked over one of those giant church candles and set the bishop's robes on fire. Churches not being places you'd find fire-extinguishers, the bishop had to roll around on the floor while some of the other celebrants reluctantly and sensually stripped the altar boys and used their vestments to put out the flames. In church circles, 'Bishop Simon Weston' became rather an in-joke, while Dave continued to make inadvertent mischief wherever he went.

I was impatient as the train clacked its way towards one of Dublin's most affluent suburbs, home to pop stars, writers, racing drivers, film directors, playwrights and Chris de Burgh. This really was alien territory we were heading into. City boys out in the leafy suburbs. Eventually, the train arrived, and we got off, iPods still on full. We walked across the footbridge and down towards the village. Jimmy tapped me on the shoulder as we passed Finnegan's pub on our right-hand side. He made the drinky-drinky motion. I was reluctant, our mission was so important, but I could feel the creamy pint on my tongue already. No, I had to resist. There would be plenty of time for pints afterwards and now we had to concentrate on the job at hand.

Less than five minutes later, we were sat outside with a pair of delicious pints. I raised my glass to Jimmy, and we clinked before taking a long gulp. I sent a text to Dave to say we were stuck on the train due to some kind of yak crossing between Sandycove and Glenageary. The evening was warm, and I watched the expensive cars go down Sorrento Road, one after the other. Ferrari, BMW, Lamborghini, Mercedes, Bentley, Porsche, Ferrari again, Lotus, Jaguar. Then some fucker spoiled it by going past in a Ford Mondeo. Jesus. The tables around us were busy, and, with the music still on, I had to lip-read the conversations. Thankfully, I had spent lots of nights watching the deaf news with the little sign-language bloke in the corner and was quite good at it.

'Can't wait for tomorrow. Folkapalooza is going to be completely middle of the road.'

'Yes, I too am anticipating a marvellous day of mediocrity. My favourite kind of ocrity.'

'Wonder what the finale is going to be?'

'...said they were talking to someone who said the

finale will change our lives for ever …'

It was clear that almost everyone around us was infected. I'd had no reply from my text to Dave but figured he just hadn't checked his phone and, with his own music on, hadn't heard it either. I sent another text to say we'd been delayed even further but to let us know if our quarry moved on from his current position. No panic. I motioned to Jimmy 'One more?' and got the 'Go for it, but this time get me a little chaser with it as well would you? Oh, and a packet of Scampi Fries' gesture back.

An hour later, we decided we'd better move but had another quick pint for the road. After that, we had another one for luck, and then we set off. Going through the village we realised we were absolutely starving so stopped off for a quick curry at a fashionable Indian restaurant that served complimentary poppadums. Once we'd finished, we were on our way again. There was still no word from Dave or Pete when I checked my phone, so I figured I'd better try and ring one of them. We passed by the Queen's pub on the right-hand side and up the downward-sloping hill out of the village. When I was sure there was nobody around, I turned off my iPod and rang Stinking Pete. It rang for quite a while before he answered.

'Well, what's the story?' I asked.

'I could ask the same of you,' said a voice I'd never heard before.

'Who is this? Floella Benjamin, the ex-*Blue Peter* presenter?'

'I think you know quite well who it is, Mr Major. If that is your real name.'

'You,' I said.

'Yes, me,' he said. 'I must say, I am surprised you are not dead. The Italian has done such good work in the past. I will have to make a point of killing him very slowly indeed when all this is over.'

'Well, it's not over yet, pal. What have you done with my friends?'

'They're all right … for now. But they will not be all right if you keep up this ridiculous chase. There is nothing you can do to stop what is going to happen.'

'What is going to happen?'

'Well, first the concert will take place, then— Your linguistic skills almost forced me into telling you what was going to happen, but I am no fool.'

'What?'

'You know very well what I mean. I shall let them go when it is all over. At that point, it will not make any difference, and I am not a vindictive person. Although I really am going to get that Italian, but that is more to do with the fact that he took the money for a job he did not do.'

'We'll find you, you freak. And when we're face-to-face we'll get the information we need from you.'

'Hah. I am no guidebook. Or tourist information office. Or Wikipedia page. Or instruction manual. You can-not just read me. The information you need is inside my head, and I will not share it with anyone. Never. The great leader has given me so much, I will not betray her now.'

'Who is this great leader?'

'A lady with soft eyes, a warm voice, pencil-drawn videos.'

'Wow, that's sounds like … erm … what's her name again?'

'Well, duh, it's … oh fucking hell. I'm hanging up now.'

And he did. I began to feel a little bit guilty. If Jimmy and I had just got straight off the train and gone to meet the lads, they wouldn't have been captured by the ginger albino. How horrible it must be for them to have to share space with that monster. On the other hand, he was probably finding the noxious funk that comes off Dirty Dave in waves a little hard to cope with too. As well as that, we hadn't got the first clue where they might be. It's not like they'd have left a Hansel and Gretel-style trail of breadcrumbs to show us the way, so we were pretty much stymied.

'Right so,' I said to Jimmy, 'this isn't really what we had in mind.'

'Look on the bright side,' he said, 'it might have been us who got captured, and then we'd be relying on those two to free us.'

'Good point.'

'You are right though. We are as buggered as a gay man in Michael Barrymore's swimming pool. We can't risk asking anyone if they saw anything because they're probably infected and will give us some guff and flapdoodle about Folkapalooza, and, to be honest, I have a pain in my beautifully smooth scrotum with Folkapalooza. I'm thinking that if we can't find out what's going on, we simply blow up the stage. Sure, lots of people would die, but I wouldn't know any of them so I could live with myself quite easily.'

'It's the last resort all right, but we have to try and deprogram all the people who are bewitched by this spell. Simply blowing them up won't do that.'

Just then, my phone bleeped. It was a text message from Dirty Dave. The ginger albino wasn't as clever as he thought. He had taken Pete's phone when it rang, but he'd forgotten that Dave would also have one. Or, more likely, he wasn't prepared to get close enough to him to rifle through his pockets to take it out. And he was probably afraid of what was in Dave's pockets, and he'd be right too, for Dave always carried his snotball with him. A perfect sphere of his own bogies that he'd been shaping and cultivating for the past eight years. It was now about the size of a tennis ball and just as bouncy. I looked at the message: 'we're in a rink gourd us the gill beside a pound eons'.

Oh, that was just classic Dave. Completely unintelligible.

'Have you got any idea what this means?'

Jimmy looked and shook his head. 'I rarely know what Dave's on about, even when he's standing in front of me.'

'Well, he's obviously trying to tell us something. I can almost picture him texting behind his back to make sure he's not seen.'

'Maybe it's the predictive text gone wrong or something.'

'Jimmy, you are a genius. All we have to do is figure out what word he actually meant to use and not the one his phone chose.'

A couple of minutes later we had it. Like the fucking geniuses at Bletchley Park, we had cracked Dave's Enigma code using our own phones. What his text actually said was: 'We're in a pink house up the hill beside a round door.'

It took us less than five minutes to find the place. It wasn't that it was the only pink house, there were loads of them. Someone had obviously gotten a shipment of knocked-off 'Salmon Velvet' one day and trawled the neighbourhood. (It reminded me of when Jimmy used to do a bit of painting-and-decorating in the past. He'd turn up to give the bored housewives a look at his colour charts and would recommend a beautiful and high-quality 'Twilight Cream' he could get for a very good price. Then he'd go out, buy a shitload of regular magnolia and make a fortune.) It was the round door that told us we were at the right place. It was dark now, and, as we stopped outside, we could see a bright light burning in a small window on the top floor.

We made our way around the side of the house and found it, and all the rooms, in darkness. The garden was soft and mushy underfoot. From upstairs, I could hear a strange noise. A sort of a swishing and, shortly after, a cry. I thought it was probably human, or a fox, although no matter how hard I tried, I could find no explanation as to why there might be a fox in the upstairs part of the house. I tried the back door, and it opened. We went inside and crept towards the stairs. There was no moonlight, and the streetlights at the front were blocked by the enormous trees in the front garden, so it was dark. I took out a packet of Swan Vestas, struck one and mounted the stairs, taking great care not to cause any creaking, the shadows caused by the burning match making weird shapes on the wall beside me. The swishing was becoming clearer now, and it was apparent that the noises following it were human and not the cries of a fox, which made a lot more sense and comforted me in a strange way. Not that I have anything against foxes, but finding an animal inside a house that should really be outside is always a bit disturbing, isn't it? I mean, what would happen if you opened a cupboard, for example, and in there was a lemur? Or you went to sit down in your favourite chair to find it already occupied by small pony? So, the idea that it was Dave and Pete that were being whipped, while not exactly nice, was by far a better option than a screaming fox.

Standing outside the door from under which the light streamed, we could hear it even more clearly.

Swish thwack 'Ooooh.'

Swish thwack 'Aaaah.'

Swish thwack 'Emmmm, yaaaaaaaa.'

What the hell was going on in there? I signalled to Jimmy that we'd go in on the count of three, rescue the lads and get hold of the ginger albino. I counted. One ... two ... two and a half ... two and three quarters ... two and fourteen fifteenths ... three! We kicked open the door, ready to perform heroics.

We took one look and knew it was too late.

23

Inside the Pink House

Dave and Pete were slumped on the floor, and there was blood all over their faces and the floor. They weren't moving, and the position of their bodies was unnatural, with arms and legs akimbo. That bastard. He'd promised he wouldn't hurt them. Now they were dead. Never again would we be entertained by the witless drunken conversations of our two fallen comrades, soldiers in the battle against really crap, boring music. Never again would Pete ask questions like, 'Do wasps have hands?' or 'Do ants have antlers?' Never again would Dirty Dave ask me which one of three implausible choices would I prefer to be and why, before telling me which one he'd choose to be and for what ridiculous reason. I couldn't help but feel a little bit guilty, what with the stopping off in the pub, drinking pints and whiskey and then gorging on Indian food while they were being tortured and killed, and possibly raped in the face, by our evil foe.

On the other side of the room, which was much bigger than I had expected it to be, was the ginger albino, topless, his white back flecked with wiry-looking orange hairs. He was kneeling in front of the bed and thrashing himself over his shoulders with what appeared to be either guitar strings or really long, thin, hard worms. He didn't turn around and acknowledge our presence, even though he must have heard us come into the room and Jimmy say, 'Oh shit, that cunt's only gone and killed them.'

Swish thwack 'Uuuurg.'

Swish thwack 'Boilk.'

I extended my index finger and put my thumb in the air as if my hand was a gun.

'Get up, put your hands in the air and turn around really, really slowly,' I said.

The ginger albino moved his head slowly from left to right, and his neck cracked like ice under a skater who knew that young Damien Thorne was actually the son of the Devil himself. He put down the guitar strings and raised himself up. He was a big man, at least six foot six, and he was extremely muscled, like a wrestler, a bodybuilder or a camogie player's thighs. He turned around carefully with his hands in the air. He had a face like Britney Spears' minge, wide and badly shaven.

'Don't move or I'll blow your fucking brains out,' I said, pointing my hand at him.

'With what? That is not a gun.'

'Are you sure about that, though? Perhaps I was rebuilt like the Six Million Dollar Man and my right hand is now a fully functional Colt .45. Are you willing to take that risk?'

'I think I might be,' he said, as he charged towards me.

'Oh fuck,' I thought, 'why didn't we at least bring some kind of bat?'

Now, I've never been hit by a train, but I can only imagine it feels like it felt when the full might of the hideous mutant crashed into me and sent me flying across the room.

'Ouch,' I said, when I landed some moments later.

'Oi, you giant Hucknall-looking, carrot-topped cunt,' said Jimmy. 'Pick on someone your own size.'

'Okay then,' he said, turning his attentions to where Jimmy was standing.

'What are you looking at me for?' Jimmy said, 'pick on someone your own size. I'm not your size. There are giants that aren't your size.'

'Oh well, I will take what I can get,' he said before moving with the kind of speed you wouldn't expect from such a big man. He grabbed Jimmy in a headlock and started punching. Jimmy retaliated by biting a big chunk out of his arm and spitting the flesh across the room. For some reason, this seemed to enrage him even further, and they traded blows for a while. Now, Jimmy's a fine scrapper, I've never seen him lose a fight (even when he was claimed by that entire troop of boy scouts in Portumna), but this was going to be his toughest battle yet. I figured I'd better give him a hand and looked around the room for any kind of weapon I might use. There was a chair by the table, and, when the ginger albino had his back to me I picked it up and smashed it down on his back as hard as I could. Now, my understanding of this action, based on television and film, was that the chair would crack into lots of little pieces and the baddie would crash to the floor, at which point we would easily overpower him. Not so. It just sort of bounced off him and remained perfectly intact. Again, this seemed to increase his ire. Jimmy had been thrown to the far corner of the room, and, before I knew it, I had been picked up and thrown over there too. I slid down the wall on my face, thankfully it was nicely wallpapered and not rough stone or it might have affected my good looks. Bloody beards just aren't in anymore. I had more than my beautiful face to worry about though.

He wandered over, his enormous pecs glistening with the effort, and his three and a half nipples standing proudly erect like a braless woman outside in the cold having a cigarette. Jimmy was trying to get up again, but he'd suffered a series of kidney punches and a Chinese burn that looked horribly raw. I was still upside down and kicking my legs to try and get right side up, like one of those little armadillo insects you find in damp places. This was not good.

'They say if you want something done properly, you have to do it yourself,' he said. 'I never really subscribed to that theory because I was always very vigilant about who I outsourced to, but I have been let down badly this time. People just do not take any pride in their work these days.'

'It's all the Government's fault,' I said, trying to buy some time.

'You know, you are right, little man. How can anyone really be filled with any pride in what they do when they see an administration like this one? Crooked, duplicitous, money-grabbing cheats and liars, the whole lot of them. Especially that so-called Tea Shock, but then people voted for them knowing fine well what they were like. Their apathy renders them insignificant. Anyway, soon there will be no need for pride.'

'What are you going to do with pride?'

'Nothing. I just said there'll be no need for it, nor any of the other seven deadly sins: lust, gluttony, wrath, greed, sloth and Terence Trent D'Arby's second album.'

'But why not? What are you planning?'

'Look, you might have nearly caught me out before, but I am not so stupid to tell you exactly what the plan is before I kill you. Somehow, you will escape at the last minute and thwart it, then I will end up either dead or floating through space in a giant mirror of some kind. So, here's the thing, I shall tell you when you're dead.'

'That's not really very fair,' I said.

'Neither is Funderland. Now, prepare to meet your maker. Kick the bucket. Pass to the other side. Do the fandango.'

He came at us his with his hands in the strangley-strangley position. Which one of us would he kill first? This really wasn't how I'd imagined my death would be. I'd sort of thought it might be like that bit at the end of *The Lord of the Rings*: me in a comfortable bed, golden light shining through the windows, warm air blowing through the room, the linen drapes wafting gently, my friends around me, and then being strangled, but not this.

'Looks like it's curtains, Jimmy.'

'It does that,' he said. 'Cheerio, Twenty. It's been fun.'

'See ya, old pal.'

I closed my eyes and waited for the feel of his shovel hands around my neck. My life flashed before my eyes, and I was at around 1973 when I realised that the strangling hadn't begun. He must be killing Jimmy. Oh the humanity. I cracked open one eye and saw Jimmy unstrangled as well. When I opened two eyes I saw the ginger albino flailing around the room with what appeared to be the ghost of Dirty Dave around his neck. I turned myself the right way up and looked again. It wasn't a ghost. It really was Dirty Dave, and he had leapt from his position on the floor, onto the monster's back and had thrust his armpit over his face and mouth. Now, there are some things that smell bad – cat piss, old people, that weird Asian fruit, cabbage and tramps' arseholes – but Dirty Dave's armpits are like all them mixed together then sprayed with manure before being left out in the sun and vomited on by a bear. Prolonged exposure to such a stench could cause nausea, dizziness, paralysis, blindness and even death. And that's exactly what Dave was doing. He was hanging on with all his might as the ginger albino's efforts to rid his air supply of these toxic fumes became weaker and weaker. He tried to bash Dave into the walls and spun around like an epileptic Wonder Woman, but there was no budging him. The beast sank to his knees, making muffled sounds and retching like a dog. Still Dave covered his face with his mephitic armpit, and soon his opponent toppled backwards, completely and utterly unconscious and with a little bit of sick around his mouth. To say my flabber was gasted would be rather an understatement.

'Dave, you're alive! And you saved my life. And Jimmy's life.'

'Of course I'm alive. What made you think otherwise?'

'Well, I came in, and you and Pete, who I assume is also alive, were covered in blood and lying motionless on the floor. I thought that freak had killed you.'

'Not at all,' he said. 'He was just flogging himself with his strings and then we both got a nosebleed at exactly the same time and then passed out because we're really tired and haven't had anything to eat since this morning.'

'Fuck me, that's unbelievably convenient.'

'You know it. Should I wake Pete up?'

'Yeah, we've got a lot to do.'

Dave wandered over to where Pete still lay, now gently snoring – how odd that I hadn't noticed that before – and kicked him in the small of the back as hard as he could.

'GIVE ME BACK MY PANTS LINDSAY LOHAN,

YOU CUNTING SLUT!' exclaimed Pete, sitting up sharply. 'Oh. I think I was dreaming. What's happening?'

'Dave armpitted the ginger albino into a coma, it seems.'

'That poor fucker.'

'Jimmy, you all right?'

'Yeah, my wrist is really rather chafed, but I'll survive.'

'Okay, we need to get this guy immobilised. Pete, stop holding your back like there's something wrong with you and go see if you can find some rope and some of that brown tape they always use when they tie people up.'

'Who?'

'Who what?'

'Who ties people up?'

'I don't know. It was just a general "they", Christ.'

Pete wandered around the creature's house to see what we could find to tie him up with. I looked at him lying there on the floor, his enormous tongue lolling out of his mouth. I have to say, I felt a bit sorry for him. To suffer both albinoism and gingerosity was a cruel twist of fate. No wonder he was so aggressive, it was probably to cover up his feelings of inadequacy. It was sort of like fat people being really jolly to cover up the fact they're physically less attractive than normal people and more likely to die young from any number of illnesses and associated complications. I didn't feel sorry for them though, they could just stop eating so many cakes and do some exercise, the intemperate gluttons. This fella, like handicapped people and Protestants, couldn't do anything about his affliction.

Dave wandered off to find a bathroom to wash the blood off his face and soon Pete came back with some old rope, some sheets ripped into strips, a ball of twine and a doormat that said 'Weclome'.

'Hahaha, look at this doormat!' he said.

I ignored him, and we hauled up the slumbering brute and, using the rope, sheets and twine tied him to the unbreakable chair.

'Now what?' said Jimmy.

'Now we find out what the fuck is going on and how we can stop it.'

24

Inside the Room in the Pink House

(Late at night)

It took us a while to bring him round from the deep, deep sleep he was in. He whimpered once or twice, probably at the memory of what had just happened to him, but when he was fully awake, he just sat there staring ahead, his face emotionless. There wasn't a peep out of him, no matter what we asked him or said to him.

'We need information from you,' I said, 'and we're going to get it out of you. Everyone has their weak point, and we'll find yours.'

I was sure I saw the hint of a smile on his face, but his eyes remained fixed on the wall. He was ignoring us and mentally preparing himself for whatever was to come. He'd obviously perfected his technique over the years, like a yoga guru, a Green Beret or a gang member from Blanchardstown. Now, normally I'd never have a problem getting information out of people, especially when their hands and feet are bound and they're tied to a chair. At home, we'd have made use of the various tools and implements stored in my shed, but a search of the house had turned up little more than a couple of spoons, a tiny Phillips-head screwdriver and a bucket. Of course, you could insert the spoons and screwdriver into places they weren't supposed to go, but nobody was quite willing to go down that road so early in the proceedings.

I lit a cigarette and smoked as Jimmy took revenge by administering a Chinese burn so ferocious that afterwards you could have used the skin to stir-fry prawns for your chow mein. The ginger albino didn't even flinch. Pete put the bucket over his head and then played it like it was bongos, but, again, there was nothing doing, even during his patented Manu Chao manoeuvre. Dave punched him in the balls fifteen times. I yanked hairs from his nose. We slapped his face, boxed his ears, kicked his shins, poked his eyes (although that was minging as they were all squidgy and slightly damp, and I'm sure I got a bit of retina under my fingernail) and pulled him up by his sideburns. This was a move perfected by years of being pulled up by my own sideburns by a vicious old priest nicknamed 'Cow' when I was in school. He'd straddle the corner of the desk you were sitting at, only his hindquarters-brown priest's smock between you and his undoubtedly enormous and leathery balls, and gently lift you from your seat by your locks. Some lads, not so dedicated to looking cool, even did away with theirs altogether, but then he just used your ear, twisting as he lifted.

We went through the whole repertoire of physical torture, and, when I pinched that bit of skin on the back of the upper arm without raising so much as a squeal, I knew we had to try a new approach. The physical stuff just wasn't going to work. Perhaps we needed to fuck with his senses. Pete farted in his face, but, after suffering the depravations of Dave's armpit, it had no effect, bar making the rest of us retch. Dave threatened him with his armpit again, but he sat there impassively. I figured it was like chicken-pox – you got it once and after that you were immune. Jimmy found an old fork and scraped it up and down a plate repeatedly, but that just made Stinking Pete put his hands over his ears and begin to weep softly. Downstairs, we found a portable stereo and bombarded him with commercial radio. Nothing. Then, it being late at night, they were replaying some of the day's earlier shows. An onslaught of Gerry Ryan, Pat Kenny and Ryan Tubridy would have been enough to reduce any man to a gibbering wreck, screaming with his God for mercy, but it had no effect whatsoever. Fuck, this was going to be difficult.

I lit another cigarette and tried to think. Perhaps music

might annoy him, but all we had were our iPods with completely awesome tunes on them. How could he possibly be broken by the best the 80s had to offer? I sent Dave and Pete to scour the place to see if they could find some music, and they came back with some CDs.

Brothers in Arms by Dire Straits, *The Best of Phil Collins*, *Westlife Sing the Songs of Foster and Allen*, Lily Allen's album and Simply Red's *Greatest Hits*. Whoever lived in this house was obviously tone deaf and possibly retarded, too. This surely had to do it.

'Right, iPods on lads,' I said as I began to inflict this so-called music upon him; there was no point in us suffering too. It took me back to my days of being a DJ on playlisted radio stations, except this time there was no Frances Black. No matter how much information you needed from somebody, there are lines you don't cross, and Frances Black is one of them. Even now, hearing the slightest chord of a Frances Black song makes me break out in a cold sweat. Cruel and unusual punishment, isn't it? 'Walk of Life' did nothing. 'In the Air Tonight', the most tedious and maddening of Collins's songs, did nothing. Westlife's computerised harmonies on 'Do you Want Your Old Lobby Washed Down?' might as well have been real music for all the effect it had. Lily Allen's cockney slag accent left him unmoved, and when I played him every single Simply Red song at top volume, I expected him to will himself to death to escape the horrible sound of Mick Hucknall, but he did not. Perhaps it was a shared ginger thing, but this was our trump card, and it had failed, completely and utterly.

Time was running out. It was now nearly 3.00am, and, with Folkapalooza about to start that afternoon, we had to find a way to make him talk.

'What the fuck are we going to do?' I asked.

'Beats me, we've tried everything, and he's impervious to it all. It looks like we'll just have to blow up the stage,' said Jimmy, eager to just blow up the stage.

'Look, blowing things up is great fun, but this can't be solved by simply exploding a stage. Sure, we'd kill the performers, but what about the rest of the people? What about the ringtone that's still out there and will just infect more people?'

'Yes, but we'd kill the performers.'

'It's very tempting, I'll admit, but for once we've got to look beyond the short-term hilarity and try and solve the bigger problem.'

'I suppose you do have a point.'

'I might have an idea,' said Dirty Dave.

'What's that?'

'Well, remember when my brother Shiny Simon (so-called because he has the world's shiniest forehead) decided he would refuse to speak to anyone after his collection of Roy of the Rovers comics got thrown out?'

'You mean when you threw it out? And instead of throwing it out, you set it on fire in the middle of his bedroom while he was recovering with a broken leg after being knocked down by a stolen car that you were driving? Yeah, what about it?'

'Well, after that shocking and unprecedented incident he changed from being a happy-go-lucky young kid who loved nothing better than to get knocked down by cars and having his head split open by golf clubs to a sullen, uncommunicative individual. He refused to talk to anyone, he'd sit staring at walls like yer man there is doing, he never cracked a smile, and nothing we did managed to change that. We tried entertaining him with puppets and funny news stories about natural disasters in faraway countries, but nothing worked. Then one day I got him to smile, laugh and make noise for the first time in nearly a year.'

'What did you do?'

'This,' said Dave, as he walked towards our orange captive. '*Cooochie-cooooochie-cooo*,' he said as his tickling fingers went to work. At first, I thought it was just another one of Dave's cretinous ideas, like the black lightbulb or the anti-Scot spray, but after a couple of seconds, the previously stern visage cracked. The ginger albino was trying hard not to laugh, his lips pursing and unpursing and his head moving where before it had been completely still.

'Quick,' called Dave, 'it's working! Everyone come help.'

Dave continued to tickle his underarms, cackling stuff you'd cackle at a baby. I worked that area just above the knees, Jimmy got his ribs, while Pete took off the shoes and went at his feet with his hardened yellow fingernails. Soon the room was filled with roars and laughs and screams and shrieks. At first, they were unintelligible, but soon we could make out what he was saying.

'Arrrrgggh ... eeeeeeeeeeeeeeeh ... stop it ... Jesus ... hahahahahahaha ... oooooooooh ... stop, please ...

stop it! Stop it! STOP IT!'

'No chance,' I said, 'not until you tell us everything we want to know.'

'Ahahahaha … I will! I will tell you everything. I promise. Just stop for the love of Gary Numan, stooooooooooooooooop! Please stop tickling me.'

We stopped. He sat in the chair, his chest heaving, sweating profusely. Eventually, he calmed down. It was time to get some answers.

25

In Exactly the Same Place as the Last Chapter

'Now then,' I said, 'it's time for you to start talking because if you don't, we'll just start tickling again. In fact, I think I saw a feather duster on the way up here. Imagine that on your feet.'

'No. I will tell you. I will tell you whatever you want.'

'So, what's your name?'

'Seamus. At least that is what I have been called for

as long as I can remember. Before that, I cannot remember because I can only remember back as long as I can remember.'

'Right then, Seamus. Why did you kill Tom O'Farrell? He was my friend and that's why this thing is personal now.'

'I was under orders from those above me. They have me enforce the parts of their plan that involve dirty work and dangerous mischief. Unfortunately for your friend he would not comply, and I was left with no choice but to shoot him in the belly.'

'That was your first mistake. You should have shot him in the head, then he wouldn't have been able to leave us a clue written in his own blood.'

'Ahhh, I was wondering how you had stumbled onto things.'

'But what was your plan? What would he not do that made it necessary to kill him?'

'He simply had to increase his stock of the likes of Damien Rice, David Gray and such. Perhaps a little display like a pyramid of CDs on the counter or a small poster on the wall over by the second-hand twelve-inch singles to increase their profile.'

'You monster. How could you ask such a thing of somebody who loves music?'

'I am indifferent to music apart from that of the great master. Her harmonies and subtle textures soothe my troubled soul. I simply had no choice; he was suspicious and that would not do. Suspicion leads to nervousness; and nervousness leads to tell-taleness; and too much had been invested in everything for it to be spoiled by one suspicious, nervous tell-tale.'

I lit a smoke, offered him one, which he took in his mouth as his hands were still tied, and carried on.

'Okay, well what we have figured out is that this ringtone is infecting people, making them like and buy crap music and, somehow, the finale of this Folkapalooza thing is going to be like some kind of Armageddon.'

'Oh yes, the finale. It is going to be like Armageddon all right.'

'The bad kind of Armageddon or the kind from the film with Bruce Willis?' asked Pete.

'Shut up, Pete,' said Jimmy, 'they're both the bad kind. A regular Armageddon or one where a giant meteorite is about to destroy the world. What's the difference?'

'Well—' began Seamus.

'Well, pardon me for breathing,' said Pete. 'I was just asking a question.'

'What is going to hap—' tried Seamus again, and the cigarette dropped out of his mouth and between his legs.

'Pete, so help me, I'll come over there and beat you like a ginger stepchild if you don't shut it.'

'At the end of the conce—'

'Yeah, yeah, whatever,' said Pete, obviously delirious with the tiredness as he was making the 'yakkity-yak' gesture at Jimmy. This wasn't wise, as Jimmy, still sore from being beaten by Seamus, moved to thump him.

'DO YOU WANT TO KNOW WHAT IS GOING TO HAPPEN OR NOT?' shouted the ginger albino, tired of people interrupting him when he was trying to explain.

There was silence for a couple of moments.

'Yeah, carry on. Sorry,' said Jimmy.

'Sorry about that,' mumbled Pete, blushing madly.

'Just before I start, could somebody please remove that cigarette from between my legs. It is burning my scrotum. Ahhh, thank you, the one they call Dirty Dave. Now, as you have figured out the ringtone is the starting-point. Knowing that Irish people rely on their mobiles for every little thing these days and cannot go anywhere without them, it was the perfect tool to unwittingly infect them.'

'With what though?'

'We discovered, well, that Alan Smithee,' he said the name like he was spitting tea leaves after a mouthful from the end of the mug, 'he discovered that a combination of tones played at the right frequency could completely brainwash a person. When you laid some background music over it, you could force them to become fans of whatever type of music that was. So, this could just as easily have been a death metal or drum 'n' bass epidemic.'

'So, why Damien Rice and that kind of crap?'

'Easy, because Mega Gigs owns them.'

'It *owns* them?'

'Sort of, yes. You see, many years ago, when these guys were just boring nobodies in their own bedrooms bashing out ridiculously shite music that nobody would ever hear, the great master grew bored. Worldwide success and enormous wealth were not enough. This became her big project, and, having invested in Mega Gigs and become its major shareholder, she simply purchased any artist making this particular kind of music. It was a challenge –

to make everybody in the world a fan – and it was a big challenge when you consider that anyone who even vaguely likes music dismisses these kinds of artists as inconsequential. Investment in them in terms of professional studio time, marketing and promotion would bring them so far, but their inherent crapness would ensure their fan base remained limited. Using Mega Gigs as promoters of their gigs allowed her to fund Alan Smithee, an evil man who wants power and will stop at nothing to get it, and his ringtone was put into development. Until she put her financial weight behind it, he was just a frustrated marketeer, now he is mad with power.'

'So, this has been planned for a long time?'

'Of course, something this convoluted and compli-cated doesn't just happen overnight. In fact, it was foreseen by a great seer in the 1980s, but no heed was paid to him.'

'Who was it?'

'Billy Ocean.'

'Billy fucking Ocean?'

'Yes. He had a gift of foresight. A sixth sense, almost. He inherited it from his father, who was killed when he was hit in the head with a hatchet one winter in a Colorado hotel. He went on to write a song called "Ginger Albino" and a limited number of seven-inch singles were pressed. It wasn't a chart success, however, and passed under the radar. He later released it as "European Queen" and later again as "Caribbean Queen", at which point it became a massive worldwide smash hit. Over the years, the copies of the original have all been bought up and destroyed by those who wished to protect the project, but one or two still exist. In fact, your friend Tom had one for sale in his shop. He did not realise it was anything but a song until he saw me. The lyrics said, "Ginger albino, he will come and you will know, that our hearts will be as one, lots of acoustic fun".'

'No wonder he changed it to "Caribbean Queen".'

'Yes, but if you listen to the rest of the lyrics, it warns of the arrival of the ginger albino and how all music, bar introspective acoustic folk sung by men with high-pitched reedy voices, will be destroyed for the benefit of an evil being.'

'So, that's why poor old Tom was so desperate to warn somebody of what was going on. And, after Ireland, this thing could be rolled out across the UK, the rest of Europe and then the world. The whole planet would become a giant hive of miserable worker bees. Except without the sweet, sweet honey.'

'Yes, the effects of the ringtone will pass on genetically to future generations, so at some point there will be no need to infect people, it will simply be the norm.'

'My God, and all because somebody has too much money and is bored? But what about you? How come you're not infected?'

'I am immune due to the vaccination developed in tandem with the ringtone so that the great leader, Alan Smithee and some assorted other VIPs, such as famous residents of Dalkey and Paul Williams of the *Sunday World*, would be free to carry on living normally.'

'Why Paul Williams?'

'Well, after everyone is infected, there will be no crime, and without crime to write about and nicknames to invent for the criminals the police tip him off about, Paul Williams becomes insignificant.'

'I'm beginning to think we might be better off just leaving everything as it is. After we blow up the stage, of course,' said Jimmy.

'We've been through this, Jimmy. Look, here's what we'll do. We'll find a way of stopping this that includes blowing up the stage. Or if we can't, you can blow up the stage afterwards. How's that?'

'I suppose that will have to do.'

'Right then, Seamus. As you probably know we've discovered a way of deprograming people affected by the ringtone. Whatever the timbre and frequency of those evil tones, they could not withstand the might of 80s synth pop.'

'Indeed, that was the one weakness of the plan. Nowadays, when people talk about 80s music, they all say they liked the Jesus and Mary Chain, Pixies, That Petrol Emotion and the Sisters of Mercy, when in reality they all loved Harold Faltermeyer, the Thompson Twins and Imagination. But with nobody willing to admit it and even less willing to play that kind of music, we didn't think anyone would crack it. But there is always one, isn't there?'

'Yes, indeed. We are those pesky kids to your Scooby-doo baddy. Now, we know how to deprogram them, but we have to find the great leader. Tell us who it is.'

'I … cannot,' said Seamus, remembering all the good times since his life had been changed.

'Cooochie-Coooochie,' said Dave, his fingers wagging in the air.

'Oh God. Okay, okay.'

He told us who it was. A world-famous reclusive singer whose music was rich with layered vocals and ambient noises and was perfect for background music in films, lifts, gents' toilets and hotel lobbies. It was as inoffensive as a cute puppy holding up a sign saying 'Please flip off.' Good lord, it could only be one person.

'Enya!'

'No, not Enya.'

'It so is!'

'It's not.'

'Who is it then?'

'It is Mariposa Cachimba, the Spanish singer who has lived here, in a castle right next door to Enya's, since the late 1980s.'

'Ahh, her. Wow. I am shocked. She always struck me as a fairly normal person, if a little reclusive.'

'Oh, she is very nice. You have just got the wrong impression.'

'Seamus, she has made Damien Rice the best-selling artist in Ireland. That's about as evil as it gets.'

'Well, once you get past all the evil, she's very nice, I assure you.'

'That's as may be, but we've got to stop her. There's no way I'm living the rest of my life surrounded on all sides by Damien Rice fans. Can you imagine? That'd be worse than living downstairs from an eighteen-year-old wannabe house DJ who can't beat-mix and plays his music really loudly at all times of the day and night. Lads, we've got to figure out a plan.'

'You do what you have to do, but I warn you, do not underestimate Alan Smithee. He is the one with the most to gain, he can just put on concert after concert and all the brainwashed people will buy tickets. From his percentage, he could become the richest man in the world. And when that happens, well, he'll make Doctor Evil from Austin Powers look well balanced.'

'That'd be frikkin terrible!' quipped Pete.

There was silence in the room, and we all just looked at our shoes. Pete did say something funny once, but nobody can remember when or what exactly it was. It's probably best that way. We had to now try and make the most of our talents, such as they were, to prevent the finale of Folkapalooza taking place. Further discussion with Seamus revealed that the finale, scheduled for 10.00pm, when the crowd had been beaten into submission by a whole day of boring music, would feature David Gray, Damien Rice, James Blunt and special guest Bob Dylan, who would sing that Damien Rice song about not taking your eyes off of something. The subtle harmonies created by their voices, on top of the infection people were carrying due to the ringtone, would make the damage permanent, and no amount of classic 80s tunes would be able to reverse it.

'Truly,' said Jimmy, 'they are the four folksmen of the apocalypse.'

It was now close to 4.00am, and everyone was very tired. We had until 10.00pm to stop things, so it was decided that we'd all better get a few hours' sleep. We'd take it in turns to keep an eye on Seamus, who remained tied up and to the chair. I said I'd take first watch. When Jimmy relieved me an hour later, I went downstairs to the sofa, turned around three times and promptly fell asleep.

26

Early Monday Morning
(The Pink House)

I woke up with a stiffy. My neck always gets like that when I don't sleep in my own bed, and this wasn't the world's most comfortable sofa. I checked my watch, 8.30am. I felt sore all over from being beaten and launched across the room by Seamus. I sat up and groaned slightly as the aches and pains kicked in. I checked my pockets for the emergency supply of painkillers I carry everywhere, but I must have lost them. I walked gingerly into the kitchen to see what I could find, but the supplies were few and far between. The cupboards were more or less empty, except for a tin of mushy peas and some red curry paste. I checked the fridge, but, apart from an old lemon and tubs of natural yoghurt, it was completely empty.

A bad start. I needed coffee to get going, and coffee would have to be procured from somewhere. I roused the others and suggested we head into the village so I could get coffee and we could get some breakfast.

We left Dirty Dave to keep watch on Seamus and promised to bring him back a breakfast roll. We reminded him that he was prone to making stupid decisions if left to his own devices and warned him not to let the ginger albino get up under any circumstances.

'What if he needs to go to the toilet?'

'He can go where he's sitting if he's that desperate.'

'Hah, I know that one,' said Dave.

Walking down the hill towards the village, the air was warm and the sky clear. When we got there, it all seemed very quiet. There wasn't the hustle and bustle you'd expect for a Monday morning, bank holiday or not. Some cars passed us by, but the streets were more or less devoid of pedestrians. Looking up, I saw some curtains twitch, and I began to feel very uneasy. As we walked through the village, it became clear that nothing was open. No shops, no cafés, nothing. This was obviously very odd but also very bad. Where was I going to get coffee now? We decided to walk up as far as the DART station to see if there was anything stirring there, and that's where we saw the people. The northbound platform was packed. The entire population of the village seemed to be there. As we stared at them from the other side, they seemed, en masse, to become aware of our presence, and all the heads turned our way. They stared blankly at us. We stared blankly back. From behind, we heard footsteps, and a young man was running towards the footbridge with the train coming in the distance. As he went past, Jimmy stuck out his foot and tripped him up. He went flying forward, arms flailing, and came to a stop when he hit the top of a step with the middle of his forehead. He just sat there, looking puzzled, as the blood began to flow from the gash.

'What are you all doing?' Jimmy asked him.

'Folkapalooza. Must go ... to Folkapalooza.'

Then he got up, leaving a trail of blood behind him, and ran across to join the others. The train, which was far longer than a normal one, pulled in, and they all got on. Those sitting by the window continued to stare at us as if we were the freaks until the train pulled away and headed towards town.

'Well, that's very strange, I have to say,' I felt compelled to say.

We decided to wander back into the village and see what we could dig up for breakfast. There was no way we were going to get everything done on an empty stomach. Luckily, I had that set of skeleton keys that came in so handy before, and I set to work on the front door of a small café. Jimmy, not having the patience for me to try a hundred keys, simply kicked in the glass of the front door, and we got in that way.

'There's nobody around anyway,' he said, 'and even if someone came, we'd just tell them they were going to miss Folkapafuckinglooza, and they'd run off wailing.'

Inside, we got the coffee brewing and started frying sausages, bacon, pudding and eggs for the sandwiches.

🎧 🎧 🎧 🎧 🎧

It was a few days after the tumultuous finale that Dave relayed to me what had happened after we went in search of nourishment and hot black liquid that wasn't a cup of Chinaman's blood. While we went to the village and encountered the strange scene at the train platform, back in the pink house, Dave and Seamus fell into conversation.

'So,' said Dirty Dave to Seamus, 'if you could be a pair of headphones, would you prefer to be those big ones that cover your entire ear or those new-fangled ones that get shoved all the way into your eardrum?'

'I think the big ones. I am not fond of having things inserted into me.'

Despite having been bound for hours, Seamus didn't need to go to the toilet; Dave urinated in the bucket a couple of times.

'Your friends talk to you like you are stupid. Why do you put up with it?' asked Seamus.

'Well, to be honest, I am stupid.'

'You should not be so hard on yourself. I have met many people more stupid than you. Also, you should not let people talk down to you.'

'Oh, I don't mind. It's better than nobody talking to you at all. These guys have been my friends for as long as I can remember, and I've never made any new ones. When I was a kid, I used to get teased a lot by the other kids, but my father was the worst. He abused me, not up the bottom though I should add, but abuse comes in many different flavours, you know?'

'Yes, I do know. For I too was abused by my father, as well as mercilessly derided by other boys and girls who thought my physical appearance merited such behaviour.'

'I understand. I remember seeing a programme on TV once about a beetle whose father used to hit him, and he went off in search of other beetles to play with, but none would put up with him, and, in the end, he took to just crawling around until one day he discovered something that would benefit every beetle, and then he became a beetle hero and everyone loved him.'

'I never knew beetles had such interesting lives.'

'Well, I kind of made up the story myself. I was forbidden from turning up the volume on the TV, so I had to make up my own stories. Luckily, I have a good imagination. In fact, I had an imaginary friend for a few years, but he got hit by a bus and died. I've been kind of lonely ever since. Every evening the same – nobody to go home to, nobody to look after or to care for. But I have the lads, and they've always looked after me. Apart from pulling the odd prank on me, like sewing up my Jap's eye after knocking me out with ether, but it's all in good fun.'

'You know something? I do not have any friends at all.'

'I can't believe that's true. A big strapping fella like you?'

'It is true. My father beat every ounce of confidence out of me. He made me feel so terribly worthless, and this affected my ability to interact with other people.'

'But everyone has at least one friend. Have you ever seen that mad woman who twirls and twirls on O'Connell Street?'

'Yes. I have.'

'Well, to look at her, you'd think she'd have no friends at all, but she does. I know for a fact she is friends with that woman who carries the anti-abortion sign and that old bearded tramp who sleeps on the bench outside Rathmines swimming pool.'

'That does not make me feel any better. If a mad twirling woman can have two friends, how dreadful must I be not to have even one?'

'Well … I … er …'

They both looked at the ground in silence for a time.

'Maybe … we … no,' said Dave.

'What?' said Seamus, hopefully.

'I was thinking, you know, maybe we … could be friends? I know it's a little awkward what with you being all tied up and tortured because you're a murderer and you killed one of Twenty's friends, but still …'

'I was just doing my job. I am just like anyone else. Like a train driver, a doctor or a suicide bomber. They all have to do their jobs and nobody holds it against them.'

'Yeah! You're right. This could be cool. We can go places like the joke shop beside the Gaiety and try on mad wigs and masks and get itching powder and that snap chewing gum. That always gets me!'

'Yes, for years I fooled myself into taking a piece of my own gum. That is how very lonely I was. But now, as we're friends, you could untie me! We could play travel Scrabble, there's a set downstairs. And – call me Seamus.'

'Hah! I'm stupid, but I'm not a complete mong.

You know I can't do that until the boys get back. And you call me Dave.'

'I think,' a new voice said from behind Dave, 'that you had better untie him right away, unless you want me to shoot you in the anus.'

Turning around, Dave came face to face with Alan Smithee, the head of Mega Gigs, who was pointing a gun at him.

'Move over to the far wall, turn around and face it,' he said to Dave.

Dave did as he was told.

'Look at you,' said Smithee to Seamus as he went over and untied him, 'you're supposed to be big and strong and you've been overpowered by one bloke. You're weak. Weak, I say!'

'There were three more of them, they have gone out but will be back shortly.'

'Who are they?'

'The men who came to your office that day.'

'Twenty Major and Jimmy the Bollix? I thought you had solved that particular problem.'

'So did I, but you can never fully trust other people.'

'Good God, can't you do anything right? Well, we'll just have to put aside your incompetence for the moment and wait for them to return. When they do, it's time for them to be put out of the picture for good. Let's see if you can't carry out one simple task.'

Seamus clenched his fists, inwardly raging at the tone of voice directed at him, while Dirty Dave, still facing the wall, farted in terror.

🎧 🎧 🎧 🎧 🎧

We made our way back up from the café with breakfast rolls wrapped in tinfoil and cups of coffee in those takeaway cups with those tops on them with little holes that you're supposed to be able to drink out of but which burn the roof of your mouth as you tentatively try to take the first few sips. We had thought about leaving some money to pay for the damage and the food we'd taken, but we were sure the café-owner wouldn't begrudge us our breakfast on the morning we had to try and save everyone from impending doom. The plan was to get some food into us, then head off to the house of Mariposa Cachimba before heading back across town to try and stop the finale of Folkapalooza taking place. I rang Splodge and told him we'd need his help. He told me it was too early in the morning to worry about it and to call him back later that afternoon and to never call him that early again or he'd make me pay for it. Some people really are cranky in the mornings. Then I rang Lucky.

'Lucky, have you got a sniper rifle?'

'No, I'm a do all my sniping with a shovel.'

I had to admit it was a silly question. An assassin without a sniper rifle would be like Anne Doyle appearing in public without her make-up. I explained what was going on and told him we might need him to snipe some of the artists on stage at the concert, in case we couldn't stop it by other means.

'How a much?' he said.

'What do you mean how much?'

'Cazzo! What do you a think I mean?'

'You want to be paid? Lucky, this is serious, it could lead to the end of the human race as we know it.'

'If is so a serious, then surely can a pay for the hire of assassin. I'm a not work for free. Do you work for a free? In a fact, do you a work? I have known you a long time now and I have a no idea what you do.'

'I'm a shepherd, Lucky. We'll pay you, don't worry. I'll call you later with more info. Just polish your bullets and be ready.'

'Ciao, Twenty.'

'Ciao indeed,' I thought to myself. I sipped at my coffee, burning the roof of my mouth, and continued in silence until we got back to the house. I called out to Dave as I went up the stairs and he answered in a strange voice. Something was wrong. I figured he'd managed to fuck it up somehow and the ginger albino was now escaping like a Red Indian from a mental hospital. I certainly didn't think I'd come face to face with Seamus and Alan Smithee, who was pointing a gun right at me.

27

Folkapalooza Day
(10.00am)

The four of us, arms tied behind our backs, stood against
the wall, herded over there by Seamus, who now stood
alongside Alan Smithee. His short, stubby gun was
pointed at us.

'So, we meet again,' I said.

'Perhaps now you will understand the power I have.'

'Maybe I will. Maybe I'll choose not to, just to
frustrate you.'

'It was a nice try, but there was no way you could
possibly have outwitted me. When Seamus failed to
respond to our text messages we knew something was
wrong, so I thought I would pay him a visit. Finding only

your pungent pal here, it was easy for me, with a gun, to take control of the situation. Now, I have all of you right where I want you, and it's time to ensure that none of you interferes with anything I do again. This whole event has been far too carefully planned for you to destroy it now. Granted, you should never have had the chance, but this hideous freak here beside me fucked it up – and not for the first time either.'

'I do not think it is quite fair to say—', began Seamus before being dramatically shushed by Smithee.

'But—'

'SHHHHHH, I SAID!' he hissed before turning to us again. 'If it wasn't for the fact that you don't know exactly what's going on, I'd shoot you dead right now. As it is, I've got something much worse than that lined up for you.'

'Ooooh, sir,' said Stinking Pete, with his arm in the air like a schoolboy in class who, for once, knows the answer to the teacher's question. 'Ooooh! Oooooh!'

'What?' said Smithee.

'We do know everything. About you, Mariposa Cachimba, the ringtone, the finale of Folkapalooza and everything.'

'Fucking hell, Pete. Did you not just hear him say he'd have shot us if we knew all that?'

'I thought he said that he'd have shot us if we didn't know it.'

I sighed, deeply.

'Shit,' said Pete. 'When will I ever learn to keep my mouth shut?'

Smithee turned to Seamus. 'You told them?'

'They tortured me.'

'After all the How to Cope with Torture courses we sent you on? Well, those were a great waste of money. Christ, it's a shame your mother didn't choke you with her fanny as she was ridding her body of your disgustingness.'

'Do not talk about my mother,' snarled Seamus.

'Smell your ma,' said Smithee, as he raised his middle finger, 'then shut your mouth and help me get this sorted.'

He took out his mobile phone and held it above his head.

'You know what's coming, don't you? That's right. I could just kill you, but that would hardly be much fun at all. Seeing all of you succumb to the ringtone and mindlessly buying and enjoying music I know you hate would be far more enjoyable.'

'You complete bastard. If my hands weren't tied and I could do more than waddle over there like a penguin, I'd take that gold chain from around your neck and strangle you with it,' I said.

He gave me a simpering smile, took the phone down and began to press some buttons.

Menu > Settings

'Once you have been exposed to this, you will make your way towards the Phoenix Park, anxious to see the dazzling array of talent that Mega Gigs has put on display for you. And for free as well. What a great bunch we are, don't you agree? Of course, when the finale takes place and the damage becomes permanent, all the music you buy for the rest of your lives will be by artists whose concerts are promoted by, yes, you guessed it, Mega Gigs. It means that instead of selling out crappy venues like the old Ambassador cinema and gay old Marlay Park, we'll be able to do concerts in the Phoenix Park all summer long. One a week, a million-plus people at a time, only these ones won't be free. There'll be the cover price, then a handling fee. "Handling for what?" you might ask, and the truth is I don't have a clue. It just sounds good and nobody ever questions it. Call it "unnecessary supplement" and people would bleat and wail, but "handling fee" sounds all technical and official. Either way, I'm creaming it in, and you're not.'

Tones > Ringing tone

'You do the maths, or, if you're American, the math. One million people by €100 a ticket is ONE HUNDRED MILLION EUROS. And that's not even taking into account sales of merchandise, programmes, food and drink and CDs and DVDs, of which Mega Gigs gets a large percentage because of our "investment" in these artists.'

Open gallery > Alert Tones/Ringing Tones

'In just a couple of months, I'll have amassed a fortune greater than anyone on the planet and, as I'm sure you know, in this country, first you get the money, then you get the power. At some point after that, I believe you get the women, but I'm not entirely sure. The people of Ireland will be my playthings. I might even turn Offaly into a giant concert venue that could attract even more people than the Phoenix Park. And once Ireland is totally under control, there is nothing to stop me doing the exact same thing in every country in the world. It might be difficult in poorer countries where mobile phones aren't present, but I might just develop some kind of a virus instead. Perhaps spread by having sex with monkeys. There's always a way. Oh, it's going to be such fun. And it'll all be thanks to people like you, and your smelly friends. I'll live in luxury, with this monster here to do my bidding and wash my feet and make me grape sandwiches, and the rest of your life will be miserable.'

`Select tone > Thetone.mp3`

'Right then, enjoy yourselves at Folkapalooza. Don't forget the finale now!'

I could see his thumb moving towards the button, but there was no way I could get to him in time. Having been infected by this thing before, I knew how awful it was. My knees were trembling, and I felt like vomiting more than usual. I looked at the lads. Pete was looking at the floor, Jimmy stared straight ahead, while Dave was mouthing silent words. What was he doing? I couldn't really see what he was saying, but it appeared be something like '… friends … friends …'. Quite how he found the gumption to talk about a poxy sitcom in the final moments of his normal consciousness I do not know, but for some reason it seemed to spark a reaction from Seamus, who yelled 'Noooooooooooo!' and swiped the phone out of Smithee's hands. To say he was shocked is rather an understatement.

'What do you think you're doing, you stupid fucking idiot?!' he yelled at Seamus.

Seamus didn't even reply, simply picking up Smithee

under the arms and raising him up in the air in front of him like a bully lifting up a small kid to steal his lunch money.

'Put me down! Put me down!' Alan Smithee shrieked just before the ginger albino's forehead connected at great speed with his face. Again. And again. There was blood and bits of teeth flying all over the place. After another couple of good butts, he dropped him to the ground where he lay, groaning, barely conscious. Seamus went over to where the phone had fallen and stamped on it with his giant Doc Martens-covered feet. Then he untied Dave's hands, ran over to the corner and started weeping. It sounded like a donkey's bray crossed with the mating cry of a manatee having a difficult shite. A haunting, plaintive sound, let me tell you. Dave untied us, and Jimmy picked up the gun.

'There, there. Yer all right. You did the right thing, you know. That bloke's a proper wanker,' said Dave, trying to comfort the blubbering beast.

'BLEEEEEURRRGHHAAAAAFFFFIIIRRRFFF,' wailed Seamus.

'Better give him a few minutes to get his shit together, Dave. But why did the bloke who hired Lucky to kill me and Jimmy just save us?'

'He wanted to go to the joke shop beside the Gaiety with me.'

'What?!'

'It is because,' shouted Seamus, with his hands still covering his face, 'that Dave was the first person to show me real kindness in years. Not since my mother died, when I was so young, so very, very young. Sure, my life was terrible, and the great leader was kind to me and allowed me to feast from her, but she wanted something in return. I always had to do something. Hurt somebody. Oh, the things I did. Threats I made to radio stations to get them to play the records in the early days. Intimidation, people's families were at risk, small children. I killed people. Rival artists who looked like they might get successful got knocked off before they could make a name for themselves and take sales away from Damien Rice and David Gray and the rest of them. Just like my father abused me, I became the abuser. The bullied became the bully. The enforced became the enforcer.'

There was silence in the room for a few moments until Jimmy spoke.

'Gay,' he said. 'But a good kind of gay, like the love between two men, and not the bad kind of gay, like the love between two men.'

'I am sorry about your friend,' Seamus said to me.

'Look,' I sighed, 'nobody here is whiter than white. We've all killed somebody's friend at some stage or another. You can make it up to us by helping us stop this madness. This crazy, crazy madness.'

'I will do what I can. I promise. And Dave, when it is all over, we can go to the joke shop.'

'If you want to help,' I said, 'get us inside Mariposa Cachimba's castle.'

28

Outside Mariposa Cachimba's Castle

(11.00am)

We left an unconscious, bloodied and somehow urine-covered Alan Smithee securely tied to the chair in the pink house and made our way towards the castle. Outside, we stood there looking at what appeared to be just an ordinary brick wall, but Seamus had assured us that there was a way in. He told us that anybody who came to the castle to do work was informed they were not to speak to

Mariposa or any of her staff. In order to minimise her contact with them, they were not allowed use the main doors of the castle, and so it was that we all used her tradesman's entrance. It was dank and dark brown but surprisingly roomy. We stopped outside a door that Seamus said led to a tool room, from where we would come out into the main hall. Her room was up a set of slowly winding stairs, and that was where she spent her days, writing music and sitting beside an open window, letting the breeze blow through her auburn hair. From time to time, she would call a maid, who would bring food, drinks and sometimes Reese's Pieces peanut-buttercups, to which she had a mild addiction.

'Okay, lads, get your iPods ready. We may need them.'

We went into the tool room where we got, literally, tooled up. I took a lump hammer; Jimmy took a monkey wrench and a Polyfilla gun; Pete took a long screwdriver; and Dave took a packet of those things that you use to fasten saplings to stakes and that everyone, at least once in their life, has put on their finger and pulled the plastic thing too tight, and you can't make it go back the other way because of the way it's made, and all the blood starts getting cut off, and your finger goes all purple and swollen until you finally manage to hack the plastic thing off with a key or a nail scissors. Before leaving, we had a final run-through our plan and then walked out into the main hall. It was resplendent in chandeliers and thick, full-length, velvet curtains that hung across the alcoves and wind chimes that made that really annoying wind-chime noise. Which was only to be expected, I suppose.

Apart from that, the house seemed very quiet, so we tiptoed our way towards the enormous staircase. It curved upwards from left to right, with a gigantic bay window offering a remarkable view. As we passed by it, on the midway point up the stairs, I could see Ireland's Eye, the Spire on O'Connell Street, the Customs House and the Hellfire Club. Talk about having it all when you're rich. Seamus led the way, and, as we got to the top of the stairs, we could hear what sounded like a choir singing.

'That's her,' whispered Seamus. 'She's practicing for her new album of Damien Rice cover versions, which is to be released some time in the late autumn.'

'My God, is there no end to the evil?'

We continued onwards until we saw her sitting with her back to us, arms waving as she sang. It was incredible. It was like she had fifty vocal cords instead of whatever normal people have, which I'm sure isn't fifty. It's probably two, but I can't be arsed to look it up. Anyway, it's not important. We walked into the room, and the singing stopped. She turned around, and if she was shocked to see us, she hid it well. She was dressed in a floor-length fur coat made of something that was probably extinct now.

'Seamus,' she said. 'I see ju have bought some friends for tea.'

'It is more than tea they want, great leader,' he replied.

'Very good,' she said, before reaching behind her, ringing a bell and calling quite loudly for a maid called Anne, who came almost straight away. She was a small woman with white hair and a kind face.

'What can I get you, Mari?' she said.

'Hola, Anne! We will take six mojitos and six sambucas. And make sure ju tell whoever it is we've got working the bar these days that I want my lima in the bottom of the glass and not anywhere else. Or he is fired.'

'Okay. That's six mojitos and …?' Anne left it hanging as if her forgetfulness was just a part of her endearing character.

'Sambucas.'

'Oh, you'll turn into a sambuca if you don't stop. Back in a jiffy!' she said.

'Lovely woman,' said Mari, 'but she is, as ju say here in Ireland, dooleettle.'

'Doolally?'

'Yes, theeeees.'

'Look, you mad Spanish harlot, we've come to stop you. What you're doing is monstrous. It's more monstrous than the offspring of Grendel and a minotaur.'

'Oh darleeeng, ju don't should be so up your tights about it.'

'How can I not be up my tights? The whole country is on the brink of being turned into a nation of cretins and halfwits that the rest of the world would make jokes about because we're so stupid. We'll be the new English, and nobody wants that. That's leaving aside the fact that you're using the world's most horrible music to do it with. We're going to stop this, and there's nothing you can do about it.'

'Yeah,' said Jimmy, 'we've already incapacitated your right-hand man.'

'Theees leetle one, he think he's so important and powerful. Is like a Yorkshire Terrier. A lot of bark, but if he bite, you can just kick across the room. Ju don't think it all rely on him, do you? This is the beauty of it. The plan is made with lots of parts coming together, but if one or two don't should make it, then is no problem overall. Soon I am totally the most awesome person in all of the land. Even more than Enya, who live next door.'

This was pretty bad. To be faced with the terror of a life surrounded by acoustic half-wits was bad enough, but, to compound it, we'd have a person in the country more awesome than Enya. Soon Anne came back into the room, pushing a drinks trolley on which sat six delicious-looking mojitos and six shot glasses filled with sambuca, which were more flaming than a towering inferno filled with drag queens.

'Let us take something together,' said Mariposa handing us each a mojito. 'Ju need to accept what will happen, will happen. Que sera, sera, as they say in some strange language which I don't understand. Is probably Catalan. Focking Catalans. I speeet on them. Filthy unwashed peegs.'

I sipped my drink. It was good. Refreshing and minty, like an Aquafresh enema.

'Look here, lady,' I said, 'while I appreciate your hospitality, a well-made cocktail won't change our minds.'

'Is not so much a question of changing your minds, it's a question of which one of you got the poison coptail!'

'Erm ...' said Jimmy, eyes moving left to right like one

of those Action Men with a thingy on the back of his head for moving the eyes.

'I'm kidding, of course,' she said. 'They're all poison.'

'Gah…' I began and immediately put my fingers down my throat, vomiting all over the carpet. 'All of you do the same,' I shouted, and the lads, well used to vomiting indoors, spewed the contents of their stomachs on the ground. The room stank of carrot and sweetcorn and bits of breakfast rolls. Only Seamus didn't vomit, preferring to stand away to the side a little bit. We had to just hope that whatever this poison was, it was all gone from our systems. I kicked myself that I hadn't thought of calling in to Rick's Remedies, my mate's shop in Stoneybatter. He has an all-in-one antidote that worked for any kind of poison (apart from politician's spittle).

'Now look at your carpet!' roared Dave. 'It's ruined. You'll never get the stain out. It's worse than red wine.'

'Carpet, eschmarpet,' said Mariposa. 'Anne, please to tell the carpet-cleaners to come in in a little while. You can go now.'

Anne left, muttering something about being promised to not have to serve poison mojitos again. She lit a Benson and Hedges, looked at me and smiled as she walked out of the room. I never saw her again.

Meanwhile, Mariposa shook her head, smiled ruefully, and one by one downed the shots of sambuca. She fluffed up the sides of her hair, as if fixing it, and sighed deeply. She turned her back to us and said, 'Ju have left me with no choice. I would say I am sorry to do this, but I am not sorry at all.'

From somewhere nearly off the scale, I could hear a faint sound. High-pitched, but very, very powerful. What the hell could it be? It was only when she had turned around again that I realised she had begun to sing. A glorious melody filled the room, so many vocal parts combining to create a wall of sound, layered strands of a musical tapestry, and it was bewitching. Pupils dilated, stomach rising like coming up on an E, her mouth a perfect 'O', large enough to put your whole fist into if you'd wanted. Enchanted, I could see the guys beginning to lose it and move towards her. But why? Beyond her was the window, and, as we were at the top of the castle, there was bound to be a long drop. That was it. She was going to make us throw ourselves out the window with her siren's song, as if she was a rock star, this was a hotel room and we were all televisions. I really missed the days when my biggest worry was whether to have an onion ring as well as a spice burger on the way home from Ron's. All this nearly-getting-killed business was becoming a pain in the arse. Imagine everywhere you go someone is trying to knock you off. It gets depressing after a while. No wonder Jason Bourne was always so very angry.

'Lads,' I shouted, 'iPods on. Now! Track 3, full volume.'

My shouts seemed to do the trick and soon the lads all had the extended twelve-inch mix of Wang Chung's 'Dance Hall Days' blasting away. We could now take our baby by the ears, and, more importantly, we could no longer hear the wildly enchanting warbles of Mariposa Cachimba. She ran from one side of the room to the other, singing as loudly as she could. Glass shattered, Seamus, who was iPodless, lay on the floor with his hands over his ears, and I was sure I could see blood seeping from between his fingers; but no matter how much she shrilled, crooned or caroled, she could not break through the sound barrier provided by our own music. At one point, her face was just inches away from mine. I could see that little punchbag thing at the back of her throat vibrating like an Ann Summers shop hit by lightning, but it did her no good at all. She slumped back into her chair. But, if we thought we'd escaped, we were sadly mistaken. Worse was yet to come, much, much worse.

29

Mariposa Cachimba's Chamber

(11.30am)

We stood looking at her, while Dave cast anxious glances at Seamus, who didn't seem to be moving. I was just about to move on her with the lump hammer when she pushed a large red button on the arm of her chair. I could hear the rumble of something mechanical and turned down my iPod to get a better listen. The wall at the far end of the room, where stood a huge four-poster bed, began to revolve and a war room-style computer screen and a large console with lots of buttons on it took its place. To the left, a small cage, covered by a yellow silk cloth, extended on a kind of robot arm. On the right was a bigger cage, at ground level, which was also covered in silk. Mariposa got up and walked over, punched a few buttons on the control panel, and the screen was filled with graphics and windows like you see on *CSI*, but which exist in no operating system known to man. A map of Ireland was slowly filled in with a golden colour and a percentage figure beside increased in a timer style. It stopped at 99.999999999999 per cent.

'This,' she said, 'is the percentage of mobile phones in Ireland that have the virus. Ju people account for the 0.000000000001 per cent. All of these people are on their way to Phoenix Park, already at Phoenix Park or, for those for whom travelling that distance was not an option, getting ready to enjoy Folkapalooza on the TV or radio. There's blanket coverage across the nation. Ju couldn't miss it if you wanted, but none of them want to.'

'You're a fucking lunatic,' I said. 'Have you not considered how this will affect people? There'll be no personality, no other music, no humour, writing, nothing that might be creative or interesting. Of course, that would mean a thunderous twat like Barry Egan would no longer bother us with his tedious shite, but still.'

'I don't care. For me is a good way to make sure I don't have to speak to anyone. Plus, I get one up on this beeeetch next door. In fact, she was one of the first we infect with ringtone. Hahaha, stick that in your Orangeloco Flow.'

'I don't really care what you do with Enya, to be honest. And if you don't want to speak to anyone, can't you just content yourself with being a recluse instead of hatching dastardly plots like this one?'

'Yes, I could, but is so boooooring. And, Mr Beardface or however ju are called, you are boring me now. It is time to end this thing, once and for all.'

'Bring it on, you festering geebag. Do your worst.'

'I will.'

'Come on then.'

'Okay, I am bringing it,' she said, fixing her hair again. She pressed a button on the console, and the silk covers fell off the cages. I couldn't believe my eyes. On his own in the tiny cage on the left was the lead singer of a world-famous band and, to the left, his band-mates. She pressed another button and the cages snapped open and he waddled out, his large hat and sunglasses on his head, his high-heeled boots clicking on the floor. He bared his sharpened teeth (crowns when out in public do wonders), waiting for a signal.

'Go! GO!' roared Mariposa, 'Fly my pretty. Devour them all.'

And that is exactly what he tried to do. His tiny little legs pattering on the ground, he moved like the Alien scuttling about the corridors of the spaceship. We moved quickly to try and get out of his way, but he managed to grab onto Pete's leg and sank his teeth into the flesh just below his knee. I ran over to try and get rid of him, but he scuttled off shouting about world debt and starving children in Africa. Jesus, famines are so 1985. Didn't Live

Aid cure all that? Then, he ran across the walls and launched himself at Dirty Dave, trying to bite his neck, but Dave shooed him off like you'd swat a wasp away from your can of Fanta on a hot summer's day in the park. The other three stood more or less still, trying to look menacing. One of them was smoking a joint, another was fixing his blond quiff, while the guitarist stroked his pointy little beard (which was quite nicely trimmed, I have to admit) and played a jangly riff of an unknown Damien Rice song with his other hand. I knew it was Damien Rice's song because it was absolutely shit. So far, though, they were nothing but a nuisance, and now the singer was hanging from a curtain gnashing his teeth and saying, 'Nobel Prize. Wants it we do. Yeeeees.'

'Is that all you've got?' laughed Jimmy.

'That, amigos, is just for starters,' she said, pressing a series of buttons. At first, we couldn't see anything, but then from a shadowed doorway emerged four attractive sisters with raven hair, carrying tin whistles and fiddles. They were all clad in identical black cocktail dresses and walking towards us.

'Ju can hit them and beat them, but unless ju kill the male, then they will regenerate and multiply. Each time ju hit a female without killing the male, a new one will appear from the doorway,' laughed Mariposa.

'Fucking hell!' said Jimmy. 'How the fuck can we tell which one is the male?'

'I know!' said Dave. 'Punch them all in the throat.'

'How will that tell us which one is the male?'

'Well, the male will have an Adam's apple, won't he?'

'Come to us,' they whispered, in their north-eastern seaboard accent. 'Come to us. Play our harps of love.'

'Oh fucking hell. This is shit. That cunt up there on the curtains, now this lot. What's next? A small battalion of Christy Moores?'

'Oh, I wish I had thought of that, but no. This is what's next!' and with that she moved a lever from the up position to down, and a large door opened over to the right-hand side. At first, nothing came out, but soon there was a hideous stench. A stench that even somebody who has spent most of their life with Dirty Dave and Stinking Pete would find objectionable.

'Oh no,' said Pete, 'The Hothouse Flowers have reformed.'

But it wasn't them. It was the members of Boylife, a famous boy band of whom 20 per cent were gay, fused into one giant creature. It was as naked as a porn star's baby, and it lumbered out of the doorway, sniffed the air and roared, 'LEEWIIISSSSS.'

'That's right, darleeeeng. Lewis is here. There he is, with the beard. And there he is, smelling badly. And there he is, well, they are all Lewis. Now, go. Do to Lewis what ju have always wanted to.'

Due to the physical limitations of being one beast made of five young men surgically combined to each other, it wasn't exactly the most nimble, but it possessed great strength and certainly posed a danger.

'Okay,' I shouted, 'we're going to have to split up and deal with these separately. Dave, you get that little fucker with the glasses and the hat. Jimmy and Pete, you find out which one of them is male. Do whatever you have to do to find out. Whatever you have to. What happens in this room stays in this room. No questions asked. I'll take care of this big thing here.'

I needed all my ninja reflexes about me as the huge creature came galumphing towards me. With only my lump hammer as a weapon, I had to be faster and use my speed to outwit it. The only thing is, I'm not very fast. Years of smoking delicious Major cigarettes has decreased my athletic potential. Still, I figured I'd be faster than the thing chasing me now, so I ran to the far end of the room. Ten seconds later, I was convinced my heart was going to explode in my chest and I stood crouched with one hand on the wall, wheezing like an asthmatic in an attic full of fibreglass. Why is that exercise is shit when you have to do it and not doing exercise is shit for you when you should have done it? It came towards me, kicking out a gnarled foot that I just about ducked away from. I skipped through its legs and smashed the lump hammer as hard as I could on the bone on the side of its ankle. It roared and threw its hands in the air before spinning around and staring down at me, those ten eyes combined into two, like a stillborn spider. I went back through its legs before it had a chance to bend down and did the same to its other ankle, and it roared again. It hadn't knocked it down though because its ankles were as thick and hardy as a Galwegian nun. I landed another blow on each ankle, but I was definitely going to need something else to take it out with. As I scoured the room, looking for another weapon, I could see Dave fighting the little big-mouth, who was imploring his bandmates to join in. They, however, seemed content to just stay in the background. Years of conditioning, I figured. He'd left them out of the limelight so often, he could hardly expect them to jump up just because he clicked his fingers.

Pete and Jimmy were in a big pile on the floor beneath the sisters who were writhing and moaning and groaning like a nurse during a slow dance at a tacky city-centre nightclub. Unable to land any blows in case they increased the number of opponents, they appeared to be grabbing between the legs of the sisters, which did nothing to stop them writhing and nothing to make it any easier to tell the difference between the male's obviously tiny penis and the enormous clitorii the girls possessed.

Then the naked Boylife thing took a swing at me. I only saw it at the last minute, and it knocked me backwards towards it. As I lay on the ground between its legs, my head reeling, I looked up and couldn't believe my eyes. As well as having a normal arse, it seemed to have another hole where men had their 'taint. It had to be because 20 per cent of it was gay. That was it. It was a mangina. That must be its weak point. I shook my head and quickly got to my feet and ran over to where Jimmy was. They seemed to be struggling with five of them now, but I could help them in a minute. On the ground was the Polyfilla gun, so I picked it up, and, running as fast as I could, I scrambled up the leg of the beast. Without thinking too much about it, I rammed the gun into the mangina and shot as much of the sticky grey muck up there as I could. The screams that came from the monster can barely be compared to any sound I could describe. If you possibly can, imagine the sound of a hippo having a fiery moose inserted up its arse by Hellraiser's head, then you're nearly there. It span around and tried to kick me off, but I knew I only had one chance and kept going as long as I could. I'd nearly shot my full load when it managed to flick me off its leg, and I went flying across the room, luckily landing on a pillow-covered chaise longue. The monster was spinning around like it was Kylie Minogue and wailing. Oh God, the wailing. It's a sound I hope never to hear again. Not until I go to the National Inserting Fiery Mooses in Hippos' Arses Championship in October anyway. Its knees were beginning to buckle, so I got up and ran over to Jimmy and Pete, helping them to their feet out of the pile of writhing sisters that now numbered seven.

'Get out of the way,' I told them, 'that thing is going to come crashing down any second.'

We ran as far down the room as we could, and the sisters, now aware of the threat posed by the toppling creature, began to get themselves out of the way. Soon there was just one left, who seemed quite keen to just continue writhing around. Despite the frantic warnings and orders from the others to 'Get up, get up now!', the writhing continued, and, when the monster let out one final, blood-curdling cry and came crashing down, it landed right on top with a hideous splat. There was no more writhing, and, significantly, no new sisters appeared. That must have been the male, just trying to have a lie-in and not listening to the constant nagging. That meant we could go to work on the rest of them. Pete went straight over with his screwdriver and started stabbing them in the neck, while Jimmy and I battered them with the wrench and the hammer. Soon, they were nothing but bloodied corpses at our feet.

'Wow,' said Jimmy wiping bits of brain off his face. 'It's been too long since I did that.'

'What about Dave?' said Pete.

He was under the giant curtains while the little man scurried around his feet, taking snaps at him when he wasn't shouting and roaring at him.

'Dave, just ignore him!' I shouted. 'He won't be able to stand it if he thinks nobody's listening.'

So, Dave turned his back on him, and the evil hobbit grew frantic, his shouting ever louder.

'Listen to me! We can wipe out all world debt. It'd be awesome. Then I can be King of Africa. Peace. Prisoners of conscience. Environment. Global warming. Red iPods. WORLD DEBT. GREENPEACE. WORLD DEBT. GLOBAL BLOODY WARMING. STARVING AFRICANS.'

He wasn't concentrating now, intent on making sure Dave heard his every word about every subject, so he didn't notice when I came up behind him and caved his head in with the hammer. There was silence in the room.

'Well, thank fucking God for that,' said the guitar player, throwing down his axe. 'Come on, lads, let's go make that Aslan covers album we've always wanted to make.'

I took the body of the little man and threw him out the window. I walked over to where Mariposa Cachimba stood by her control panel, her fur coat wide open to reveal her in lacy underwear. It was like seeing a giant walnut dressed in lingerie.

'Your pretty has flown, you miserable old wagon. Now, it's time for you to fear the reaper.'

'Dios mio! Ju are going to rape me?'

'Eww. No. Ree-per. Ree.'

'Oh, thank goodness.'

The other lads came over. Jimmy with his bloodstained wrench, Pete with his screwdriver, Dave had picked up the guitar and was swinging it around like a club, while I slapped my trusty hammer into my palm. We were about to go to town when a shot rang out and a bloody hole appeared in the middle of her forehead. A look of surprise came upon her face, and she fell, face-first, onto the ground in front of us. Spinning around, we saw Seamus, struggling to stand, the gun barely clinging to his fingers.

'Something … I … had to … do,' he gasped.

Dave ran over and caught him just before he fell to the ground. He lowered him gently and supported his head on his legs. He'd been almost pulverised inside by the singing our iPods had protected us from. There wasn't an orifice that something wasn't leaking out of, which wasn't the most fragrant situation I'd ever been in.

'Shhh, you'll be all right,' said Dave, wiping a lock of ginger-white hair out of his eyes.

'D-Dave …'

'Don't worry. We'll get you help. Won't we?' he turned to me with hope in his eyes. 'Won't we, Twenty?'

The look on my face told him everything he needed to know. The hope was gone, replaced by anguish, his heart beating madly in his chest as he realised what he already knew.

'Dave,' said Seamus, reaching blindly with his hands, '... are we going ... to ... to the ... joke shop?'

'Sure we are, Seamus. Sure we are.'

'Dave? We'll ... always be ... fr ... fr ... fr—'

'Francium, atomic number 87?'

'Friends.'

Seamus breathed once more and died. Dave let out a small sob, which echoed around the now silent room.

'Right so,' said Jimmy, 'will we see if we can steal a few beers from an empty pub before we sort out this Folkapalooza thing?'

30

My House

(3.00pm)

Given the fact that we didn't really have a lot of time and still had a lot of work to do, we only had three free beers in the Queen's, but we worked up a thirst smashing the door down. I stole loads of cigarettes from the machine as well. The village remained deathly quiet; like the night before Christmas, nothing was stirring. Except this wasn't the night before Christmas, and no fat man in a red suit was going to lavish gifts on people.

After we had our refreshing pints, Jimmy hotwired a car, some kind of Mercedes I think, and we headed back towards town. On the drive in, the roads and dualcarriageways were almost deserted as well. Houses were left with their doors wide open, a child's swing swinging back and forth in the breeze with a little teddy lying underneath it just to make you fully aware there was nobody around because no little child would go off without their teddy. The swinging was just to make it a bit eerie, I think. There was hardly enough wind to make it move on its own. As we got closer to town, we did see some cars passing by, all speeding to get to the Phoenix Park. Pedestrians were few and far between, but those we saw, single and in groups, were all heading the same direction as the cars – to Folkapalooza. The plan was to meet back in Ron's in an hour to formulate a plan. In the meantime, we could shower, shave, and get a change of clothes. I hadn't exercised that much in about, oh, ever, so I was somewhat 'manly'-smelling, and I prefer to be slightly more perfumed than that. I called up Lucky and Splodge and told them where we'd be.

I checked on the dog and the cat. They were fine and delighted to see me. Bastardface leapt around woofing, while the cat showed he was glad to have me back by spitting the half-chewed corpse of a giant rat at my feet. I gave them enough rubs to calm them down and fed them. A wild boar for Bastardface and the offal I'd plundered from the corpses back in Mariposa's castle for Throatripper. I decided I'd check my emails and have a look around the blogs. It seemed ages since I'd done that, but I should have known what I'd find. Every single Irish blog had posts about Folkapalooza: the line-up at

Folkapalooza, maps of the concert area, details of bloggers meeting up together at Folkapalooza and generally just post after post talking about how Folkapalooza was the best thing ever. Political bloggers started agreeing with each other tech bloggers stopped making snippy remarks about each other because they were jealous of their rivals' ideas the most highbrow consorted with the great unwashed and people even paid attention to sports bloggers. Just when you thought Folkapalooza couldn't get any worse, you discovered that it manages to damage something so inherently wonderful and awe-inspiring as blogging.

If it wasn't previously, it was certainly on now. Oh yes. It was on.

🎧 🎧 🎧 🎧 🎧

When I walked into Ron's, everyone else was already there. There were fresh pints on the counter, and I picked one up and took a big swig. Ron's pints of Guinness really were the best in town.

'Right so, Twenty,' said Ron. 'What's the plan, then? I was trying to watch *Dr Phil*, like I do every afternoon, and … what? What? He has lunatics on who make me feel better about myself. Anyway, I was trying to watch, and there's nothing on but Folkapalooza.'

'Blow up the stage. I've got Semtex!' said Jimmy waving a small rucksack in the air.

'But if we blow up the stage, people will panic and run off. As well as that, you'll have destroyed the link between the giant banks of speakers and the sound-desk, meaning we can't play the music to deprogram the people. You can blow up the stage afterwards, I promise. Lucky, do you reckon you could snipe them as they come on stage to do their solo performances before they all come back on together?'

'Is a piece of piss, as you Irish a say. But I'm a ask you. Is a not the same problem?'

'Whaddya mean?'

'If I a shoot one, the people they a panic and run away.'

'Shit. You're right.'

'Looks to me,' said Splodge, 'like the only possible way to do this is to get backstage and somehow stop them coming on stage to do the finale. Otherwise, people will get suspicious, the way they do when performers get shot in the head by somebody sitting up a tree 500 metres away. Also, they could easily see where the shots were coming from, and this is a pack you don't want chasing you. They'd rip Lucky limb from limb for spoiling the ending. Once you've delayed them or whatever, someone can take control of the music desk and get the tunes playing.'

'Okay, that sounds pretty reasonable, I have to say. I keep thinking there's something we're forgetting, though.'

'I can't imagine what it might be,' said Jimmy.

SCRAAAAAAAAAPE went Ron's nails down the small blackboard that had his Cocktail of the Week on it. (Ron's Cocktail of the Week was a pint of Smithwick's, and it hadn't changed in six and a half years.)

'I'll tell you what you're missing. See, if you manage to cure them, right? Clear that shit out of their heads? They come to and realise what's happened, what's been happening. What's the first thing they're gonna do?'

'Hug each other, glad to be alive again, and then laud us as heroes for saving the day?' ventured Pete.

'Nope. They're just going to start phoning each other and say stuff like, "Did that happen to you too? Yeah, it happened to me. That was weird, huh?"'

'Oh fuck,' I said, 'they've all got that ringtone on their phones, and it will just start the whole thing over again.'

'Exactly, Columbo.'

'Looks like we have no choice but to blow up everyone there along with the stage,' said Jimmy.

'You're forgetting all the people at home watching and listening.'

'Arse. So I am. And we hardly have time to blow up everyone in the country. That would take a bit more planning.'

'Well then, how do we do it?' I asked.

'Gotta use the phone networks,' said Ron. 'You either send a signal to every phone to shut itself off, or you shut down the networks themselves.'

'Well, we're fucked then because nobody here has the first idea of how to do anything like that. We're men of manual trade, honest trade and, sometimes, rough trade. Dave, you're good with computers, can you do it?'

'I doubt it, they're hardly the same thing, are they?'

'Actually,' said Ron, 'I've been doing an Open University night course in mobile telecommunications. It's not much, but it's all we've got.'

'A night course? Don't you already work at night in the bar?'

'Dealing with you cunts every night leaves me hyperactive at closing time. I've tried all kinds to chill out. Drink, drugs, violence, strange sex, stodgy food, Neil Jordan movies. None of it worked. Then I found studying. Christ, it's seriously fucking tedious, but it gets me to sleep.'

'So, what would you have to do?'

'I think the best way is to get to the core transmitters for each network. It is feasibly possible to write a mobile application that we could force download onto every phone that would wipe out all the ringtones, but I don't think there's time for such hardcore coding. You see, when you switch on your phone, it automatically finds two servers: the Media Gateway and the Mobile Switching Centre. They then send signals to the Home Location Register, which knows where you are until you move to a different location. I suppose we could try and divert all calls through a Legal Interception Gateway, but that could be difficult. Basically, we've got to cut out the signal between the MGW and MSC so it can't send a signal to the HLR. Once the MFI has been routed through the PCP, then it should be easy enough to change the frequency on the JWT so the BPM can't recognise the PPV when it tries to transmit to the EBS.'

'And in English?'

'Basically, I'm going to blow the shit out of the main transmitter for each network.'

'You might need this then,' said Jimmy, handing him his backpack. 'I've been saving this for a special occasion. It's Semtex that I bought when the IRA pretended to throw down their arms. They had to get rid of most of the stuff, so I took it off their hands. You know how it works?'

'Jimmy ...' said Ron.

'Yeah. Sorry about that. Have fun with it. I'll miss you, semmy.'

So, over a couple more pints and a bottle of Jameson (real stuff, not the tourist Jameson bottles filled with VAT69), we cemented our plans. Ron was going to blow up the transmitters of the phone networks; I gave him the keys of my Honda 50 to zip around town on. Thankfully, a quick Google search showed they weren't located too far apart. Me, Jimmy, Pete and Dave were going to try and get backstage and stop the finale. Splodge, who spent a long time as a DJ in the Temple of Sound on Ormond Quay, was going to take over the sound-desk with Lucky, who was going to compassionately assassinate anyone who got in the way. Just so he wouldn't get miffed about working for free, I promised to pay him €10 for each person he killed. He brought a cigar-cutter with him to provide me with the thumbs as evidence for payment, like cocktail sticks in a Basque tapas bar.

Soon it was time to get moving. I gave Splodge an iPod containing the playlist that would cure everyone, then Ron locked up the bar, and the lads headed on their way. I had to make a short trip into town to pick up a couple of things and arranged to meet them later on in the Phoenix Park.

It was time to stand up and be counted. As I was already standing, I said 'One' and headed towards town.

31

Clanbrassil Street
(5.30pm)

It was the strangest walk into town I'd ever had. No cars, no traffic at all, no sounds, even the birds in the trees were silent. It was like something out of *28 Days Later*, where that bloke wanders around London on a bank-holiday weekend or something. I called out and heard my voice echoing back from the buildings.

'—unts
nts
ts
s'

The shops were closed; pubs were closed; no church

bells rang. I could hear a dog barking somewhere, its pitiful woofing query answered only by deafening silence. As I continued down towards St Patrick's Cathedral, I thought I could hear a car in the distance but paid it no heed. As I walked on, I realised I could definitely hear it revving its engine, taking advantage of the empty roads, and screeching around corners. It was coming this way. Suspicious that anybody operating normally had to be in league with the Folkapalooza people, I stood into a doorway and tried to stay out of sight. It came closer and closer, turning up from Malpas Street and around the corner, down New Street towards the traffic lights. I was on the left-hand side of the road and peeked out from behind the doorway. I recognised the car from somewhere but couldn't place it. I went back to hiding, but I had been spotted. Shit. I could try to escape, but I couldn't outrun a Matchbox car, let alone a real one. It screeched to a halt right in front of me, and the window went down. I braced myself, expecting to hear the crack of gunfire before everything went dark, for ever. I was getting really tired of expecting to die at any moment. So, you can imagine my relief when a voice shouted at me.

'Hey, Beardface. Need a lift?'

I opened my eyes.

'Grace Jones Taxi Driver!' I said.

'Hahahaha. Jump in!' she said, and I did.

'It's good to see you, Grace Jones Taxi Driver, but how come you're not affected by the madness like everyone else?'

'Bwa ha ha ha ha. This crappy spell not work on

someone who come from de land of real witchcraft. Haha. Stupid people. Where we go?'

'Exchequer Street, please.'

'Okay. Hang on.'

And hang on I did as we turned down Kevin Street and then careered onto St Stephen's Green. She went all the way around the Green, taking the corners at around 90mph, laughing all the time, before mounting the pavement and accelerating down Grafton Street. I have to say, there are many nights when a trip down Grafton Street has passed in a flash, but this was something else. With no pedestrians to get in the way, she floored the accelerator, and I estimate we were going five times the speed of light when we got to Brown Thomas, at which point she pulled a handbraker around the corner onto Wicklow Street and up the wrong way onto Exchequer Street.

'Here, please!' I said, and she rammed the car to a halt outside Music Maker, a finer emporium of musical instruments you'd be hard pressed to find. 'Hang on here, I'll be right back.'

'Bwa ha ha ha. Meter's running. I don't care how long you be.'

The front door of the shop was closed, but the two main windows looked like they might just break if I hit them hard enough. I went back to the taxi and grabbed the tyre iron from the boot and smashed in both windows. Taking care not to slice my hands or wrists, I clambered through and made my way to the guitar section. If we were going to get backstage at

Folkapalooza, we had to at least look the part, so I grabbed four acoustic guitars, some plectrums and a tambourine. I brought them down and put them in the back of the car before going back inside and robbing all the money from the tills. Hey, I don't work for free either. Getting back in the car, I told Grace Jones Taxi Driver we were headed for the Phoenix Park. I don't need to tell you she told me to hang on, do I? Continuing the wrong way up Exchequer Street, she turned onto George's Street, took a left up Dame Street, then took a right and went the wrong way down Parliament Street and onto the quays, where we picked up speed. Red lights made no difference, and I kept my fingers crossed we didn't encounter some late comer as we flew blindly through the stop signals.

'What you gonna do with the guitars? Bore someone to death? Bwa ha ha ha ha!'

'Something like that. If we don't stop it, then the whole country is completely fucked.'

'It's fucked anyway. Have you seen the crime statistics recently? Ho ho ho ho!'

'At least with criminals you can put them in prison where they're rehabilitated through anal rape and heroin. If this isn't stopped, then it's curtains for everyone. Even you.'

For once, she had no answer. We sped past the Guinness brewery, a building that summed up all that was great about Dublin and its people: it looked ugly, smelt funny, but tasted great. She heaved the car across the river and turned up Wolfe Tone Avenue. How old Wolfey would have loved this scrap. Turning up Parkgate Street, she sped up the hill and towards the gates of the park, where cars lay abandoned, doors open, some with their engines still running.

'Can't go no further. Stupid cars!'

'Right, well, I'll take it from here. Wish me luck Grace Jones Taxi Driver.'

'Good luck, Beardface, €11.50, please.'

I gave her a €20 note from the money I'd stolen and told her to keep the change. As she pulled off, she ran over an old lady who had emerged from a nearby house and was heading towards the concert. 'Stupid old lady. Get new hips. Bwa ha ha ha ha!' I could hear her roar as the car sped back towards town. Leaving the old lady to drag herself towards the gates with her now useless legs trailing behind her, I gave Jimmy a quick ring to arrange a meeting place. I hauled the guitars up the road and through the maze of cars, vans and small trucks that blocked the way. The lads came down Chesterfield Avenue to meet me at the gates of the park and I handed them a guitar each.

'What's this for?' asked Dave.

'If we have to get backstage, then we have to pretend to be either staff or a group that's supposed to be playing. As Lucky is going to be going around killing as many Folkapalooza staff as possible, we don't want any mix-ups. We're going to pretend to be an acoustic folk group that just got a phone call at the last minute to replace someone who couldn't show up.'

'I can't play the guitar though,' said Dave. 'I learned the first few chords of "Hallelujah", but I'm pretty sure

I've forgotten them now.'

'Don't worry, we're not going to have to play. Where are Lucky and Splodge?'

'Just up by the Obelisk, trying to find something to eat, but it's all tofu burgers and soya noodles. Lucky was talking about shooting a deer and roasting it behind Áras an Uachtaráin, but I don't think we've got time for that.'

'Right, well, let's catch up to them.'

Throwing our guitars over our shoulders, we walked up the avenue. The sun was still warm, and the park looked beautiful. We could hear the distant but undoubtedly monotonous strumming of some bloke whose singing voice was as strong and powerful as the Progressive Democrats. There were people around, but all of them seemed to be hurrying back towards the stage area, which was just in front of the Pope's cross. Old JPII had attracted a big crowd back in 1979 when some people in Ireland still believed in God. Now they believed in the Celtic Tiger and Nokia and Microsoft and the bloke who could get them an eight-ball for €150. The crowd was far bigger than the one for a giant mass all those years ago, but without so many people having sex in the bushes. They were all facing the stage, enthralled by the music. Lucky had given up trying to find anything decent to eat and was swigging from a bottle of fancy-looking grappa, which he passed around.

'Mmmmmm, petroly,' said Pete.

We hung back a bit, making sure everyone knew their role and the signals required. I called Ron and finalised things with him. He knew how vital his part in all this was, and, as he was going to blow up the mobile-phone networks, we would have no way of contacting him once it was done. We just had to hope he could do it all in time. Ron has good experience of blowing things up, although since the Pillar he's laid low, pretty much.

'Splodge, Lucky, good luck. Lucky, you probably won't need it as your name is enough, but Splodge might. Just remember when we give the signal to cut the sound from the stage to the sound desk and get that playlist on the iPod going. We've only got one shot at this.'

'You don't a worry about us. I've a got a my killing head on.'

'Hah, like Worzel Gummidge.'

'Who?'

'Never mind.'

We did that up-in-the-air handshake that footballers do just before a match and slipped into the crowd. Old and young, fat and thin, and all that, immersed in music and the event. Rich and poor mingled. I saw the famous mixing with the hoi-polloi, although Gay Byrne dirty dancing with a pregnant teenager from Shankill is nowhere near as arousing as you might imagine. We had to find our way to the artists' entrance after battling to the front (quick tip: raking the heel of your shoe down the Achilles tendon of someone in front of you at a concert will give you the personal space you desire) and then around to the side, where we found a couple of bouncers guarding the backstage area. They looked like your typical bouncers: short hair, bomber jackets with a 'Gammon Security' logo (which was a cartoon pig with sunglasses on showing his mighty biceps), ear-pieces, slack-jawed and completely and utterly disinterested in everything. Dave and Pete were under instruction to not do any talking, under pain of death, so I went up to one.

'Hi, we're The Separated Bags. Last-minute replacements for ... erm ... Jeff Buckley and ... uhm ... Elliot Smith.'

'Don't see your names down here,' he said, looking at his clipboard. 'And as you well know, if your name's not down, you're not coming in.'

'Like I said, last-minute replacements, so we are.'

'That's all well and good, but you're still not coming in.'

'But we have to perform. Alan Smithee told us specifically we had to come to the backstage area to get access.'

'Who?'

'Alan Smithee. You know, the head of Mega Gigs. Bloke who employs you, pays your wages and so forth.'

'Never heard of him,' said the first bouncer with a smug look on his face. 'Have you heard of him, Tony?'

'Can't say I have,' he smirked.

'And now that you mention it, we were told to be extra vigilant in case anyone tried to get backstage as they might be planning on sabotaging the finale. You wouldn't have any plans to do that, would you?'

'Well, I hadn't thought about it, but now that you mention it, it sounds like a decent idea. I'm joking, of course! We're just here to play our unique brand of tepid folk music. Do you want to hear a song?'

'No, thanks. Move away from the door, please.'

'But we—'

'I said, move away from the door. You're not coming in and that's final.'

'No, this is final,' said Jimmy, as he shot the first bouncer in the heart.

'Jesus Christ,' said the other bouncer seconds before Jimmy shot him in the face.

'No time to waste,' said Jimmy.

'But I have the pepper spray here, and Pete was going to chloroform them.'

'Look, Twenty,' said Jimmy, 'you promised I could blow up the stage. Then I had to give my precious explosives to Ron, which means I can't do that and I was really, really looking forward to it. You have to let me have a little fun here.'

'Okay, fair enough, but give me that gun now. No more shooting people till we finish this.'

'Aw …'

'The gun …'

He handed it over reluctantly, and I put it inside my coat pocket.

It took us a couple of minutes to kick the corpses into a dark corner, where they simply looked like a pair of drunkards who happened to be sleeping, if you overlooked the fact that there was a big pool of blood and one of them had no face where his face used to be.

We slipped backstage.

32

Backstage
(8.00pm)

There were only two hours until the finale that everybody was waiting for like a pensioner waits for that winter day down at the post office when they collect their fuel stamps and finally heat their home. Backstage, we discovered a lush area with marble tables, hot spas and as much food and wine as you could possibly imagine. Whatever you wanted was there. The decadence was, I have to admit, rather wonderful, and, one day, I promised myself, I'd find a job so big that I could live life every day in a house by the sea where the evenings were warm. I dreamed of Skerries often, you know.

On the wall, pinned to a noticeboard, was a schedule of the artists due on stage. James Blunt was on at the moment, which explained my background irritation, like living next door to somebody who drills a lot early in the morning. He was to be followed by David Gray, then Damien Rice, then came the finale with special guest Bob Dylan, who had played earlier in the day. We had to let Gray and Rice play, as much as that might burn our ears, and take them out on a one-by-one basis. It was decided that Pete would get into the dressing room of James Blunt when he came off and incapacitate him. Dave would do David Gray, Jimmy would track down Bob Dylan, while I'd detain Damien Rice. The timing had to be right. We synchronised our watches – Pete's watch was also a calculator (cool!) – and wished each other good luck. Jimmy and Pete went off to track down their prey, while Dave and I had to continue mingling around until our foes had finished their sets. With our guitars and our facial hair, we fitted right in, and nobody so much as gave us a second glance, too busy were they in their trances and generally ligging about the place taking as much free stuff as they could.

'Twenty?' said Dave.

'What, Dave?'

'What the fuck is after happening the past couple of weeks?'

'You know what, Dave, I don't have a fucking clue.'

We found a bar area, and there were VIPs galore there. There was that weatherman from TV3, whatsherface off the News and that bloke who was in *Father Ted*.

No, not Ardal O'Hanlon. He was the equivalent on Ted's rival's island. Yeah, that cunt. Some gin and tonics were in order, with a slice of orange, of course, and we sipped on our drinks while trying to avoid anyone and everyone. We got ambushed by Simon Carmody, who insisted on talking to us until Dave said, 'You still get backstage at these things?' and he seemed to take offence and buggered off, his fake leopard-skin coat – yeah, *that* fucking fake leopard-skin coat – billowing out behind him.

Eventually, David Gray's doctors ordered him off stage; his constant head-wobbling caused such problems to his spinal cord that he was only insured for forty-five minutes a night. Dave went off to do what he had to do, and I ordered another drink at the bar. I kept to the sidelines, away from the crazy rock 'n' roll kids doing all their drugs, red eyes and red noses and brown tongues from talking so much shite. I'd gotten another couple of drinks down me when Rice did his final song. I skipped around to where the dressing rooms were and slipped inside Damien Rice's. I hid myself in the toilet and waited. It wasn't long before I heard the door open and a voice say, 'Yes, after the finale we can do it,' then the door clicked shut. I peered around the bathroom door, and he was standing there with a towel around his neck, fixing himself what appeared to be a glass of Ribena. Creeping up behind him, I karate-chopped him in the neck, and he slumped to the ground. Oh, no, he didn't. He just turned around and said, 'Ow, what was that for?'

'Your first album,' I said, karate-chopping him in the neck again.

'Ooooooooow,' he yelled, 'what was that for?'

'Your second album,' I said and karate-chopped him again and again and again and again and again and again, until he lay dying at my feet.

'What …was … that … for?' he gasped.

'For the sake of future generations,' I said, and karate-chopped him once more, and he was still at last. Phew. That was fun. I dragged his body into the toilet and, just for laughs, drew a big clown face on his stomach, with a permanent marker that had been lying on a table, and shut the door. I checked the drinks cabinet, and there was nothing stronger than Lucozade. I wished I could bring him back to life just so I could kill him again. As I came back out, there was a knock at the door. It opened a crack, and a voice said, 'Five minutes till finale, Mr Rice. Five minutes.' Luckily, these people never look in. It's just in case you're shagging a groupie or having a midget suck you off or something. Your man from Something Happens told me that one night in the Baggot Inn. He said he had more minge than Hitler, which was pretty fucking impressive. Hitler must have had all the schnatch he ever wanted.

I took out my phone to try and ring Jimmy, but there was no connection. Ron must have taken his network down. Mine was still up and running. I tried Dave, who was on the other network, and his was gone too. That meant there was just mine left, but there wasn't long for Ron to blow up the final transmitter. I'm not a religious man, but I said a little prayer that he could do it in time. Then, hedging my bets, I implored Satan to make sure it happened. So, this was it. The final few moments. I felt like Rocky before a fight, except I wasn't wearing a big flannel and praying while the Penguin kept rabbiting in my ear. All or nothing now. So much was out of our hands. We just had to hope that Splodge and Lucky were in control of the sound desk. We had to hope that Ron could shut off the final mobile-phone network or else all the hard work could be undone within moments of curing everybody.

I thought of the way Dublin had always been a cool city for music. We had everyone from Goths to punks to new wave to Cureheads to Emos to disco girls whose idea of what was cool came from the DJ at Annabel's to mods and the I-don't-know-what-you-call-them people who are into dance music. We had personalities these people made the city vibrant, different, colourful, heaving with characters that everyone remembers from their own generation of growing up out on the town in Dubin city centre. Even if you thought most of them were wankers, they were a lot better than having everyone be the same, boring, coma-inducing cuntbutlers that we had at this moment. We had to do this. No matter what the cost. You could end up a true Dublin hero, like Barney Rock or Fortycoats. And then, I could just get back to doing the normal day-to-day stuff without having to worry about people trying to kill me as much. There was another knock on the door. I expected a further countdown update, but the door burst open, and there stood Alan Smithee, his swollen face contorted with rage. He looked at me, just one eye open, with such hatred he might have been a person with half a brain looking at a copy of the *Sunday Independent*.

He stood there without saying a word, just shaking with rage. I stood and stared back at him. It was a stare-off, obviously. I didn't even blink. He stood. I stood. Eventually, he spoke.

'You … ruined … EVERYTHING,' he said slowly, before shrieking, 'I'm going to kiiiiiiiiiiill you' and launching himself at me. I was ready for him though and sidestepped, but one of his flailing arms caught me right on the bridge of the nose, and you know how much that hurts.

'Ow,' I said, my eyes watering. Just watering. I definitely wasn't crying, if that's what you're thinking. As if. I spun around as Smithee came at me again, lowering my head and butting him in the stomach. He fell to the ground, winded. Excellent, this was going much better than the last fight I was in. I looked around for something to beat him with, but there were no heavy ashtrays, and the Lucozade bottles were those plastic ones, not the old-fashioned glass ones with that weird plastic wrapped around the top of them. I had to get rid of him, and there wasn't a moment to lose. There was a knock at the door, and the voice told me there were three minutes until the finale. I ran to the bathroom and began to wrench the arm off Damien Rice's corpse so I could beat Alan Smithee to death with it. It was no good, though. Unlike an Action Man or a Steve Austin action figure, a real person's arm is quite hard to rip from their torso. I heard a noise behind me, and, all of a sudden, the crazy man had jumped on my back and was trying to claw my eyes out of my head.

That would not do. I needed my eyes. I tried to shake him off, but he clung on tightly, and now he was strangling me like I was a Tory politician with an orange in my mouth and a Sainsbury's bag over my head and he was a rent boy. I was finding it hard to breathe, and slowly the light was fading. I tried my hardest to rid myself of him, but he was like a man possessed. He would not let go. As the darkness approached, I heard a voice in my head.

'Use ... force ...'

What was it trying to tell me?

'Use the ... force ...'

Star Wars? Fine, it was, seminal movie experience and one of which I was rather fond, but I couldn't see what the escapades of a bloke with a cool sword who nearly shagged his own sister had to do with anything. The darkness came ever closer.

'Use the ... force, Twenty.'

'What fucking force?' I thought.

'The fucking magnum force, you thick cunt. You've got a gun in your pocket.'

The gun! I'd forgotten all about it. With the very last of my strength I reached inside my coat pocket, contorted my hand backwards and pulled the trigger.

Alan Smithee fell to the ground, screaming. Loudly. Something about me shooting his cock off, but I wasn't paying that much attention. The knock on the door told me there was a minute to go. I had to stop him screaming. I realised that most people would assume the high-pitched, off-key wailing was simply Damien Rice warming up, but I couldn't take any chances. I stuck the gun in his mouth.

'Eat lead, fucker. This is for Tom,' I said, before pulling the trigger and blowing his brains all over the room. I like to have my moments, you know? My throat was on fire from the strangling, but I had to act quickly. Grabbing the marker, I quickly wrote, 'I did it. It was all my idea. Nobody else was involved' on a napkin and left it beside the body. Fingers crossed the cops would buy it. The door was rapped once more.

'Time, Mr Rice.'

'K,' I said.

This was it. Time to do this thing. I have to say, my heart was pounding in my chest. That might still have been the thrill of murder, but I figured part of it was that this whole episode was nearing a close. One way or another it was all going to be over, at last. I took a few drags of a refreshing Major, shook my head and walked out the door. To the right, I could see Jimmy outside Bob Dylan's dressing room with what looked like a mop head placed on his head to look like Dylan's curly hair. It was quite convincing actually. Beyond him, Dave stood proudly, and to my left was Pete. We held our guitars in front of us like musical instruments none of us had a clue how to play. No words were spoken, but we did that manly, lips-pursed head nod at each other that meant, 'Come on, lads. Let's fucking do it.' So, we did. We took the steps up to the stage where even the staff seemed in a daze, eagerly awaiting what was to come. As we were walking up, and DJ Rick O'Shea, compère for the night, was working the crowd into a state of mild excitement, I spoke to Jimmy.

'Any hassle?'

'No,' he said. 'All good. Let's hope Splodge and Lucky are in place.'

'How'd it go with Dylan?'

'Grand.'

'Kill him?'

'Ah yeah. Of course. Collateral damage, some might call it. I'd call it the opportunity of a lifetime.'

'You're not wrong there.'

'Rice?'

'As dead as Kurt Cobain crossed with Jim Morrison.'

'Good stuff. Let's hope the lads did what they had to as well. It's all or nothing now, Twenty.'

'Sure is.'

'Best of luck, mate.'

'Yeah, you too.'

'Need a new lead singer, I hear,' said Jimmy.

Well, if you can't laugh …

We made our way out on stage. The lights were blinding; all we could see was this enormous bank of people, and every last one of them staring at the stage as if this was the moment they'd been waiting for their whole lives. There were four mikes set up, and we made our way to one each. It went deathly quiet, mouths were open, gaping, waiting.

'Two,' said Pete, 'Two. Two. One. Two. One Two. Two. Two. Testing. Tssswo.'

'Pete,' my voice boomed, 'I mean, James Blunt …' I moved away from the mike. 'Shut the fuck up, for fuck's sake.'

I went back to the mike, checking my mobile phone. The network was still up.

'Now the moment you've all been waiting for,' I said in my dullest voice, 'the finale of Folkapalooza.'

There was a ripple of mild applause.

'That's right. I, Damien Rice, and them, James Blunt, David Gray and special guest Bob Dylan, will perform, for the finale of Folkapalooza, a song that will change your lives for ever, FOR THE FINALE OF FOLKAPALOOZA!!'

The mild applause was interspersed with a few shouts of 'Champion!', 'Capital!' and 'Trem!' I looked out into the crowd, and far away, in the middle of them all, I could see the sound desk. There appeared to be the odd flash of light down there, but I couldn't hear if they were gunshots or not. I could only hope that innocent people were dying. They'd be heroes, but they'd never know it. Please let them be pupils of Blackrock College, I thought. Nits make lice, and all that. The lads were looking across at me. The backlights went dark, and four spotlights picked us out of the blackness. I coughed into the mike, the sound travelling across the night sky. Jimmy burped really loudly into his mike. I laughed into mine. Burping is really funny. Damn, had to pull it together. The audience was silent; I picked out the C chord on the guitar, the only chord I knew, and gave it a mighty strum. There was a small gasp from the crowd, and I shouted into the mike, 'Sploooooooooooodge!' That was the signal. Isn't that better than some random yet vaguely appropriate phrase? There was a loud noise, like somebody plugging something in, then music began.

The faces in front of us became confused, then irate, when the opening bars of 'Safety Dance' rang out. This wasn't what they were expecting, and they looked at us as if we'd pissed on their cornflakes. With blood-flecked urine. When Yazoo came on, you could see the infection in them fighting against the remedy. Some of them came towards us, and we broke their heads open with the guitars. I checked my phone. Shit, the network was still up. There was time, though. There just had to be. By the end of that song, their sense of ire had given way to curiosity, and the next three songs saw all those but the strongest dancing around and doing the robot and trying to remember that little bit of break-dancing they knew.

Then it began. The seminal tune, the one that even a spotty pirate radio DJ couldn't ruin for ever, no matter how abysmal and embarrassing his version of it. Oh God, there were those artificial cowbell sounds at the start. It was booming from the sound system now. Those in front of the stage were bombarded with its synth bass rhythm, and within moments, the whole Phoenix Park was dancing like a coked-up Irene Cara. Across Ireland, the song blasted out of radios and televisions. In pubs up and down the land, the dancing, the rí-rá was something to behold. During the 'la la la la la la la la' bit in the middle, they geared themselves up for the guitar solo and fell to their knees, playing air-guitar. Old and young were at one, and the nation moved and grooved and danced, quite literally, like they'd never danced before. It had worked. Thank God. Or Satan. It didn't really matter. The important thing was, we'd done it.

I signalled to Jimmy, Pete and Dave that we had to go. We legged it down the stairs and headed out past the barriers into the park. Leaving the guitars behind us, we ran towards the monument in the middle of the road that seems really close when you enter the park but gets further away from you the longer you drive. The song was still playing. There was about a minute left. I checked the phone. Still network. Dammit. Come on, Ron. We kept running. I say running, but it was more a continuous, wheezing shuffle. With just thirty seconds of the song left, we arrived at the monument. There was still network. Come on! Splodge and a blood-covered Lucky came running over.

'Well?' he shouted, as he threw the bag of thumbs over his shoulder.

I put my hand up. Staring at my phone now. Come on, Ron. Twenty seconds left. Come on. Ten seconds. Five … four … three … two … and then.

'No signal. He did it!' I said as I held the now useless phone in the air. 'He did it!'

'Ooooh, mama!' said Lucky.

'De do Ron Ron!' gibbered a clearly over excited Dave. 'Order has been restored.'

'Now,' I said, 'let's get the fuck out of here before the crowd starts spilling out and they catch sight of us.'

'Don't worry,' said Splodge. 'I bought us a bit more time.'

'How?'

'Listen.'

I heard the first bars of Madonna's 'Crazy for You' come on.

'You old dog. Slow set. Good thinking.'

We legged it down Chesterfield Avenue as quickly as we could while behind us people came to, blinking and staring around them. Some of them vomited, the release, the blessed release, so powerful that it washed over them like a chunky-carrot tsunami. There were emotional scenes as people returned to their former selves, feeling as if something terrible had happened but they couldn't quite figure out what. But soon, couples were spinning in the moonlight, digging the romance of feeling good again. Even the spotty lads who lurked in dark corners in school discos got a dance. We got to the gates of the park and headed towards the quays. Our work done. There was only one thing on my mind now, and that was beer. As we got to the bottom of Parkgate Street, I heard a familiar engine screeching towards us, and a car pulled up in front of us.

'Beardface! Bwa ha ha ha. Looks like you save the day.'

'We sure did Grace Jones Taxi Driver. Will you take six?'

'Six? Sure! In my country we get fifteen before we go anywhere.'

And so the rest of the lads experienced the driving of Grace Jones Taxi Driver. Even Lucky Luciano, who has experience of driving in Rome, thought she was 'a craaazy biiiiitch!'. Soon we were at the front door of Ron's. She took her money and left, back towards the park where she could make a killing taking fifteen at a time before the rest of the city's wonderful drivers could get their bellies behind the wheels of their cars. This time, she didn't shout anything out the window, but I couldn't help but feel I hadn't seen the last of her. Not long afterwards I heard the trusty sound of my Honda 50 approaching, and a slightly charcoaled Ron pulled up. It was time for some pints.

'That was close,' I said.

'Yeah. I stopped off in town to blow up a few pubs, lost track of time a bit though. Now that fucker on Dawson Street whose bar nearly has the same name as mine doesn't have a bar anymore. Hah.'

He opened the door, flicked on the lights, locked the door behind him and got in behind the bar.

33

Ron's Bar

(Bank-holiday Monday night)

'Well, lads,' I said, 'that was the worst thing we've ever been through. Even worse than that time we had to spend a weekend with Sting and those weird Indians with ashtrays for mouths.'

'Those were tough times, indeed.'

'We did well, though. Nobody will ever know the heroic feats of heroism we performed, the sacrifices we made, the emotional baggage we'll always have to carry around with us, but what matters is that we saved Dublin and, less importantly, the rest of the country.'

'Nobody can argue with that, Twenty.'

'Hey, cazzo Irish pig. How much a for these?' asked Lucky as he emptied dozens of thumbs onto the bar in front of us.

We all roared with laughter, the horrific act of cutting a finger off a corpse breaking the ice and reminding us that we had come through what was sure to be the most exciting and ridiculous adventure we'd ever be part of. Until the next one.

At this stage, Ron had a round of pints poured, and we took one each. They were picked up in the air, and I thought I'd better say something.

'Here's to never having to go through this again,' I said. 'What a fucking pain in the hoop it all was. Cheers.'

'Cheers,' resounded the other voices, and we drank, and it was good. The stories were flowing, and I got to telling them about my old mate Stan, who had a rather unusual hobby.

'You see, when Stan was a very young man, he very much enjoyed the television program Dick Turpin, *which was about a highwayman. As he grew up he had this romantic notion of the highwayman. The life of a daring, adventurous, risk-taking bandit was one he longed to lead, but in these modern times, it was not possible. In fact, Stan grew up to be as far removed from that kind of lifestyle as possible. He became a chartered accountant, following in the footsteps of his father, who was also a chartered accountant and who had followed in the footsteps of his father, who was a boring old bastard.*

He got married and had a couple of kids but soon realised there was a great big hole in his life. His kids had grown up and moved away, and his sex life was practically non-existent. His wife had gone through the change and was no longer interested in his mickey. He tried to have affairs, not out of badness, just out of the need to have sex now and again, but he found he was suffering from a severe erectile dysfunction disorder. Remembering an ad he saw on TV starring Pelé, he went to the doctors and got a prescription for Viagra. He thought this would be the cure for his problems, but Viagra did not work. He then tried the many and varied Viagra-style drugs that are available via the internet, but none worked.

He was resigned to a limp, sexless life until one day he somehow discovered a way of getting it up, keeping it up sticking it in (and out again more than three times), and he was overjoyed. It all harked back to his obsession with Dick Turpin, you see. He was a bit vague on the details, but he told me that if he was travelling along a road through some woods in an old-fashioned horse-drawn carriage while eating internal organs which he had dressed in sharp clothes, he could then ravish the woman he was sharing the carriage with. Now, as you can imagine, it was difficult for him to get too many women to agree to go along with this. Most women understand men have fantasies like threesomes or tying the lady up or wearing tight-fitting rubber garments, but it took a lot to convince a woman to go along with the idea of eating kidneys dressed in plus-fours and frilly cuffed shirts in a horse-drawn carriage in the middle of the woods.

Now, Stan had confided in a neighbour about his problems, and the neighbour, taking pity on him, decided to try and help him out when he heard of the upcoming date. Knowing of Stan's fondness for highwaymen, he hired a horse from a bloke down in Smithfield, bought a set of old-fashioned pistols and set off on the same day wearing a black cape and a mask. Later, things were going wonderfully well in the carriage. The lady that Stan had convinced to go with him was a horny housewife who loved unusual things. As he set about devouring his plate of offal, which he had kitted out in a Victorian gentleman's outfit, the lady was stripping off, her weighty bosoms bouncing as the carriage sped along the track in the Wicklow Mountains. He couldn't believe his luck. He was as stiff as a poker and could barely contain himself. The windows were steaming up, and he was perspiring slightly. There was no rush though. The longer they waited, the sweeter it would be. All of a sudden the carriage came to a stop, with the horse whinnying in terror. Stan was beside himself. What could have happened, he thought. He was about to get out and see what was going on when the door was reefed open, and there stood a highwayman right in front of him. Looking first at the woman, then at the plate of food, the masked raider spoke.

"Stan! Dandy liver. Your money or your life."'

'Oh, for fuck's sake,' said Ron. 'I need a pint of poison now.'

And so the night carried on like that, good spirits and tall tales. Shortly before midnight, Jimmy came over.

'Have to go, Twenty.'

'What? Why?'

'Johnny's operation tomorrow. Got to fast from midnight.'

'Fuck Johnny, man. This is the best adventure we've ever had, and I include that time we got kidnapped in Venezuela and in exchange for our own lives we told them three aid workers were in the IRA and they let us go and arrested them.'

'Look, I promised.'

'Aw, come on. Johnny is a cunt.'

'He's my brother, Twenty.'

'Yeah. Okay. You do whatever you want, Jimmy.'

He finished off the pint in his hand and, without saying a word, took a key from Ron and let himself out the front door. I have to admit it slightly soured the night. We should have all been there celebrating together, and, though we'd saved the lives of thousands of cunts we didn't know, I was slightly unhappy that the life of one cunt I did know, and hated, was to be spared.

'What's a the matter with Jimmy?', asked Lucky, who had now managed to wipe most of the blood from his face so he only vaguely looked like a child from *Lord of the Flies*.

'Family shit,' I said. 'Fuck it. Let's get drunk.'

And we got drunk. All of us, Ron included. There was laughing, there was some dancing, quite a lot of singing, including Pete's heartbreaking version of 'Dirty Old Town'. Heartbreaking because it's so out of key, it might as well have been sung by a deaf monkey. I know it was bright when I left, but, after that, the fresh air destroyed what was left of my memory. I must have been a sight, stumbling through the Blackpitts towards my gaff while so many flocked home from the Phoenix Park, chattering madly about what could possibly have happened.

I woke up the next morning on the sofa in the sitting room, an empty carton of Bird's Custard on the floor and Bastardface snoozing at my feet.

'Morning, big fella,' I said, as I rubbed his enormous head. He licked my hand. I cracked my neck, left to right. It probably shouldn't have made the noises it did. I made my way to the fridge and took a big gulp from a bottle of orange juice and used the liquid to throw back 1,200 milligrammes of Spanish Ibuprofen. The back door was open; I must have gone out there when I came home, and I looked around for the cat. Soon he came jumping down from the tree and wound his way in and around my feet while the dog vigorously gnawed an orphan's bone he'd been working on. I sat down on the bench and lit a smoke, watching the blue sky above me and knowing that my town was safe. No matter how far away you go, no matter how long you spend there, this is home, and good things happen here.

I sat smoking for a while, then went and checked my email and the blogs. People were back. Once again, there were arguments, scraps, snobbishness and mild retardation. Thank fuck things were back to normal. For now, at least. We had to hope that there was no way of connecting us to the carnage that had taken place and that people's memories were so affected it was hard to separate fact from fiction. Otherwise ...

♫ ♫ ♫ ♫ ♫

Friday, 6.40pm, Ron's bar.

I sat there, sipping on a pint of Guinness and reading the Evening Herald. Well, it's the only evening paper, isn't it? Anyway, I stole it. I wouldn't pay for it.

Officials and Gardaí are still at a loss to explain the events of last Monday night when the entire nation woke from what felt like a hypnotic trance. It is believed that the gigantic free concert, Folkapalooza, was somehow behind it. The company responsible for the concert, Mega Gigs, is currently under investigation, and Mega Gigs, MD, Alan Smithee, appears to have committed suicide backstage with a note admitting the whole thing was his idea.

Detective Larry O'Rourke (35) gave the following statement. 'For legal reasons, I cannot divulge too much information, but what we do know is that Mega Gigs and Alan Smithee were involved in a scheme which sought to brainwash the people of Ireland. Thanks to a group of individuals, who we believe to be dead and into whom no further investigation is to be made, the plan was thwarted, resulting in Smithee's suicide. Links between Smithee and famous Spanish singer Mariposa Cachimba are currently under investigation. Ms Cachimba was found dead in her Dalkey mansion three days ago. She had been shot by a strange ginger albino creature, who we believe to be responsible for the death of record-shop-owner Tom O'Farrell. The ginger albino was also found dead at the scene, suffering from what the State Pathologist calls "complete and utter organ failure". At this moment, I can confirm that we are investigating the deaths of a number of the artists involved in Folkapalooza but cannot provide any further information at this time.

Following an anonymous tip-off, it was discovered that a mobile-phone ringtone was the cause of the brainwashing. The explosions at the mobile transmitter devices have rendered the networks useless, and the Government has introduced emergency legislation to prohibit all mobile communication until all traces of the ringtone have been removed for ever. Even after just three days, some citizens have spoken of how much freer their lives are without being in constant contact with everyone else at all times.

Mystery surrounds this group of people who saved the day and rescued Dublin and, nearly as importantly, the rest of the country from this terrible fate. Some say they were like the A-Team; others say there was little or no chance that one of them was a burly black man wearing lots of gold who hated to fly. Whoever they were, we should be grateful to them for their bravery and fortitude and we should count ourselves lucky that such a decent, honourable and moralistic band of brothers happened to be the ones to save the day.

Despite the reluctance of the Gardaí to discuss the famous people who may have died, the *Evening Herald* has learned that the body of Damien Rice was discovered backstage at Folkapalooza with a clown's face drawn on his stomach. We believe it could be the work of a serial killer and have dubbed him 'The killer that draws a clown face on your stomach killer'.

Just then, the door opened, and in walked Jimmy. He had a stick with him, and he limped badly, leaning to one side.

'All right?', I said, as he painfully lifted himself onto a stool beside me.

'Yeah. I think.'

'Pint.'

'Course.'

I gave Ron a nod, and he dropped them down.

'Cheers,' I said and raised my glass.

'Cheers,' he grimaced.

'Johnny?', I asked.

'Dead.'

'What?!'

'Yeah, when the doctor cut that bit off my knee all those years ago, he told me that if my brother ever needed an urgent transplant I should make sure to tell him that having that piece of bone removed all those years ago rendered my bone marrow poisonous and would result in almost instant death.'

'Oh. You must have forgotten all about that.'

'Funny the things that slip your mind, eh?'

'Sure is, pal.'

We sat there, enjoying the pints and reliving the fun times we'd had on the way. I went out and brought some food back from the chipper. A selection of chips, battered sausages, onion rings, scampi and spice burgers. Haute cuisine, Dublin style. I didn't really notice when the old rotary dial phone behind the bar rang and Ron called Jimmy over. I was having a laugh with Dave, who had just asked me, 'If you had to be a pen, a pencil or a piece of chalk, what would you be?', when Jimmy came over.

'Need a word.'

'Okay, what's up?'

We moved away from the rest down towards the other end of the bar.

'The phone. That was them. They want to meet Monday.'

'Monday?'

'Yep. And these aren't the kind of people you stand up.'

'Monday it is then.'

Monday it would be.

ACKNOWLEDGEMENTS

So many people, so little time.

I know I'm going to forget somebody here so, if it's you, don't be all offended: it's simply that my brain doesn't work as well as it used to, and it's certainly nothing personal.

Or is it?

To 19 and the running lady, my thanks for being the best soundboards in the history of soundboards. Without your fertile imaginations, ridiculous ideas, fine advice and pints of beer, this book wouldn't have been half as good as I'd like to hope it is. It's a two book deal though, so see you in the usual seats soon.

To the man with the white beard. I hope you don't cringe too much reading this. Well, this part won't make you cringe, but the previous 300 pages might. That game at Lansdowne Road changed my life and I thank you for it. Without it I'd never have appreciated the artistry of swear words.

The gork, you're such a gork and you're gay and you smell. But I quite like you. Even if you do have the plague.

To Bernard from runningwithbulls.com for invaluable information regarding mobile phone networks. As such, any inaccuracies in anything I say about them can be blamed on him and not on my severe bending of reality, truth or facts.

Hat tip to Damien Mulley for putting me in touch with Bernard and his constant championing of Irish bloggers.

The fearsome duo from Crumlin, cheers for the evenings, food, wine, gin and old whiskey. But fuck you for the fucking hangovers.

My editor Ciara Doorley deserves a big round of applause and one of Ron's special cocktails, not only for her hard work in making this book the best book I've ever written, but for her boundless enthusiasm for the whole project. I'm sure there was a lot of pressure after she'd convinced them to give a bloke who says 'cunt' a lot a book deal on the back of a sketchy idea and three chapters – so thanks for being willing to take that risk: and to Breda Purdue for running with it.

Thanks also to my agent, me. You rock, you handsome, fragrant bastard.

Finally, the biggest thanks of all have to go to the people who have helped make this book possible – the readers of the blog. Without your visits and comments and everything else this would not have happened. It's still a pleasure to write something every day and I look forward to producing lots more crap on there before the next book comes out.

Thank you all, you magnificent cunts.